THE MANLY PARADOX

MAX STEINER

authorHOUSE®

AuthorHouse™
1663 Liberty Drive
Bloomington, IN 47403
www.authorhouse.com
Phone: 1-800-839-8640

Published by AuthorHouse 10/15/2012

ISBN: 978-1-4772-7299-2 (hc)
ISBN: 978-1-4772-7300-5 (e)
ISBN: 978-1-4772-7301-2 (sc)

Library of Congress Control Number: 2012917657

THE MANLY
PARADOX

ATHENÉ IS A PICTURESQUE UNIVERSITY PERCHED on a hill overlooking one of the finger lakes in central New York. Founded in the late 1800's by an idealist, it was the first coeducational institution within the elite group to which it belongs. In the 1960's, Athené's administration made a successful effort to recruit more minorities, and to this day, its student body remains racially, economically, and even internationally diverse. Students come from all over the United States and from as many as 38 foreign countries. There are 12,000 undergraduates and a total of 6000 students seeking advanced degrees.

Athené is a large university with 13 distinct schools including a school of arts & sciences, an agriculture school, a school of architecture, a veterinary school, a medical school, a law school, a hotel school, and an engineering school in which the division of computer sciences is lodged.

Architecturally, the university campus retains the grand character to which it was originally built, ivy-covered stone buildings more than a century old - most of the rock quarried at Enehta - or Athené spelled backwards. Attempts at modernization and expansion have generally been accomplished without affecting its character although there have been several universally acknowledged mistakes.

Generations of students have loved the hill as it is often called. Rich and poor have attended here sometimes keeping to themselves in ethnically defined or perhaps socioeconomically defined groups but more often they have mixed creating lasting friendships and changing the shape of a society.

The student union itself is named for an orphan who went on to marry the daughter of an extremely wealthy family.

It is certainly still possible for a poor young man to meet and marry the daughter of wealth and privilege. Such a union may not be met with instant approval by the young woman's family. Many adults who have a comfortable financial position in life begin to think that they are entitled to their special status. They may even begin to think that they are somehow different than other people. They believe they can protect their children by keeping them within the circled wagons. Money is security. There is safety in numbers if the numbers are dollars. There is prejudice.

Sometimes children rebel. It is not necessarily intentional. Young people often form friendships and bonds without considering the needs of their parents.

The fall in upstate New York can be stunning. Often forgotten, it shares New England's beauty in the changing seasons. Fall brings the students back to the hill. The majority of undergraduates are returning as sophomores, juniors, and seniors but, of course, 3000 are newly arriving freshmen and women. There is excitement in the air.

Kyle Manly, beginning her first year, arrived with her mom. The two shared a special warmth that was missing from either's relationship with Kyle's father. Mary Manly had been unsure about leaving her daughter to begin college. Although she had attended an elite private school, Kyle had insisted on being a day student and had never lived away from home before. Mary and Kyle were both quiet, thoughtful women who were comfortable by themselves and, for the most part, comfortable with each other.

Mary Manly knew that Kyle was self sufficient. Growing up in a large urban center, Kyle could travel the city alone and could acquit herself well at large obligatory social events. She knew that her daughter had no interest in alcohol or drugs and that she was a virgin. It worried her that Kyle was so reserved.

Mother and daughter did the usual things. They had deliberately arrived a few days early to explore the environs. They shopped, went out for dinner, and spent hours walking together. The countryside around Athené has several state parks with waterfalls and Kyle loved them instantly. She felt that she and her mom could be truly alone, surrounded by the roaring rush of falling water. And she worried about her mom. She didn't want to confront her mom but wanted desperately to know the answer to why her mom seemed to be keeping something from her.

"Don't you think this is beautiful?" Kyle said to her mom. "And it makes me feel that you and I are totally alone. Surrounded and alone. No one can find us here. The waterfall protects us." Mrs. Manly smiled. "I will be sad when you leave" Kyle continued. "I love you, mom."

Kyle then added cautiously. "You're the reason I never wanted to go away to school when I was in high school. Seems silly, huh? I didn't want to leave my mom. And sometimes I feel like there is some terrible secret that you need to tell me." There, she had finally said it. She turned and smiled at her mom, giving her time to answer.

Mary Manly looked at her daughter and thought to herself. "God! How I wish she would remain a child forever, but I am glad she is becoming my friend." Mary Manly steeled herself against showing the emotional content of her answer. "I love you, too, Kyle. More than anything." There, she had told part of the secret. "You must forgive me. You are right there is something I must tell you, something you must know. But I am not ready. I will tell you soon. Life is never as simple as it seems. We all make terrible mistakes. I will tell you as soon as I can. I am just not ready."

"I can tell you one thing, Kyle," she continued. "You are the most thoughtful and insightful daughter and friend I could have ever imagined. Still waters do run very deep" and then changing course, she continued "so unlike this waterfall that is full of spray and noise and rushing away without a thought as it moves by us."

Kyle didn't want to hurt her mom and suspected the secret had to do with her father. She sometimes wondered, they were so different. But more than anything, as Kyle realized she was becoming an adult, she wanted to be her mom's friend. She sensed that her mom really needed that. "Don't worry, mom. I'll always be your friend. I will be here when you need me."

Mary Manly looked at her daughter and thought her special. Perhaps as all mom's do. She saw in her daughter intelligence, thoughtfulness, and loyalty. But she also knew that someday soon she would have to tell truth about the one thing she had hidden from Kyle.

Chris sat in his jail cell and thought about Kyle. The kidnapping charge had surprised him. Perhaps he wasn't as clever as he had thought. On the other hand, the kidnapping charge might really work to his advantage. While he would be expected to ask for bail on the other charges, kidnapping might be used to prevent bail. He didn't want anyone to find out that he had no way of making bail. There also might be another hidden advantage for him. He might actually be safer in prison. Then again he might not be safe anywhere. He had a powerful enemy and he was the only one who knew why that enemy was so angry. He knew that Kyle was safe. She was surrounded by people who would protect her at all costs. He hoped that she had forgiven him for not telling her where she was going. She had gone without a fuss because of her trust in him.

The first day of orientation, Kyle was immediately happy she had chosen to have a roommate. Jennifer had a shy but engaging smile and Kyle liked her instantly. They seemed suited to each other in temperament and style. Neither was a show off. Kyle also knew she and her mom would have to bend the facts for her father. It was clear that her new roommate wasn't rich. John Manly would be unhappy that a suitable roommate had not been found for his daughter. Kyle and her mom had talked about this contingency and were prepared to lie. They understood each other. It was not a problem. They did not share Mr. Manly's feelings on class and privilege. And they didn't share their doubts with him.

Kyle and her mom were not ostentatious about their wealth, and they had chosen a rented car over one of the limousines. It was a far less conspicuous way to travel. But Jennifer's mom had twice advised her daughter. "If you think you need more money, let me know." Kyle never discussed money. She had so much it embarrassed her. She had learned to become an inconspicuous child of the city. No one ever knew she could afford absolutely anything, anytime, anywhere. Sometimes she was just another girl on the subway. She had chosen very simple clothes for college. When questioned by her father she said she would want new clothes for parties. She hated to lie but it was so easy.

Jennifer and her mom also mentioned they had come by bus. Mary Manly asked Jennifer's mom if she would accept a ride back. Both mothers would be lonely and need someone with whom to talk. Kyle loved her mom for the grace with which she made these arrangements. Both mothers had come early with their daughters and both were prepared to leave immediately as a gesture to the independence of the new generation.

Kyle and Jennifer couldn't have found a better match. Kyle knew that early on she would have to tell Jennifer the truth about her wealth if only so that she wouldn't have to lie. She would wait until they were better friends. She was concerned that her last name or her pushy father or an ingratiating university official would make the secret hard to keep. But if she wanted to be friends with Jennifer she would have to show her new roommate who she really was before it became clear who she was supposed to be.

7

Chris sat on the cot, leaned against the wall and looked at the bars on his cell. Chris Krail was an orphan. He had come of age early. When he was five, his parents had a second son. The younger brother, Jason, had multiple congenital abnormalities. His parents loved both children and Chris had learned to love a brother who could communicate only in the most primitive ways. It had helped make Chris sensitive to the needs of others. Indeed, Chris had grown into a kind and patient man who on the outside seemed a model of middle class reasonableness. The younger brother had died when Chris was thirteen, shortly after a memorable birthday. Chris thought of this birthday as a focal point in his life. A symbolic coming of age might that have been the last time he was a member of a happy intact family. His brother's death taught him far more about being an adult than any other event in his life.

Chris had received a birthday gift that he treasured above all others. His parents gave him his first computer. It wasn't much compared with the marvelous systems he had encountered at Athené but it allowed him to escape. He learned to program, he indulged his fantasies, and he learned about the fine line between the truth and the virtual truth. With his computer he withdrew into himself and he tried to recreate his younger brother. He had a talent and was able to create an interactive game for himself in which he and his "brother" would spend hours together. It was not too much of an extension for Chris to invent grandparents. All of his had died before he was born. So he created them. Chris was in his element with the world of computers. He knew he could probably create enough facts about his mythical grandparents to actually have them issued social security numbers and credit cards, but he wasn't yet ready to cross the line between fantasy and fraud. That would come later.

Kyle and Jennifer went through orientation together and each hoped the other would become the sister, the friend, the confidant each had always wanted. Both cautious and self contained, they opened up slowly and it was through conversations about school, the news, and politics that they learned about each other. They were both from Gotham, both wanted to major in anthropology, and both signed up to learn rock climbing to fulfill the requirement in physical education.

Neither Kyle nor Jennifer were interested in popularity. Neither wanted a lot of friends. Each wanted a few good friends. Jennifer was one of the best looking young women to ever appear on the hill. She often had mixed feelings about her good looks. While Kyle had immediately seen the shy child within, most of her peers thought her a little unapproachable because she was so stunning. Jennifer loved the space. Kyle would often be approached about her roommate but would be deliberately vague.

Both of them dressed simply, mostly in dungarees. Jennifer to hide her looks. Kyle to hide her money. Kyle deliberately borrowed something from her roommate hoping it would make it easier for Jennifer to also borrow.

One sunny fall afternoon they were sitting on the wall outside the library. It was Jennifer who opened the first personal subject. "You know, Kyle, I was glad my mom rode back to the City with yours. I spoke to her and she likes your mom. My mom really needs a friend."

"My mom's real special" Kyle responded hoping Jennifer would continue. She did.

"My dad died about a year ago" Jennifer said. "He was much older than mom. He was so warm, he was like a father and a grandfather all rolled into one. He always made me feel like all he cared about was our happiness. Like he had no needs of his own. You know, this year on my parents' anniversary it suddenly dawned on me that they didn't get married until mom was more than seven months pregnant with me." Kyle was a good listener.

Continuing, Jennifer added "Sometimes I think my mom is going to tell me. When she wanted to come here a day early and stay in a motel, it was like she wanted to spill some big secret. Maybe she just wanted to spend time with me. She has had to work really hard since dad died. I almost didn't go to college because I was afraid she wouldn't have enough money. But she keeps telling me not to worry. I need to look for a job soon."

Kyle was anxious. This was a really critical moment in their relationship. Kyle really wanted to pull it off. So she did what she thought best. "My mom also has a secret. She admitted it to me when I asked her on our trip here. I wish it was as benign as that I was conceived out of wedlock. Somehow I think it is much darker. There is something really wrong and I don't know how to help her. I just told her I'd always be there for her. But I think her secret must be awful and I do think it is about my father. She says she just can't tell me yet."

Kyle stalled and changed the subject. "I gotta ask you a question. What do you like to be called? Jenn? Jennie? Jennifer? I've been calling you Jennifer because that's how you introduced yourself but I thought it was OK to ask this year instead of waiting 'til just before we graduate."

Jennifer laughed. "I think of myself as Jennifer because that's what dad called me. I even asked mom to call me Jennifer after he died. I wish you could have met him. You would have loved him, too." She paused. "But I have kind of an outrageous idea."

Kyle smiled and said "yeh?"

Jennifer blushed and said "We're gonna be together through a lot of time and a lot of changes. Whaddayathink we call each other KJ? It'll always remind us we're close friends."

"I love it, KJ, but nobody else calls us that unless we add them to the roommate list."

"Agreed." They both laughed.

Kyle said seriously. "Listen, KJ, there is something you need to know about me. But first I have to ask you for a favor. If I tell you my own personal secret, will you promise that you'll still be my friend? I'm serious, I am very embarrassed about what I'm going to tell you and you are going to have to help me keep this secret. Somebody will figure it out sooner or later but you need to hear it from me."

"Don't worry" Jennifer said. "Now that were both the same person I have to take care of you. And I knew we were gonna be best friends the moment we met."

Kyle also knew she had chosen the right person for her friend and was overwhelmed with gratitude for whomever had set up the roommate program. She began. "My father is not at all the man you describe as your dad. He is appropriate but distant. He is very structured in what he wants for me. He can be rigid. He never shows his temper but I believe down deep there is one lurking. He always behaves properly but he is controlling. My mom and I know how to get around him. When I think about him what I really hope is that he is secretly more caring toward my mom in private. She deserves so much more than I see. It's not that I don't love him. He is my father, but sometimes I feel like a trophy. My mom is my friend." Kyle paused, then continued.

"The real issue with my dad is that he is obsessed with work. He is the founder, president, and largest shareholder of Global Financial Transfer. Global Financial Transfer is the dominant provider of electronic fund transfers in the entire world. Some people say that my father directly or indirectly controls 80% of all the money on the planet. He no longer works to make money. He has more than anyone could ever count. He just likes his position."

"And there is more. His politics are incredibly conservative, I find them embarrassing to the point of pain. He is always talking about how other people should live. He is intrusive. If he weren't so busy with his company I am afraid he would run for office - maybe as a Nazi. If I ever don't invite you to my home, it is only because I am sometimes so embarrassed."

Jennifer didn't know how to respond so Kyle continued. "So there it is. I was brought up having everything. I have worked hard to be myself regardless of my father's wealth. I try to buy only what I need. At the same time I am lucky. Money is never an issue. So do me a favor. If you're going to get a job, find one where we can both work together. I think a job could be fun. But don't ever worry about money. It's you and me, we're both KJ, we're going to need to share a lot of things."

Kyle waited. She hoped by emphasizing that the real problem was her father and her concerns about her mother, a few billion dollars wouldn't be a big deal.

Finally Jennifer said "Well, maybe we could do something nice for our moms."

Some events had taken place on the hill about 18 months before Kyle told Jennifer her little secret. Destiny was moving toward the young woman who would one day inherit the bulk of the Manly fortune.

Walter Black was the head of the anthropology department at Athené and he had a problem. His favorite student puzzled him. He had talked it over with his wife Marcia and they had agreed to invite him to dinner. Dr. Black valued his wife's impressions of people. Chris Krail was a computer science major who was seen as a genius. Chris Krail was also interested in anthropology where he excelled. But Dr. Black had discovered that he was either a young man in trouble or a dangerous psychopath.

They had first met at the request of Chris who wanted to take an advanced course given by Dr. Black for which he did not have the prerequisites. Since he had done so well in introductory anthropology, Dr. Black waived the usual requirement. He was pleased that he had done so since Chris unlike many undergraduates was intellectually engaged, always came to class, and often had a novel point of view. Chris was the best student he had taught in years.

Dr. Black loved nature and it was his interest in the outdoors that led him to what he thought of as the Chris problem. His wife had bought him a pair of snowshoes for Christmas so after the first big snowstorm he was out before dawn. He knew all the forest land around Athené and loved the gorges and the rock cliffs. He was thinking that the heavy drifting snow and the snowshoes were letting him go into an area where ordinarily the underbrush wouldn't let one walk. There were a few animal tracks but otherwise the unbroken snow was exhilarating. He was not prepared for what he found.

Chris was sleeping under a rock face. Chris heard him and looked equally surprised. Chris woke quickly and extemporized that he was into winter camping. He had grown up in the city and had come to love the outdoors after he had moved to Athené. He said the night had been tough but waking outdoors on such a beautiful morning made it all worthwhile. Dr. Black really liked Chris and was pleased to find a kindred spirit.

It was only after leaving Chris and heading home that Dr. Black had second thoughts. He had heard hundreds of excuses from countless students over the years and he had a sixth sense about bullshit. He knew it when he heard it. "Well," he thought, "maybe he was just hiding something he didn't want to tell me."

A couple of weeks later, Dr. Black wanted to tell Chris that he had loved the paper submitted for his course. He didn't want to embarrass him in class so he picked up the student phone directory. Oddly, the only phone number was a campus computer lab. Why didn't Chris have a phone? Couldn't he afford one? Usually students would give up food before a telephone. There was something odd about the home address but he just couldn't place it. After dinner he asked his wife to go for a drive. The home address was a commercial mailbox that allowed its boxholders to write an apartment number in lieu of a box number.

Dr. Black was not a really suspicious man but he genuinely liked Chris and wondered what was going on and where Chris really lived. Maybe he had a girlfriend. He relied on his wife who pointed out that he was going to the city on business. Why not see if Chris' parents lived where they were listed. It was the trip to the city that got his attention. He not only could find no listing for the parents but neighbors said they had been killed in a car accident when Chris was in his last year of high school. They said Chris had just turned 18, and as soon as he graduated moved out and left to spend the summer before his freshman year in summer school at Athené. Dr. Black talked to the neighbors. They were not helpful, they all liked Chris but didn't know of a single living relative.

Back with his wife, Dr. Black told her that he knew few students like Chris. Chris was a junior and was already being actively recruited by the faculty who wanted him as a graduate student in computer science. Yet Chris had found another intellectual interest as well. He was polite. Yet he was hiding something or from someone. The Blacks knew that they were instinctively supportive of students and they were a little afraid to be taken in by someone who was so obviously not telling the truth about something. They would invite him to dinner.

Kyle and Jennifer, KJ and KJ, didn't intentionally exclude other students. They made friends, interacted in the dorm and went to classes. Only half their classes were together. They clearly had their favorite. Rock climbing. They loved athletics. They jogged together. They met between classes. They studied together in the library or in the room. More than half the dorm thought they were lovers.

The rock climbing gave Kyle a chance to show Jennifer she was serious about sharing little things like a lot of money. The classes were indoors on a wall, but there was an optional weekend field trip by bus with an overnight stay. The fee was $175. Kyle knew that Jennifer could never afford the trip so she signed them both up. She told Jennifer after rehearsing in front of a mirror for about two hours. Jennifer hesitated and then said: "Hey, you said we could do something for our moms."

So, it was decided. The first foliage weekend after the rock climb they would have mother's weekend. Kyle deferred. "How do you think we should do this?"

"I would really like it if they would drive up together. Wouldn't it be nice if they could be friends, too. But look, KJ, do you really have so much money that I could borrow some to get my mom a nice place to stay instead of the dorm?"

Kyle knew that Jennifer was being polite. She had clearly told her roommate that she was rich. She only hadn't said how rich. And she was independently wealthy. Her father had given her stock when she was very young. She had gained unrestricted access to millions on her eighteenth birthday and would easily have over nine figures at her disposal by her twenty-first. In retrospect her father would probably never have willingly given away this control if he could have foreseen the future.

Kyle wanted to share but didn't want to hurt or embarrass her roommate. "KJ, we, you and I, have so much money to share that if we don't spend some soon, my father will get suspicious and send us a full time maid. How can I tell you that it is just money and the cost is no object? If we need to do anything we can, if we want to do anything we can. Let's just decide what we should do for them. But please, I am so embarrassed by it all. I'm just learning how to share with my best friend so don't make it worse by trying to give it back."

Jennifer finally caught her drift. "I'm sorry. I'm making it hard for you. I tried not to really listen when you said you were rich. But here I am making it difficult. You don't want to feel stingy and I don't want you to think I'm a leech. Just promise to tell me if I screw up."

Kyle wanted to make it easier. "Would you let me set up a joint checking account? Then we could pay each others bills and make sure that each of us was spending exactly the same amount. We'll each have our own money for emergencies but we'll pay living expenses and gifts for our moms out of the joint account. It would help me if you and I would never have to mention money. Just know that giving money is just as difficult as taking it."

They walked to the commercial section next to the campus and did just that. Jennifer awkwardly inquired about a ladies' room when the banker asked how they were going to fund the account. Kyle was grateful and was able to set it up so that any overdraft would automatically be replaced from her personal account. Things got worse when they left. Each got a checkbook and a credit card. Jennifer said "So how do I know if you cashed a check? How do we keep track of the balance? What happens if we overdraw our account? Suppose we both cash a check on the same day?"

Kyle looked at her roommate. "As long as you only take what you need for yourself and your mom the account will never run out of money. Now we did this so we wouldn't have to keep talking about money. But just this once I am going to tell you how embarrassed I am about all the money. You don't need to make any effort to keep track of what you spend. If each of us took $1000 per day out of this account for all four years of college, no one would notice. We are in this together. Right, J?"

"Right K." Jennifer still couldn't quite bring herself to believe she had just been given unrestricted access to an unlimited amount of money.

They walked to a bed and breakfast. They made reservations for two rooms and asked if they would be able to join their moms for breakfast. Kyle made Jennifer write a check for both rooms for both nights. Then Kyle made another decision. She rented a car and drove Jennifer to her favorite waterfall.

"This is where I came with my mom before orientation. Don't you think this is beautiful? I told my mom that here we were safe. No one could find us here. The waterfall would protect us. "

"I think this park would be perfect for a picnic. By the time they get here the leaves will be changing. What do you think we'll need for a picnic? "

Jennifer added "Maybe its time you and I went to a mall and picked up a picnic basket and a few supplies."

They giggled. Kyle began to feel that maybe Jennifer would relax. Jennifer hugged her friend and felt happy. "I just never had a friend as generous as you. And I understand that its not the money. You are just sharing and you don't want to keep track of who has given more. I love you, roommate."

Chris really didn't know how the legal system worked. Since his arrest he just did what he was told. He assumed that there would be an arraignment and a bail hearing. He would be charged with grand larceny and kidnapping. While he had stolen large amounts of money, he had not stolen the money which served as the basis for his arrest. The charge of kidnapping intrigued him. He wondered if Kyle knew that he was accused of kidnapping her. He wondered if it was convenient for the opposition to get all this in the papers. Or did they want it quiet?

The first session before a judge was pretty frightening. He was brought in the room. After the charges were filed, the district attorney asked that no bail be granted because a beautiful young girl was being held for ransom by the one criminal who could also get past any security system in the country's banks and money transferring institutions. He was a public danger. The evidence was irrefutable.

The judge turned to him and said "Where is you attorney? You certainly aren't going to plea that you're destitute and need a court appointed lawyer, are you?"

Chris felt his mouth go dry. The virtual world was so different than the real world. He was out of his depth and he knew it. No one but he knew he really couldn't afford an attorney. Kyle was too far away to help and it would be too dangerous for her to try. "Your honor, this case hinges on technical expertise in *the field of computer science. I don't feel that I could be adequately defended by someone trained as a lawyer, so I will defend myself."*

But when the judge laughed Chris was scared. Judge Branson leaned forward and said "You're a stupid kid. Kidnapping is not normally a technical issue. I am going to pretend you understand the charges against you and let you defend yourself. Bail denied." Chris had good reason to be scared. He couldn't have drawn a worse judge, the deck was stacked against him.

Dr. and Mrs. Black were not nearly as anxious about the dinner as was their guest. All three, however, were having a tough time. Dr. Black instinctively felt responsibility for his students. Was Chris hiding from someone? Did he really have no existing family? Was he using his computers to hide some hideous crime behind phony addresses? Maybe he was just a kid in some adolescent trouble. Chris was as nice and polite and approachable as any student he'd ever met. Dr. Black wanted to believe in him.

Marcia Black had her own theory but she wasn't telling. She thought the answer might be one so obvious that her husband had completely missed it. She would reserve judgement. And she had done something devious. Her two adult sons had long since left home. She had arranged for one to call this evening so that she could be alone with Chris. She thought the one to one dynamic might help sort out the mystery.

Chris had been unable to say no when Dr. Black had casually mentioned that he and his wife would like him to come over for dinner. Especially after being surprised in the woods, Chris didn't want to take a chance by again lying to a professor he admired. Dr. Black had kidded that he knew that the future was computer science but he had to make one earnest effort in recruiting for the anthropologists. Chris didn't know any undergraduate who had been invited to a professor's home for dinner. Chris had always been a loner and wasn't sure his manners were up to the challenge. On the other hand, he could use the meal.

Chris shaved and showered in the locker room and walked to the Blacks. He thought to himself that the Blacks were probably just nice people trying to be nice to him. He had to just relax and accept the evening for what it was worth. In many ways it was an honor to spend personal time with a professor of Dr. Black's stature. Maybe they could talk about which course he should take next. When in doubt be honest. Just don't be too open.

They had asked him to come at six on Sunday. Chris was relieved that the Blacks didn't drink and offered him coffee (which made him feel like an adult). Dr. Black started on how interesting it was that a computer genius could be so good at a subject as human as anthropology. Chris responded that computers were his escape, while the courses he took with Dr. Black helped him understand the real world. He could create his own electronic world but anthropology was his key to understanding people and institutions. He knew he was gifted with computers. But he explained quietly that his younger brother had taught him the difference between what was real and what could be imagined. He was glad they didn't pursue that point.

The Blacks missed the opening provided by the mention of the younger brother. They were prepared to ask about where Chris lived and they were completely taken by surprise by the mention of a brother. But it was time to start serving dinner. Mrs. Black clearly missed having a family and seemed thrilled to be able to have a young man to dinner. Dr. Black took a new tangent to win the confidence of his young guest.

"Chris, you know that the way my department is structured there are never enough graduate students to serve as teaching assistants. Every semester we seem to be at least one short. I know I'll never get you to consider staying on in anthropology but I also know you would be an outstanding teaching assistant. So I have come up with a plan. If you are willing, I can pay you next year when you are a senior to be an assistant teaching assistant. When you become a graduate student in computer science, I'll hire you as a regular teaching assistant in the introductory anthropology course. I know you'll also have to teach in your own department, but I thought you would bring us an unusual point of view and besides you could make a little extra money."

Chris was smart enough to know that this was a genuine offer and that Dr. Black could not possibly know his problem. "Gosh, Dr. Black, I don't know what to say. I'd be thrilled. I'll check it out with my own department but I bet they would let me do it. They'll think it'll help with their geeky reputation." Chris knew how badly he needed the money and that teaching was much more fun than the usual student jobs. He knew he was really lucky and wondered just how open he could be with the first adults who had treated him warmly since his parents had died.

Mrs. Black fussed over Chris and kept pointing out that she had made a lot of food because she knew how much a young man could eat. And besides if there were left-overs he could always take them home. For Chris the food was a real treat and he paced himself but kept eating. During dinner he made a decision that he needed someone he could trust but he would still have to hide a few little things - like his ability to steal.

The call from the son came during the second or third dessert. As soon as Dr. Black left the room to talk, Marcia Black looked at Chris and said "My husband is concerned about you. We both obviously like you. But he found you camping in the woods one day and he says he can always tell when a student lies. We wondered if you could use a friend. I don't want to be pushy Chris. But I am a mother at heart. Where do you live?"

Chris hesitated and felt this part might look strange but wasn't a danger to him. The couple would keep this secret. "Well, I lived in the dorms for my first two years and now I kind of live in my lab and at the gym." He smiled, looked right at Mrs. Black and added "of course sometimes I just camp out. Your husband is the only one who has ever caught me."

Marcia Black wanted to cry as she asked her next question. "When did you run out of money?"

Chris picked his words very carefully, especially about the tuition. He didn't want to risk her intuition. "I have been able to finesse my tuition. I have some money left from my parents. They died three years ago just before I started here. I thought I could really cut my expenses when the computer sciences division gave me my own office. Students are always sleeping in the library, and the athletic facilities give me a place to change. I have been careful to avoid the subject with other students and I would appreciate it if you would keep my little secret."

Mrs. Black struggled with her emotions. She really wanted to hug Chris. She too measured her words. "The job my husband gave you doesn't start 'til the fall. I want you to accept a job from me as well. We are getting older and we could use some help with shoveling snow and cutting the grass. Walter has accepted a visiting professorship for the summer session and we will be away for six weeks so we also need someone to watch our house. Would you consider doing these things for us in return for room and board?'

Dr. Black returned before Chris could answer. The professor looked at his wife and said "I guess he's figured out how spoiled I am by your cooking."

They had been married for forty years and she knew she wouldn't have to explain this one. She looked right at her husband and said "Chris is willing to be our caretaker. But he wouldn't take any money because you already gave him one job tonight. So I insisted we'll swap for room and board. We'll put him in the apartment over the garage."

At first Chris felt extremely awkward about the living arrangement but essentially he was totally independent. He wondered who was really the caretaker. Especially when he would open his refrigerator and find it full of food. He was very careful to explain to his hosts that sometimes he really did stay up all night working on his computer projects. But since he was bright and cheerful and always did what he promised, they tried to stop worrying about him.

The rock climbing expedition helped Kyle and Jennifer continue to bond with each other and also to make other friends. Neither was exclusionary by nature and easily welcomed new friends into their group although not into their unique friendship. They were especially receptive to the socially inept and the pathologically shy. They went out of their way to meet the students who didn't seem to be naturally included in a preexisting group. Both instinctively felt that supporting others made them feel better about themselves. When they were alone they quizzed each other so as not to forget the names of the other students. They dreamed of becoming instructors and getting to belay the ropes for more junior students.

Joking (but not quite), Kyle told her roommate "My father didn't bring me up to help others, especially not those who needed the help. This is great."

"Oh no, you're a rebel! I should have known" answered Jennifer. She added "You once told me your father thinks of you as a trophy. It made me feel so close to you. All through high school, I was expected to be the trophy date of the football heroes. Nobody else would ask me out. My dad would cover for me by telling those young men that I had to be home by 10pm. I loved my dad dearly for protecting me from guys who just wanted to be seen with me."

Continuing, Jennifer said "It gives me this incredible sense of power now. If someone is attracted to me because of my looks, I force them to be just as nice to everyone. I am glad you're instincts are like mine. I like helping people."

Chris knew that any request for a computer would be immediately dismissed by Judge Branson. And a computer was only half the answer. He wanted access to

the net. He wanted to do a search and find out about the judge's background. Chris sensed he had somehow added yet another enemy. What he really wanted to know was why had this judge been assigned to his case and to whom was this judge connected. Maybe if he waited until the trial began he could demand a computer for "legal research." If he could get online he had a chance. Otherwise it was just an execution with him wearing a blindfold.

The other reason he had to get online was to check to see if anyone was trying to penetrate the elaborate "history" he had created for himself. He had finally gotten around to giving himself grandparents. And his new grandparents were extremely wealthy and very reclusive. Kyle had help him understand how rich people manipulated anonymous numbered foreign accounts.

He was grateful to Judge Branson for just one thing. The no bail ruling saved him from the scrutiny that might uncover what really happened when he "asked" his imaginary grandparents to fund the bail.

The summer between his junior and senior year, Chris Krail devoted to working on his personal problems. The Blacks were away for six weeks on a visiting professorship and they had added two weeks to travel and see their children. Dr. Black had thoughtfully left Chris the teaching materials to review so he would be ready for his first teaching job. Chris had the house to himself.

At first Chris had declined a summer project for Computer Sciences and then later regretted it when he knew it would make his cover a bit more difficult. He returned and told the head of Computer Sciences that he would be gone most of the summer but nevertheless he would want to keep his office. Chris had decided to do his graduate work in financial security algorithms and encryption software.

Chris had set up the appointment and reminded himself that Dr. Roberts, the head of the Division of Computer Sciences was a technician and unlike

Dr. Black would never question personal motivation. In his meeting with Dr. Roberts he said he wanted to spend the summer playing with some variations in standard programming languages. His plans were to sit out by the lake with his portable and just play with some idioms he thought might help him for his security work. But he wanted to do it with no pressure. He would be in and out of the lab to try things on the supercomputer but he wanted to be free of any goal-oriented project. He said he thought some freeform creativity might help him understand the limits of standard systems.

Dr. Roberts was secretly thrilled. He wanted to keep Chris unattached from any long term project. He was negotiating the largest private contract in the history of a university academic department. Chris was a prize student who could help make him succeed. Dr. Roberts, of course, would keep the credit for himself. The contract would come in the form of an incredibly huge grant from Global Financial Transfer, the world's largest financial institution. It was in the early stages but it was about computer security and protecting computer driven fund transfers. Chris was going to be his prize graduate student.

Dr. Roberts said "That would be fine Chris. This department really wants you to join our program when you graduate and if you will commit, I would like to work with you personally during your senior year. I think our department will be asked to work on a project of real, not academic significance, and it is just your area. I used to be really concerned about taking grants from private industry but this one comes with solid guarantees of non-interference and only very general guidelines of the area being subsidized by the grant. When you get back in the fall, we are going to start building in that direction."

Chris was grateful but had an idea. "I really appreciate your support." And then as he was getting up to leave and shaking hands with Dr. Roberts he casually added "Do you think if I have any extra time I could start reading about our sponsor?" Chris tried to act as if it was just an idea with no substance.

Dr. Roberts was only too happy to get the contract and Chris was going to spend several years working for him. Dr. Roberts made a big mistake. "Chris, I'll give you access to my file on Global Financial Transfer. You'll have to memorize the password." He provided Chris with a string of numbers and letters. "I will also authorize your account to access standard business databases so you can start poking around."

They were both gratified by the meeting. Dr. Roberts thought he had landed the graduate student who would make him rich and famous. There were small incentives in the contract and there was the unspoken promise of direct reward. Chris on the other hand got exactly what he wanted. Dr. Roberts project was his declared area of interest. He had only the most rudimentary knowledge of the world's largest financial institution but he knew it was important.

But Chris really wanted the summer to begin constructing a bulletproof fiction about his personal background. The Black's were wonderful people who had blundered on the fact that he had no money and nowhere to live. He needed to construct a wealthy background so that no one would question where he got his money. He knew it would take time but if he could fabricate an electronic trail it just might work. And Global Electronic Transfer sounded like just the opportunity. Long before Chris had known such a fiction was possible. Now he was going to prove it. In realtime.

In the meantime he needed a portable computer. He made a decision. He would pay them back when he could. Chris would steal only when there was no other way.

Chris Krail logged on the university computer. He used Dr. Roberts' password. And he was sure that the electronic trail was so well buried that no one would ever find out who authorized the campus store to issue a very expensive and complex portable computer to an undergraduate. He also authorized a smartphone through the department. He knew every penny he had ever taken like this and he would pay everyone back. Thanks to Dr. Black, he might even earn enough his senior year to pay for the computer.

★ ★ ★ ★ ★

Kyle and Jennifer thought of it as the best weekend of their lives. Two daughters and two moms spending three days discovering new depths to their friendships. The weather was unusually perfect for a part of upstate known for its long rainy season. The fall colors were vibrant. They walked, they had a picnic, they went to restaurants and a campus play. The girls not only regaled the moms with tall tales but actually made them go rock climbing on the indoor wall.

Mary Manly was happy for her daughter. She always knew that sending her away to school would free her from the constraints of a rigid father. She also knew that Kyle was mature and capable and would never live in anyone's shadow. She instantly saw that Jennifer's friendship for her daughter was sincere. She was glad that the weekend was so full that the issue of her secret could not come up. She deliberately avoided all serious conversation except once.

Kyle and her mom were walking along a beautiful gorge trail a few feet behind their counterparts. Mary Manly quietly asked her daughter "What have you told your roommate?"

Kyle quickly outlined what she had done. "I think I pulled it off, mom. Money never comes up. We are so alike in so many ways. I like to share. She likes to share. For my birthday she made my bed. Would you believe it? What a great present. Students don't need much money. And she told me that she has been approached by people with questions about me but she blows them off. What's her mom know?"

"We've had lunch a couple of times" was the answer. "Either I pay or she pays. We never split the bill. Once I asked her if she would be embarrassed if I picked her up in a limo. She told me not to worry, money was nothing to be embarrassed about. That's as close to the truth as we got until this weekend. But I trust her and we are becoming friends."

"That's great. I'm so glad you like her. Jennifer is the perfect roommate for me. Did I tell you that we call each other KJ? She's terrific. You know she hides those stunning looks most of the time but occasionally she uses them to force guys to be nice to some of our less outgoing girlfriends.

Kyle continued "I'm glad you and her mom are friends. It must be so hard to be a widow and then have your only child leave for school."

Mary looked at her daughter and marveled at both her insight and her concern. "I think that recently she has begun to see someone. She once made an allusion to someone from her past who appears to be making cautious advances. Don't worry, I won't let anyone hurt her."

"Listen Kyle, there is a problem you need to know about." Your father has been meeting with the officials of Athené since before you decided to apply here. Remember how happy he was about your choice and we couldn't figure out why. Apparently he is about to give a huge grant to this university. Be prepared. There will be newspaper articles. I am quite sure the fact that his daughter attends the university will not be overlooked. I hate to ask. Do you want security?"

"Don't be silly, mom. I'll be fine. You know me, don't worry."

"Well, Kyle, there is one other problem about which you should be forewarned. Last week your father had a little dinner party at the house. Just forty very important people in black tie including Edmund Burrows who is the president of Athené. President Burrows will probably invite you to dinner and it will be a formal dinner. He even suggested that it will be soon. He would like to do it before the big announcement. He will be inviting Dr. Black, the head of the anthropology department, so that you can meet him socially. I don't think you have any choice."

"Mom, do you think I'll be able to take Jennifer. She would never get an opportunity like this and I like to share everything with her."

"No problem, Kyle. Even if your invitation doesn't say 'and guest,' just say that you and your guest will be pleased to attend. Like everybody else, he's a little afraid of your father. Believe me, you won't have any trouble with

Mr. Burrows. I am more worried about the impact in your dorm. Think about staying off campus in a hotel and using a limo. Why don't you come home next weekend and show me what clothes you'll want. Your father will be in Europe. Bring Jennifer."

At that point Jennifer interrupted. "What are you two so serious about. Come check out this waterfall. It's amazing."

Chris loved the teaching job. He discovered that he was a good teacher. Dr. Black was thrilled. Not only had be rescued someone but that someone was giving much more than he took. He did try not to interfere in his student's life, but his wife insisted that Chris join them for dinner every Sunday whenever they were home. Chris kept his secret in the computer lab.

His senior year was full. In addition to his interest in anthropology, things were beginning to happen in the Global Transfer project. Dr. Roberts was still chasing the mother of all grants but seed money had begun to arrive. Chris had learned an immense amount about the world financial markets and how money moved from one place to another. By the middle of his senior year he knew as much about standard computer security as anyone in his department.

Chris continued to work on his unauthorized project. He was making progress on his personal family fiction. He wanted to be absolutely sure. To prepare himself for putting his 'grandparents' online he thought he should investigate a few real rich people. Without the knowledge or approval of Dr. Roberts he began to thoroughly investigate personal information about the largest stockholders in Global Financial Transfer. It started out innocently enough. He just wanted to know what someone with a few computer skills could find out about an individual. The two largest stockholders in Global Financial Transfer were John and Kyle Manly, father and daughter.

Chris spent hundreds of hours poking around. Kyle was young and pretty straightforward. The mother, Mary Manly, also a stockholder, was an obvious addition to his investigation. But his most important insight came from looking at John. Truly rich and powerful people compromise their own security by bending the rules to fit their personal needs. Perhaps their personal perception of their own importance gets in the way. One advantage Chris had with his own grandparents was that he didn't have to hide any preexisting information.

The most important thing that happened to Chris his senior year was due to the kindness of Marcia Black and her husband. Chris learned there was someone he could trust. While he couldn't tell the Blacks everything he finally had real friends. He knew he could trust them. In order to protect all his secrets he had never let another student get truly close to him. His friendship with the Blacks made him realize how lonely he had been. He still thought of his brother Jason as his special friend, but without the Blacks he would never have thought of himself as happy.

Sunday of mothers' fall foliage weekend had a goodbye brunch in the early afternoon. All four promised each other that this would be an annual event here at Athené. The brunch was most notable for its glow of fellowship, its good humor, and how easily formerly awkward secrets kind of spilled out onto the table.

The brunch took place in the dining room of the hotel school. Student managed, it was known for high quality food and high quality service. There was enough space between tables for intimate conversations. Even if they got a little loud with laughter.

Maureen Martin, Jennifer's mom had realized early some of the truth about her new friend Mary. Mary never answered her own phone. Her address spoke for itself. Maureen knew her new friendship was sincere and thought perhaps it was Mary who needed the friendship more. Sometimes rich people live in a prison she thought. If she wondered how rich, she found out quickly at the brunch.

"KJ" said Kyle "I have good news and bad." With her eyes twinkling she continued "I want you to be my date for a party. Everybody talks about us anyway, might as well fuel the fire."

"That's the good news" Jennifer responded. "What's the bad?"

"I think it is going to be a black tie affair and we have nothing to wear." This wasn't exactly true. Kyle did have appropriate clothes at home. "So like it or not, you and I are going to the city next weekend to buy dresses. Matching black dresses. If I get lucky someone will mistake me for you."

Jennifer was a little worried. "I don't know, K, we just took three days off. We can't afford to blow every weekend. What about in two weeks?"

There was a pause as Kyle desperately considered her options. She knew the invitation would not give them a lot of time. Her roommate was right. They needed to study. But Jennifer was also envisioning a bus trip and a Friday night through Sunday. She made her decision with only a quick glance at her mom.

"Jennifer, we need to have outfits in a hurry, and they will need to be altered. Not for you. You look gorgeous in everything. But anything I buy has to be fixed so I can look half as good as you. And it won't take as long as you think. Saturday morning we'll take a taxi to the airport. We'll shop all afternoon. We'll have dinner with our moms and we'll be back here in time for bed. We can study on Friday and Sunday and even on the airplane if we're desperate."

Kyle continued with a big smile, knowing that her next statement had to look really natural. "Mom will send a jet for us and a limo will meet us in the city. Just don't take more than 2 or 3 hours picking out our dresses and we'll be fine."

Mary Manly thought her daughter was probably the least snotty rich kid in the world. Definitely didn't suffer from affluenza she thought. Never spent any unnecessary money on herself but had just offered a small fortune to be sure that her friend would be included and have appropriate clothes and still wouldn't miss school.

Maureen Martin smiled at Jennifer to encourage her. She saw through Kyle's little ploy. Kyle probably has more than adequate clothes she thought. She's doing this so my daughter won't be embarrassed at the party or worse not invited to something that is obviously important. And neither Mary nor Kyle have ever before tried to use money to solve a problem. It must be very important.

Jennifer looked at her friend, then at their mothers and saw nothing but positive reinforcement. "Kyle, what's so important about a party that we need a private jet to go and buy clothes? Who would have a black tie party at Athené?"

Mary Manly answered. "I'm kind of to blame for this." Which, of course, was not true. "Kyle's father is about to give a massive amount of money to the Division of Computer Sciences at Athené. He will do it through his company, Global Financial Transfer, but unfortunately Kyle's father will also give a press conference and make this announcement. President Burrows has decided to invite Kyle to dinner at his house. He wants to do this before the formal announcement. My bet is that his secretary will call Kyle tomorrow to make sure the date is okay with her."

Jennifer looked overwhelmed so Mary tried to make her smile. "I need a favor. When this announcement gets in the papers, I am afraid someone will notice that the daughter of one of the richest men in the world is a student here at Athené. Would you protect her for me?"

This was a subject Jennifer liked and she finally smiled. "Don't worry. If I'm good at anything, it's taking care of my buddy." She thought for a second and added "when we come to the city, do you think we could get matching wigs? Maybe I could double for her."

Kyle added "there is one more thing. I'm not sure yet who will be at this party. But Dr. Black is being invited so that we can meet him socially since we've identified anthropology as our major."

"Just Dr. Black?" Jennifer asked with a very sly grin. "Is there someone else coming, Kyle? Is there something you want to share with the rest of us? It's okay, we're all friends here."

Kyle blushed and for once had nothing to say.

Chris was amazed at his conversation with Dr. Roberts. Dr. Roberts wanted Chris to work on improving the security of GFT but he also wanted Chris to challenge the security of the company.

"Chris" he said "I have been authorized to give you the most amazing project any student ever had. Mitchell Bierman is the head of security at GFT and he wants me to assign someone to try and steal $100,000 from them. He doesn't want to know who is going to do it, but then there will only be about 20 possibilities. You don't have to take it as cash. You can if you want or you can just move it. Don't get too excited about it. We will have to give the money back."

Chris grinned. "I accept. How long do I have?" He didn't need more than a week. Thanks to his little foray into the personal affairs of John Manly he already knew the fatal flaw at GFT.

Dr. Roberts already had the parameters. "Two years from the official announcement which will be in the late fall. Just keep records, secure records, and be sure we can give it back. Don't tell me anything about your progress unless you think you might fail."

Chris thought to himself. "I graduated last week. I only managed to graduate by stealing large amounts of money. Now I am being asked to steal $100,000. They got the right boy. " And then out loud he said "I'm sure it will be an interesting challenge. It will take some time. But trust me. I am the right guy for this project. I won't actually do anything until after the announcement but I'll get started on some research right away."

Chris woke up early. He was glad they were keeping him isolated and away from the general prison population. He was also glad for a passing memory of Kyle. She had once told him "I wished you talked in your sleep, then I would even know your dreams." It was reassuring to know that if anyone was listening, he slept silently.

And Chris was worried. Passive was wrong. He should be making motions before the court. He should be controlling the process. He needed to have some control over his fate. He wanted the blindfold off and his hands untied. He needed Kyle. He needed her badly. But he was doing this for her.

He drank the prison coffee and thought about how the girls had spoiled him. Between Marcia Black and Kyle and Jennifer he had to spend all his time politely trying not to eat too much. His job was making the coffee. He took a lot more pride in his coffee than whoever served the prisoners.

A guard came by and announced "Judge wants to see you in half an hour. Get dressed." Mechanically Chris began to get ready. He was worried. What would happen to him next. Had they found anything? If he was lucky the judge would just set a court date. He knew it was useless but he would ask for a computer so he could "prepare his defense." He really wanted to begin an offense.

When Chris started his graduate studies Kyle and Jennifer were beginning their freshman year. It was Dr. Black this year who was lecturing Introductory Anthropology and Chris was one of the eight teaching assistants. Kyle and Jennifer were in his section. At first he found this amusing. Then he realized that he was attracted to Kyle. He made every effort to hide his feelings. He had not been prepared to like her.

Chris knew more about Kyle Manly than anyone else in Athené. He had hunted her and studied her. She was the second largest stockholder in GFT. He tried to be non judgmental but he couldn't help but dislike the Manly family based on what he had learned. He was not prepared to like anyone that rich and he knew that her personal fortune was immense. He had known before the first class that she was in his section and he had studied her picture. He had secretly read her entire university file including her application to be a student except for her personal essay. For some reason the personal essays were not made part of the electronic database. So Chris had never seen any information about Kyle that had actually been generated by Kyle.

Two weeks into the first semester one of his other students was thrown from a horse and broke her dominant arm. Chris waited for her after class and asked her if she needed any help. She smiled at him and said "two of the girls, Kyle and Jennifer, have already started giving me photocopies of their class notes. If you would just take my exams for me, everything would be perfect." Chris laughed and said that if she couldn't write her exam, they could do it together as an oral exam.

Chris was very confused about his feelings for his student, Kyle Manly. He was totally unprepared to meet an attractive, simply dressed, open young woman who could never be described as pretentious. The only thing that made him sure that she was concerned about her wealth was her reaction when he asked the section to introduce themselves. There were about twenty students in his section. Only Kyle Manly and a stunning young woman named Jennifer Martin used only their first names in the introduction. It didn't take Chris long to find out that they were roommates.

For the first time in his life, Chris felt guilty. Despite his occasional forays into the less than legal acquisition of funds, he had very high standards. He stole only because he had no other means of providing for himself. He stole, with the intent to return, only the minimum to survive and to learn. His investigations into Kyle Manly had been part of two projects. Learning about Global Financial Transfer was one. The second, and more important project, was learning about rich people so he could create a personal family fiction that couldn't be penetrated by other computer security geeks.

As soon as Chris met Kyle he felt that ethically he should not be peeping into his student's private life. He tried very hard not to do anything improper. But Chris was intrigued and he was an information junkie. Chris also knew how to gather information without getting caught. He thought of himself as a nice guy who through personal tragedy had been forced to live on the fringes of society. In some ways he actually identified with Kyle. It didn't take him long to realize that Kyle Manly and Chris Krail both had something to hide.

Chris knew Kyle's class schedule. He knew her phone number. He knew what she liked to eat. He knew when she studied in the library. He knew she had an older laptop that was not yet hooked up to the campus computer. He knew she spent next to nothing. It took him only hours to discover the KJ joint checking account and its unlimited funding. And he knew something else. Kyle was being followed. There were two men and two women, ostensibly students but who lived off campus. He didn't think they were a threat. They were very professional and they kept their distance.

The joint checking account came as a surprise. At first he wondered whether Jennifer was a real student or a bodyguard. He computer searched Jennifer Martin and decided that she was for real. Whatever the reason he didn't understand it. The account barely moved enough money to justify its existence. What the joint checking account told Chris was that he did not understand the person named Kyle Manly.

Chris was also one of Kyle's teachers. He knew that she was a good student. She participated and did well on exams. She was thoughtful. Also, she routinely let others go ahead of her. This was true whether someone wanted to ask a question or wanted to use the water fountain. Chris knew about the rock climbing.

Kyle and Jennifer would often stay late and engage him in a dialog. They would ask him about the course content or what other anthropology courses they should take. Chris thought they were just being freshmen who couldn't get enough contact with their professors. One day as the girls were leaving, Kyle once again took him completely by surprise. She lightly touched his shoulder and said "everyone says you're the best instructor in in this course and you're not even in the department." Before he could answer they were gone.

Brunch at the hotel school was the close of a great weekend. Jennifer had found something that made them all laugh. There was something that embarrassed her best friend far more than a little money. Kyle had a crush on her instructor and had no idea how to proceed.

Kyle thought Chris Krail was too good to be true. Once she got her composure back she figured if she and her roommate couldn't share her feelings with their moms there was no hope at all.

"Well" Kyle started "it's not just that I think he's cute. I mean you can't help but wonder. Everyone is in awe of his reputation. He is a graduate student in the Division of Computer Sciences. Rumor has it he's a genius. He also has to teach introductory courses in computer science but he is the only graduate student in the history of the school to teach in two such diverse departments simultaneously. And he's great. It's not just his knowledge. He knows how to communicate. He is thoughtful and kind. He's warm, he's approachable..."

"Not approachable enough!" her friend interjected.

"He treats me like everyone else. I have never wanted to flirt with anyone before and I don't know how. I can't identify any close personal friends. I looked up his address and rode by on a bicycle..."

"At least one hundred times" added Jennifer with a smile.

"It appears that he lives in an apartment over the garage in the house where Dr. Black lives. Next time he's teaching basic computer science Jennifer and I are going to sign up for his class. The best part about President Burrows' party is I'm going to make Dr. Black let us stay in Chris' section next semester."

"What about you, Jennifer?" Mary Manly was trying to help her daughter.

"I guess we all can't be as lucky as Kyle. Not all of us can have true romance with someone whose is real nice but doesn't have the slightest clue who we are." Jennifer could not have been more wrong.

"Jennifer's problem" added Kyle "is that totally inappropriate guys drool over her. Jennifer wants a friend, not someone who thinks she is a substitute for a movie star."

After brunch the four women hugged. Maureen Martin was invited to join the dress fitting. The two moms would meet at their daughters at the Gotham airport. The girls went to the library to catch up on their studying.

The party given by President Burrows was his attempt to introduce himself to Kyle and to introduce Kyle to a few university celebrities. Kyle had sized this up correctly and had told Jennifer to remember that everyone at the party would know who Kyle Manly was supposed to be, not who she really was. Kyle's mom had been right. The dinner was only one week after the shopping trip, and two weeks after the foliage weekend.

The two of them raised eyebrows as they entered in matching strapless black cocktail dresses. The dresses had been made for them in the Manly mansion by a crew of dressmakers. Emergency shopping for the ultra rich does not actually include going to a store or standing in line. They had followed the advice of Kyle's mom and had booked a hotel room where they changed and were picked up by limousine. It was an unforgettable entrance.

The party was cocktails, introductions, and a formal dinner at which President Burrows gave a polite talk about the privilege of having Kyle as a student. It was embarrassing. Kyle just pretended she was standing in line at the motor vehicle department and got through it without missing a beat. The formal announcement would come at midweek.

One person who felt out of place was Marcia Black. Her idea of college life was having Chris over for dinner, not elegant dinner parties. She came only to support her husband for whom this was a command performance. He, too, would have stayed home and read a book if given the choice. While Marcia Black did her best to fit in with the others, one person in the room quickly sensed that she was uncomfortable.

Jennifer Martin, the self-appointed protector of the intractably shy and the socially forgotten, moved towards Marcia Black at all deliberate speed. Jennifer did not exactly belong here either. She had come to protect Kyle but Kyle had been through this kind of thing before. Jennifer giggled to herself when she saw an occasional wife chide her husband for staring at the two girls.

"Hi, I'm Jennifer Martin, Kyle's roommate" she said extending her hand. "Have we met?" Jennifer had no idea who the woman was but sensed she needed someone to talk to.

Marcia Black had hoped to get through the evening unnoticed but this young woman seemed genuinely friendly and had a nice smile. Marcia Black had always had good instincts about students. "I'm Marcia Black. Dr. Black is my husband. We were invited because you two are anthropology majors."

Jennifer felt sympathy for her new friend and asked "would you like to sit on the porch?"

While Marcia Black really wanted to escape she felt obliged to ask "but don't you want to meet people?"

"I'd kinda like to meet you" answered Jennifer. Then sensing Marcia's one true weakness she added in a conspiring whisper "and I could really use your help." Jennifer remembered where Chris lived and had a sudden inspiration.

The two women retreated to the enclosed porch. Jennifer took her arm and they found a seat away from the crowd. They would rejoin the party in time for dinner. They chatted about things in general, about the beautiful campus, and they were pleased with themselves for escaping the worst of the cocktails.

"So how can I help you?" asked the older woman.

"Kyle and I have a man problem and I was thinking you might have some insight. It seems my best buddy Kyle is infatuated with a young man and I thought you might be able to help. Do you know Chris Krail?"

The older woman smiled. Jennifer had found a friend.

Much later Chris and Kyle would laugh about it. One thing they certainly had in common was that when they were stressed about a personal interaction, they would practice in front of a mirror. Kyle had practiced her lines in the mirror the first time she spent money on Jennifer. Chris spent the weekend of President Burrows' party in an intense dialog with his mirror. He wanted to talk to Kyle. He didn't want to be inappropriate. He didn't want to violate any teacher student ethics. He didn't want to scare her off. He didn't really know what he wanted. But he remembered that she had touched him. He sensed that Kyle Manly liked him. For all his understanding he was afraid of interacting too closely with others. His friendship with the Blacks had given him courage.

In another part of his life he had been trying to make friends with a sophomore engineering student named Bill Marlin. Bill clearly had even less friends than Chris. He was a student in Chris' computer science class and he redefined the meaning of the word geek. He knew every electron of how a computer worked but he barely even knew how to use the on/off switch. He was studying to be an electrical engineer. Chris thought he could do some good for Bill and himself and Kyle. All if he had the courage to talk to Kyle.

Chris knew Kyle's schedule from memory. He knew that she had a two hour break on Wednesday afternoons and that she and her roommate usually went to the library to study. He knew how they would walk there and where to intercept them. If he had guessed wrong, if they knew about her father's visit, they would just say they were busy.

Kyle and Jennifer met as always and turned toward the library. Chris materialized and smiled at them as if the meeting were purely accidental. "Hi guys."

Kyle had never been able to figure out where Chris hid between classes and was delighted by running into him on campus. "Hi Chris, where you going?"

Chris was happy with the lead. "I'm going to meet one of my computer science students for coffee. Actually, I would love it if you both would join us. But I have to warn you about this other guy." Chris had planned every word.

Kyle was definitely going and there was no way Jennifer would desert her. She thought she could help by distracting whomever Chris was meeting. She said "We're not scared of anybody, even you."

Chris told them about Bill. "He is such a nerd I don't think he has spoken to a girl since puberty. I'm a little concerned that he is afraid of girls. But maybe its the other way around. Maybe nobody talks to him because he is a nerd." Chris was observant and had noticed that both young women saw themselves as protectors of the weak.

Kyle was not to be deterred. "My roommate told you. We don't scare. You promised us coffee. Lead on."

Chris had also planned to lead them away from the library. He had chosen a site to meet Bill that would keep them far away. On the way he continued talking about Bill. "I'm glad you're coming. I think it will be great progress if Bill can even talk to you. His social skills need a tune up." Chris genuinely liked Bill and he had similar inclinations to his two companions. He wanted to include people that no one else wanted. He was so grateful to the Blacks for including him.

He wanted to say one more thing and this was the part with which he and his mirror had struggled all weekend. Just before they arrived he turned and faced Kyle. Jennifer wasn't sure what to do but Chris didn't hesitate and she could only listen. "Kyle, there is one thing that I have to say to you before we meet Bill. I know how close you two are so I'm sure that this won't embarrass Jennifer. I am a key participant in the project sponsored by Global Financial Transfer. I knew who you were a full year before you ever met me. I am here confessing how dumb I have been. It has taken me all this time to realize that you are not who you are supposed to be. I think you are terrific." He turned to Jennifer. "So are you. I just didn't start out with any prejudices about you."

There was an awkward silence. Chris wanted to run away. Both girls were at a loss for words. Finally, Chris said "let's go meet Bill."

Bill was waiting at the most obscure corner table. He wasn't sure why Chris was there with two women but there was no escape. Chris apologized and described the accidental meeting. Neither of the roommates had recovered enough to talk but their natural senses about others drew them to Bill. They instantly believed that Chris was right. This kid had never been out of his room all semester. Jennifer tried to fill the gap to give Kyle a chance to think. Chris went for coffee. Bill looked at the floor and earnestly but unsuccessfully tried to respond to Jennifer.

Chris had correctly understood Bill. Bill was totally overwhelmed by Jennifer even though he could not have had a more sympathetic ear. Jennifer was a woman he had only seen in magazines or in his fantasies. He could not even get himself to look at her. She was so gorgeous. Bill made Jennifer feel inadequate. Her strength was her ability to make people feel comfortable. She knew Bill would need a lot more time. She was grateful when Chris returned with the coffee.

While neither Kyle nor Jennifer had understood why Chris had made his sincere declaration before entering the coffee shop, they knew he meant well. When Chris directed his next few remarks at Bill, they understood he was using them to try to rescue Bill from becoming so reclusive that he would never have any friends. Chris had chosen the right women for the job. His declaration to Kyle was absolutely necessary. First, to tell her that he liked her. Second, to tell her that he knew who she really was. And third, he was about to use her to reach Bill.

"Bill, Kyle may not be able to hang out very long. Kyle is the daughter of John Manly who is providing the university with a huge grant. Her father is about to give a speech at the library." Bill looked up. Kyle looked up. Jennifer looked up. He had their attention. "The grant is being announced in about half an hour at the library so don't be upset if they don't stay very long. Mr. Manly himself is going to give a talk on the value of corporate sponsorship for university research. I'd go myself but there are sure to be a lot of protesters."

Kyle was remarkable as she began to recover. "Chris, you are full of amazing information. It is so like my father to assume that I knew. Since you are so well informed, what are his plans?"

"Kyle, I will tell you everything I know if you and Jennifer and Bill promise never to tell anyone where you got the information." Everyone nodded agreement. "Your father is booked overnight at the hotel school. At seven o'clock he has a reservation for six in the hotel school dining room. That was easy. The guest list was a lot more difficult to obtain. President Burrows and his wife, Dr. Roberts and his wife, and you."

Kyle was quiet. She looked first directly at Chris, then at Jennifer. "I need to call my mom" she said. Chris felt badly for her. He had meant to meet her on better terms and then he wanted to protect her. It looked like all he had done was upset her. In addition, he had exposed himself by showing his ability to pry into the private affairs of Mr. Manly.

"Kyle, before you call your mom, there is one other thing. Somehow a Jennifer Martin got added to the guest list. I kind of changed the reservation to show seven people instead of six. I made it look like the request came from President Burrows' office."

Kyle hesitated as she got up to go outside with her phone. She leaned over and kissed Chris on the cheek. "Thank you, Chris. I owe you. Trust me."

Jennifer had to cover for both Chris and Bill since now neither was capable of talking. Chris was trying to believe that all the planning and all the risk had been worth it. Perhaps Kyle really would be his friend. She had asked him to trust her. She had kissed him! Jennifer was helpless. Bill was the most shy young man she had ever met. She couldn't say anything to Chris because the only thing she could think of was that her roommate had a crush on him. She tried to talk about rock climbing. It didn't work. Finally she laughed out loud. They both looked up. She said "I guess I'm just totally helpless around men." Everyone laughed, even Bill.

Kyle returned. "Mom says that since we have such short notice its okay to make a repeat entrance in our power dresses. I booked a room at the hotel school so we can change. We will not change in my father's suite! Chris, I didn't mention your name, but my mom says that she is your friend for life. She will never tell anyone where I got my information. I can sense you think you may have been intrusive but I can only see that you have done me an act of great kindness. If you hadn't warned me, my father would have simply sent a limousine to fetch me. One of my father's bodyguards would have appeared in the dorm and I would have been hopelessly embarrassed. And I wouldn't have had my buddy Jennifer to protect me. I owe you."

As they got up to leave Chris had his back to Bill and momentarily to Kyle. He apologized softly to Jennifer and said he had only interfered out of concern for two very nice young women. Jennifer said "Don't worry Chris. You did us a really big favor and I have already figured out how we're going to get even." She was going to call her new friend, Marcia Black.

After the women left, Chris worked at engaging Bill in a conversation. He apologized again for showing up with the women. He described how they just happened to be in his class and how he accidently met them on the way to meet Bill. But weren't they great. Bill said he had never seen a real person who looked like a model. Chris agreed but indicated that it was the other one that he found so interesting.

Finally Bill focused and said "Do you think I could learn how to rock climb?"

Chris was brought to the judge's chambers by two guards. He was handcuffed and in leg irons. He wondered if this treatment was designed to show him his insignificance in the process. He was not a flight risk. He couldn't help Kyle unless his case went to court.

There was a different judge. Marianne Williams couldn't have been more different from Judge Branson. She smiled at Chris over her half glasses. She instructed the guards to remove the cuffs and wait outside. The guards told her they weren't allowed to leave a violent criminal uncuffed. She instructed them to secure the leg iron to the rail and that was that. The guards waited outside.

"Molly, off the record please. Mr. Krail, as you can see a new judge has been assigned to this case. I have been assigned since I was the only judge available who has time for what appears to be a long case. We are now off the record for a moment because I want to be clear with you. Molly, the transcriptionist, and I have worked together for years. We cannot be bought; we cannot be threatened. You will have a fair trial."

"Molly, on the record please. Judge Branson has recused himself from your trial. This means he believes he has a conflict of interest. I am Judge Williams, I will now be presiding. Molly, off the record please. Judge Branson clearly had no intention of removing himself until yesterday afternoon when he had a visitor. I didn't think he was the kind of judge that would ever remove himself. I will tell you about the visitor in a moment. Molly, back on the record please."

"Mr. Krail, I see from your previous transcripts that you have decided to defend yourself. While I have no doubt that you are an extremely bright and capable young man, and while I understand the argument that lawyers can't understand the technical aspects of your work, I am going to strongly recommend that you accept a lawyer."

"Molly, off the record please. We have numerous requests from lawyers who want the notoriety of defending you. You would do better than most of them. I am going to insist that you meet with and consider one lawyer. The lawyer I want to you meet is the mysterious visitor to Judge Branson. He was only there fifteen minutes, Judge Branson withdrew, and I estimate your chances of acquittal have doubled on the basis of this one action. This lawyer is worth your time."

"Molly, on the record please. I am going to insist that you meet with a lawyer named Anthony Dragoni. He will meet with you early this afternoon. If you agree to accept him as your lawyer, I will hold another bail hearing at 3PM today. I have already notified the prosecutor. While the choice is yours, I strongly urge you to accept either this lawyer or any other lawyer of your choosing. Molly, off the record please."

"Mr. Krail, I don't believe anything in your record justifies holding you with

no bail. The evidence against you is not that strong. I know you can probably bankrupt anyone you want with one of your computers. At the bail hearing I will ask you to promise not to steal. The most compelling evidence against you is that a child is missing but there is no evidence you are holding her against her will and she is over 18. Nevertheless the state will be adamant. I have decided in advance to set bail at $10 million to appease the state. If you accept Mr. Dragoni as your lawyer, he has already raised the money and you will leave with him today. But do not accept Mr. Dragoni just because he can make bail for you. Let me tell you a little more about him."

"Mr. Dragoni has a reputation of mythic proportions. The sources of his income are only whispered about. When I was a clerk 20 years ago and he was a legal aide lawyer I saw him defend an apparently homeless girl who had killed a man. He argued self defense. He was brilliant and he fought for her night and day. He was his own investigator, he spent his own money, and he hid the girl at his mother's home. He won. After that he disappeared and went into corporate law. Some say the girl's father found him and rewarded him. He rarely comes to court. Only on pro bono cases. He has never lost. He will spend a fortune defending someone he thinks is innocent. But he is believed to be dangerous. I never thought that myself. I found him polite. But any lawyer that can make Judge Branson back down in 10 minutes is a force to be reckoned with. He only wants 15 minutes to ask you to accept him. "

"Molly, on the record please. Mr. Krail, will you accept my recommendation to meet with attorney Dragoni at 1PM today to discuss being represented by that lawyer?"

"Yes, Your Honor." Chris was very skeptical but he really wanted to meet the man who was willing to risk $10 million for the dubious honor of defending him. He also wanted to thank him for the change in presiding judge.

Marcia Black caught Chris on his way to class Thursday. "I just wanted to be sure you are coming to dinner Sunday. I invited a couple of folks who I met at President Burrows' party. They are very nice and I think you'll find them really interesting. Promise me you'll be there."

There was no way for Chris to turn her down. Actually he loved dinner with just the two of them. The more he got to know them, the more he appreciated how lucky he was to have found them. Chris loved Marcia Black and tried never to say no when she wanted something. It never occurred to him that Jennifer Martin was behind this.

On Friday Kyle caught him after class. "I wanted to thank you again for Wednesday. There are so many things you did all at once. I really owe you. I'm blushing. I'm sorry. I don't know quite where to start. I called the hotel and left a message for my father saying he didn't need to send a car. I would meet him in the dining room. You should have seen our entrance. And Jennifer can really turn heads. And then we left before dessert. Just like that. We really took control."

Kyle continued "but there is more. I knew you were in the computer department and it never occurred to me that you would be involved with GFT. Don't ever be self conscious about knowing so much about me." She paused. She remembered how well this had gone in the mirror. "Most of all Chris, I want to thank you for taking the time to think about who I am, and for not just accepting what you knew." She touched his shoulder and was gone.

Jennifer was waiting outside. "So, did you tell him you'd be his slave for life?"

"You're a jerk, J, but I love you." Kyle hugged her roommate and said "So what had to wait until after my talk with Chris?"

"Well, uh, we have dinner plans for Sunday night." Jennifer smiled at her roommate. "We were invited to the home of Walter and Marcia Black. Can you make it? Chris will be there but Mrs. Black didn't tell him who else was coming."

★ ★ ★ ★ ★

Bill Marlin was indeed socially challenged. He had never formed any real friendships in high school or during his freshman year at Athené. Like Chris he had compensated but he lacked Chris' ability to interact with others. His choice in interests was a little different.

Bill would fantasize about rescuing others. His parents indulged him by buying him a police scanner. He took it apart. He loved the elegant electronics. He also loved what it could do. He could listen to others doing the things he wished he had the courage to do. By extension he taught himself other forms of electronic eavesdropping.

He did extremely well when he took a course to become an emergency medical technician but he didn't have the courage to volunteer to actually work as one. He wanted to really badly. If someone had encouraged him he might have done it. Bill was the quiet nerd that everyone forgot to include.

He was an extremely good student. His teachers were not surprised by his science grades but they couldn't imagine how anyone with no verbal skills could do so well in written English and even other languages. The kid was a sponge for information.

While Bill liked to learn everything, his one true joy was to vicariously participate in life by listening in on not only his police scanner, but also on a few scanners he had made from scratch and which were probably not strictly legal. Having a healthy dose of paranoia, he also taught himself about countersurveillance. It was certainly unnecessary but he got in the habit of sweeping his room weekly. You never know who might be listening.

When Bill arrived at Athené he requested a private dorm room. He told himself he was worried about his expensive electronic equipment but he was actually afraid that a roommate would not like him. He was very lonely. He spoke to no one unless it was necessary for his schoolwork.

He was comfortable asking directions from a librarian or questioning a teaching assistant to help understand an assignment. He dutifully called his parents once a week and told them everything was great. Bill was all alone.

Chris Krail was about as non-threatening as a human being could possibly be. When Chris asked him to have coffee one afternoon, it never occurred to Bill that Chris might have any problems. If he were ever going to talk to anyone he sensed he could trust Chris. The fact that two girls had showed up with Chris was clearly unplanned. That they talked to him was amazing. No girls had ever talked to him except when they needed to copy his homework. He had never been noticed by any of the popular girls and no one as pretty as Jennifer had ever before acknowledged that he was alive. She had talked to him more than she had talked to Chris, her instructor.

Bill had no idea how to react. He didn't know that Jennifer would always offer her charm to the person who needed it most. He didn't know that Jennifer wanted to leave room for Kyle to talk to Chris. He only knew that the most spectacular woman he had ever seen had actually talked to him.

When confused Bill always retreated to electronic eavesdropping. A college campus is not really exciting. The standard police channels never had anything more interesting than an illegally parked car. Bill also had the scanner he had built for himself. Nothing happened at all after his meeting with Chris and the girls. He stayed up all night listening. He had never done that before.

The next day he was exhausted and went home to take an afternoon nap. As he was falling asleep he had a vague recollection of the words "the subject and Jennifer are heading for the dorm…" but maybe he was just dreaming of Jennifer.

The thought persisted when he woke. He set up a voice-activated recorder on one of the more unusual channels. He would keep rotating the channels until he found it.

After Chris agreed to meet with the attorney he thought he would be taken back to his cell. There was yet another surprise.

"Molly, off the record please." Judge Williams looked at Chris. "There is someone here who wants to visit you. Early this morning I was approached by a woman who says she must talk to you. It is clear that she doesn't want to be seen. She asked if she could see you in my chambers rather than the visitor's room. I must say I was totally surprised."

Chris was frantic. Kyle and Jennifer should never take this chance. It was too dangerous. He couldn't imagine another woman who wanted to see him. He had told Marcia Black to stay as far away as possible in case he needed her as a witness.

Judge Williams continued. "Things get stranger yet. She said to say that if you would see her she would strip completely and wear nothing but one of my judicial robes so that you would know she wasn't wired. Further she says she will tell anyone who asks that she only came to the courthouse to see if there was any new information about her daughter. Will you talk to Kyle Manly's mother? Molly and I will have to remain in the room."

Chris was taken completely by surprise. Mary Manly was taking an incredible risk. On the positive side it meant that Kyle had made no attempt to contact her. It must be so hard on both of them. "Of course" he told the judge.

Molly brought Mary Manly into the room. Mary walked directly to Chris in her floor length black robe and sat down next to him. She put her hand on his. She looked at the judge and said "none of this is recorded in any way." The judge nodded.

"Chris." She looked into his eyes. "Chris." She paused. "Is my daughter okay?"

Chris ached for Kyle's mom. There was so much he wanted to tell her. It would have to wait. He was afraid. "She's fine, Mrs. Manly. Her only problem is she wants her mom."

"Where is she Chris?"

"She's not alone. You know she has to stay hidden until after the trial. We can't let her get hurt."

Mary Manly was afraid to say more. She shared Chris' primary motive of keeping her daughter safe. She knew that this young man loved Kyle. She knew this young man was willing to go to jail to protect her daughter.

"Chris, are you sure she's safe?"

"She said to tell you not to worry, she's her mother's daughter."

There was silence. Mary Manly gave up a single tear. Chris touched her face. They looked at each other. Mary Manly got up, thanked the judge and left with Molly.

Chris remembered his first dinner with the Blacks. This one was proving to be just as awkward. He had not thought much about who the guests would be. He had assumed it would be another professor and spouse. When he came home on Sunday afternoon there were no extra cars so he took his time and showered. He no longer called in advance or knocked. He was a member of the household. With no suspicions and no chance to practice in front of his mirror, he walked innocently into the kitchen. Kyle and Jennifer had been there all afternoon and were helping Mrs. Black cook.

Chris may have had no chance to prepare but the ever mothering Marcia

Black had been working on it for days. She loved Chris and wished that he would be happy. She had worried intensely because in over a year he had never brought a friend to dinner despite her repeated hints. When she had met Jennifer she was thrilled that two such nice young women were interested in Chris. She had met Jennifer and Kyle under the worst of circumstances but with her usual intuition was quick to recognize their sincerity. She secretly admired their bravado and their power entrance.

Jennifer had called her and the dinner was arranged. Mrs. Black felt a little guilty for not preparing Chris but the girls had asked that they surprise him.

Chris was ecstatic to be with Kyle in this environment but over and over again he couldn't think of anything to say. He kept wanting to tell her that he found her captivating. He thought that was too aggressive. To make it worse, Jennifer and Mrs. Black were clearly trying to leave Chris and Kyle alone together. Kyle thought she had pretty much laid it on the line and didn't dare go any further.

Finally Chris asked her if she knew anything about the content of the grant. He quickly learned that she did not. She did, however, have a good grasp for the extent of GFT and how it worked. She was reticent on the subject of her father. She only said that he was not as thoughtful as her mom and that he needed a lot of control.

"Chris, I owe you a favor. I don't have much to offer but I will tell you this. If you are working on the grant, my father knows all about you. I am sure he has had his security team check every electronic detail of your life and a private detective has probably done a background check."

Chris hoped his electronic fiction would hold. He was grateful to Kyle for confirming his suspicions but the tone was too much like a business meeting. He took a chance. "Kyle, what would your father do if I asked you out?"

Jennifer could not have regretted her timing more. She guessed quickly and retreating said "whenever you two are ready we're going to eat."

Kyle looked right at Chris and once again put her hand on his arm. "Sometimes I am afraid of my father. If you ask me out you too might have cause to be afraid. But I would like to get to know you better. Please ask me out Chris. Just make it look innocent. Sometimes I think he is watching." Chris thought about the surveillance he had spotted and for the first time wondered if it were possible that Kyle didn't know. He would try to spend time with her but he had better learn more about the people following her.

Dinner was different. Most of it had been cooked by the girls. Marcia Black was amused that they wanted to work this hard to please Chris. Dr. Black sat back and smiled to himself. "What a privilege" he thought "to participate in the lives of one's students." One of the best things he had ever done was to help Chris.

Chris didn't want the dinner conversation to be about him or GFT or Kyle. So he thought about Bill. He thought if there were ever a group to help a lonely student, they were sitting in front of him. He mentioned his desire to help one of his computer students and reviewed for the Blacks what had transpired and how wonderful the girls had been even though they had problems of their own. He also took advantage of the opportunity, mostly for the sake of Kyle, to talk about his own internal conflicts in interfering with the lives of others. While it was in the third person, Kyle smiled to herself. She knew he was apologizing to her.

They all wanted to help Bill and unfortunately their best conclusion involved a contrived solution. Jennifer pointed out that Bill had no chance in a group of four. Their best chance was a little one on one contact. Chris would try to befriend him alone. And Kyle had a suggestion.

"Chris, can you find out the longest walk he has to take between classes? If you can figure out his schedule, Jennifer and I will each accidently run into him alone. If each of us just acknowledges him by name and walks a little way with him as if we were going in that direction anyway, it might make a difference. Jennifer and I have come to the conclusion that for shy kids sometimes you can turn them around by just remembering their name. Kids like Bill think they are all alone. Don't worry, we're subtle. One contact this week and maybe the other next week."

Chris thought to himself "I am so pleased that she is kind and thoughtful."

There would be no trouble sorting out his schedule and mapping his movements. Chris would do it from Dr. Black's computer after dinner. It was agreed that Kyle would go first because everybody stuttered when they met her roommate.

The last thing that Chris said to Kyle when she finally left was "I'd like to see you soon."

After class the next afternoon, Kyle winked at Chris and whispered "mission accomplished."

On Friday, Kyle responded to his glance. "Jennifer's on deck for the alternate route on Monday, but only if the weather's good." She was rewarded with a smile.

"I have an idea, Kyle. I've been thinking about it all week." He blushed. "Or actually I been thinking about how to ask you out all week." He was rewarded with a smile. "Call your mom tonight. Tell her you are going to buy a new computer for yourself and another for your roommate this weekend. Ask her if she thinks you should get some advice from someone like me. Then we can spend all tomorrow afternoon wandering around the campus store and talking. And a second afternoon in your room setting up the wireless for your computers. What you think?"

"Perfect" from Kyle.

"I am sorry your first date with me will cost you several thousand dollars but I'm not cheap. I hope I'm worth it." Chris made Kyle laugh. He continued. "Do you really think we need to be this cautious?"

"Yes" Kyle said. "But only because I like you." She was gone.

Using Kyle before Jennifer to contact Bill had been a brilliant strategy. Bill was completely taken aback that Kyle had remembered his name. He had read about her father after the announcement and all he could think was "wow." It took him days to get over thinking that a rich kid, not to mention a girl had actually remembered his name and had walked a few hundred yards with him. He vowed that next time it happened he would be able to say something civilized, Maybe even "it's nice to see you." On the other hand it had never happened before and he was pretty sure it would never happen again.

So when he blundered into Jennifer and Jennifer said "it's nice to see you Bill," he was lost. She had taken his line. Finally he managed to return virtually the same words except he couldn't get her name out. Jennifer filled the space by saying complimentary things about Chris like "isn't he a great teacher?" This allowed Bill to mumble his agreement.

He could not pay attention in class for the rest of the day.

Jennifer was thrilled that Kyle had a date to spend the afternoon with Chris no matter how contrived or constrained. Chris tried to amuse Kyle by describing what a computer could do in thinly disguised suggestions of human relationships. He used words like connect, communicate, and respond. She new instantly that he was trying to connect, communicate, and respond with her. He was just staying within the careful framework of the date. It was agreed that Kyle would again call her mother with conversation that made it look like Chris was a helpful teacher. Kyle knew her mom and was sure the message would be understood. Especially after the foliage weekend roast where she had been forced to confess at brunch.

When it was time to part, Chris looked at her and told her he wished he believed this wasn't necessary.

Kyle looked at him for a minute, then took him by both shoulders. "I'm afraid." Then she vanished.

Chris wondered why Kyle was afraid. He thought their date had gone well. She had laughed at his jokes and encouraged him. He liked what he saw in her. He was dreaming his way across the campus when Bill came running up to him.

Bill was sweating and upset. Bill had trouble communicating in the best of circumstances. "Chris, I've been looking for you." He really looked like he was in trouble. "There's a problem. It's in my room."

Chris could see that Bill was frantic. He couldn't imagine what was going on. Bill was agitated and clearly wanted to say more but couldn't. Chris followed him back to the dorm. Chris tried to ask but Bill just kept saying "hurry!"

When they got to the room, Bill still had trouble verbalizing. Chris was in awe. There was electronic equipment everywhere. A basic computer seemed like an afterthought. Chris didn't even know what most of the equipment did. Finally Bill looked at Chris and said "Jennifer." Chris had no clue.

Bill brought a tape recorder and put it in front of Chris. "Jennifer" he repeated. Bill played the tape.

"X1,X2, you there?" "What do you need?" "Cover me for half an hour?" "No problem." "Jennifer is heading for the wall, I think the subject will meet her there."

"Roger." "Also, I checked out that contact they both had. Don't worry, William Marlin, III. Most interesting thing about him is that his father calls him Trip, short for Triple. He's a nothing. Purely coincidental."

Chris looked at Bill. He was sure by now that Kyle would be upset to learn she was being followed, even if they were supposed to be bodyguards. "Bill, they sure got you wrong. You are something special. How did you put this together?"

With encouragement Bill was able to tell him about the voice-activated recorder, about his scanning, how he thought that once before he had heard Jennifer's name, and also that the frequency he was monitoring had no legitimate use.

"Wow, Bill. I feel so badly for the girls. We need to tell them but maybe it's just her father trying to protect her." By now he realized that if even this were true, Kyle would be unhappy. Where did they get off checking out the harmless contact with Bill Marlin? It was more like a well-organized police surveillance.

Bill said "it gets worse."

"How could it?"

"Listen to this!" The tape went back on and there was a brief conversation noting that Jennifer and the subject had been trying on wigs again. "How could they know that?" Bill asked.

Chris looked at Bill who was still completely agitated. "Bill, you might turn out to be the best friend these girls ever had. Can I use your computer?"

Chris accessed his Kyle Manly file and looked over his notes on the surveillance. He had been wrong to dismiss it as benign. When he got to his lab he would have to look for who was funding this operation. Next he accessed the university architectural files.

Before he left, he added. "Bill I can't thank you enough. This is going to really upset them but I think it would be best if we brought them here to listen for themselves. I will have them here in the next two hours. Will you be okay here 'til I get back?" Chris always knew exactly where to find Kyle.

It was too important to wait for class. Chris found them sitting on the wall by the library. He leaned forward and said softly. "I have some really distressing news. Kyle you were so right to be afraid. I want you both to go to the South Campus student recreation building. You need to go now. Go to the back of the cafeteria. Take the stairs down to the second subbasement. There is a tunnel connecting the buildings. Actually there are four tunnels. Figure out how to get to dorm number four. Back up the stairs to the basement. Then the elevator. You're going to Bill's room. It's 4404. I'll meet you there. We've got a problem. We will have to take a chance."

Then he took Kyle by both shoulders and looked at her. "You were right to be afraid, but it will all turn out OK."

An hour later they were all assembled in Bill's room. Kyle was sitting on the bed and crying. Chris was holding her. Jennifer had cornered the still agitated Bill and was telling him over and over how grateful they were for his friendship. It took Chris and Jennifer over half an hour to calm their counterparts.

Chris finally knew he had to take charge. "Okay everybody. Listen. We know who they are. We can monitor their conversations. Or we can report them to the campus police. We have a lot of options.

Kyle spoke. "Forget it. Leave them alone. This is my father's idea of bodyguards. He is always afraid someone will hold me for ransom. If we do anything we need to make them feel really secure. If they get suspicious my father will just add more guards."

Bill finally had a chance to rescue someone. "When Chris goes to help you install your computer, I'll go along to help. I'll sweep your room for electronic surveillance and I can probably defeat any device without actually removing it." It was the longest speech Bill had ever given.

Jennifer despite everything knew he still needed encouragement. "That would be wonderful, Bill. I don't know what we would do without you."

Dr. Black was by nature sympathetic to his students. He was philosophically an old-time liberal academic. Unlike Dr. Roberts he did not welcome corporate money on campus. He believed in unrestricted gifts but he didn't believe there should ever be a quid pro quo. He was privately distressed about the GFT grant. He thought it gave a private corporation too much say in the university's activity. He believed in research for the sake of research. He did not like goal-oriented research sponsored by a corporation. Publicly he said it was a commentary on the times. He tried to sound neutral.

Privately at dinner he told his wife and his young friend Chris how he really felt. These were three people who were beginning to share their secrets. Chris knew the one secret he would always have to hide was his financial fiction. But Dr. Black's discussion led exactly where Chris was afraid to take his two treasured friends.

"I can't get over how much I like that young Kyle Manly. Marcia has always had the best instincts about people. I have to say I was appalled to be summoned to the Burrows' black tie dinner where he fawned over how wonderful it was that she chose to attend our university. But he was right about one thing. We are lucky to have her. Not for the reasons he thinks."

"And I am furious about what happened today. A member of our university board of trustees appeared in my office and asked if I would personally serve as Kyle's advisor. Don't get me wrong, Chris, I would be thrilled if Kyle wants me as her advisor. It was the way I was asked. These decisions belong to Kyle! And no one should have that kind of influence with the board."

Chris's head spun with ideas. Perhaps he had found a way to see Kyle on a regular basis with a minimum of risk. "Dr. Black, if you were her advisor, would you invite her here for dinner again?"

Marcia Black knew him well enough to laugh at him. "Chris, she can come here every day if you want her. Walter, I think our friend is in love." Chris blushed.

When Chris regained his composure he asked a leading question. "If Kyle wanted to thank you for something or wanted to ask you for a favor and she invited you two to dinner, would you go?"

Chris entered the official visitors room. All the hardware was removed. He was instructed to sit at a table in the center of the room. Mr. Dragoni entered. He was tall and good looking. He wore a simple but expensive suit. He smiled at Chris, shook hands, and sat opposite him.

"Chris, I'm Tony Dragoni. I'd like to be your attorney and I am very grateful that you were willing to consider me. There are a few simple reasons I think I could help you. First, I'll give you a secure office with a computer. Second, I am sure that I can force John Manly to take the stand. If you know as many

secrets as I do we will be able to make him perjure himself even if he is a hostile witness. And third, your grandparents and I are old friends."

Chris looked at him and hesitated. He liked the attorney's direct manner. Any attorney could have guessed he needed a computer, but what did he know about John Manly. This room was clearly not the place to discuss any secrets. And this line about his grandparents - what did he know? Chris sensed that this lawyer knew a lot more than he was saying. How could this man be connected to him in any way? Then it occurred to him that he might have it backwards. Perhaps the attorney hated John Manly. He dropped that thought and began to hope that somehow his friends had sent this attorney.

Finally, he asked Mr. Dragoni. "How much will you charge?"

Tony Dragoni looked right at Chris and wondered about the question. Chris didn't want to know how much the trial was going to cost. He was looking for verification that a complete stranger was acting in good faith. He hoped they didn't have any illegal listening devices in the room. He leaned forward and spoke softly "An organization named mom has asked me to accept you as a client. It is fairly well known that I only act as a trial attorney in pro bono cases."

Chris didn't have a clue where this lawyer had come from. But he now fully understood the meaning of an offer he couldn't refuse. Three hours later he was put in a bullet proof vest and led by his new attorney and four bodyguards to a waiting bulletproof limousine.

The next Saturday afternoon Chris borrowed the Black's car and appeared at the girls' dorm room with boxes of computer equipment. He brought Bill who also had a box full of electronic gear.

Bill was full of admiration for Chris who was able to communicate multiple meanings with his words. While explaining his straightforward installation of a computer network and the two new computers, he was also a teacher. He made explanations logical. But he was also trying to connect with his girl. He was often rewarded with a subtle smile.

Meanwhile Bill swept the room for bugs. He found two sophisticated pickups in the reading lamps that were built into the wall above the beds. Clearly each microphone could listen individually or both together. Each had a built in transmitter. There was no way to tell from where they were listening.

Always good on paper, Bill wrote a note. "Do you want me to kill it? The other choice is to leave it and provide it with a little misinformation. I vote for misinformation. If Kyle wants them to feel secure, a dead bug will only wake them up."

Kyle wrote back. "Any cameras?"

Bill scribbled "absolutely not."

Kyle and Jennifer looked knowingly at each other. Jennifer wrote "are you 100% sure there are no cameras?

"Yes!" he wrote. The girls looked at each other, grabbed Bill and kissed him on both cheeks at the same time. Fortunately, Bill did not provide the bugs with a single word. Unfortunately, the girls realized they might have gone too far and could not say they were sorry. They both scribbled him notes saying how grateful they were.

Kyle looked and Jennifer and they turned on Chris. They kissed him on the cheeks. "Thanks Chris. What would we do without you?"

After they were all outside a decision was made to fool the bugs rather than destroy them. Bill clearly wasn't going to speak and kept nodding his head. Finally he wrote a note that said "when you get back from Christmas vacation I'll have a solution."

Chris was trying to flirt with Kyle using only his eyes. This gave Jennifer a chance to speak softly to Bill. "We're really sorry, Bill. We didn't mean to embarrass you. Sometimes we just get a little carried away when we're happy. Next time I'll ask first. I promise."

Kyle and Jennifer took the Blacks out to dinner. Kyle chose the hotel school dining room again. Dr. Black agreed to be the advisor for both of them. She was sure that the event would get back to her father. He would approve. That would be convenient for Kyle.

"My father wants me to go to law school. Is there such a thing as legal anthropology?" Kyle actually was interested in the law. She thought her interest in anthropology was related to a secondary interest in how the law held society together.

"Actually, not only does legal anthropology exist Kyle, but we're holding a special adult education event this summer. It's call 'Society and the Legal System.' You might really like it. You would have to be here for the whole month of July. If you're interested I'll make sure your application gets accepted.

"You really didn't have to take us to dinner, dear." Marcia Black would have far preferred staying home.

Kyle leaned forward, drawing her three guests toward her. In a low voice she said. "This is a public show for the goons from Global. This way if we were to socialize together it would look natural. For instance, we could get invited to dinner at the Blacks without raising my father's suspicions. Chris thought it up, he's brilliant."

Marcia immediately saw all the advantages. "Both of you should always consider yourself part of our family. We make a big deal out of dinner on Sunday. I would like it if you would come as often as you possibly can."

Meanwhile, Bill and Chris were having dinner alone at the Black's house. The girls had told Chris how Bill had immediately withdrawn when they kissed him. Chris was concerned. He said that he would work on Bill while they were at dinner with the Blacks.

Even though it was late in the fall, Chris made hamburgers on the gas grill. He told Bill he secretly wanted to take an outdoor cooking class in the hotel school. His goal was to be a certified grillmeister so he could impress Kyle. "Sorry, Bill, but I'm trying out my act on you."

Bill had not been himself since finding the surveillance on the girls. Chris knew he had to reach Bill as soon as possible. He had seen similar students go home at Christmas and never come back. He did what he thought best. With the exception of his financial and family fictions, he told Bill about himself.

Chris mostly talked about the Blacks. After more than two years of frightening loneliness, Walter and Marcia Black had offered him unquestioning friendship. They had given him a job and a place to live. They gave him the courage to relate to other students. Chris told Bill that it was only in his senior year when he began teaching that he realized he had a talent and could communicate with others.

It was incredibly hard to draw Bill out at all. So he talked about his work in computers. He talked about his current work in security algorithms. The technical aspects fascinated Bill who always found any kind of electronics much easier to talk about than people.

Chris offered him something. "You have taught me that without looking at the physical elements like wiring, computer security is useless. Would you like to work with me on trying to create computer devices that sweep themselves for electronic listening devices as well as the traditional searches for intruders in the software."

Bill rose to the occasion. "I would love to Chris. I have been thinking for a long time that what I really need is a computer expert to improve some of the tools that I have built. The stuff I build is clever but good computer programming would really speed them up and make them a lot more useful."

"I have never told anyone except my brother Jason what I really want to work on in the field of computer sciences. After I graduate I will earn my living in computer security. But I want to work on the application of computer assistance to physically and mentally compromised children."

"I'm a whiz at wiring and servo devices." Bill added "maybe I could help you."

Bill had gone when the Blacks returned. Chris was grinning when he realized that all four had come back to the house for coffee. "I think I finally reached Bill a little bit, but I had to give him everything I had."

"That's the way it is" Kyle looked directly at him. "If you want to reach someone you have to be willing to take some risk."

"Speaking of risk, Chris, what would you say if I told you I agreed to be the faculty advisor for the two prettiest freshmen on campus?"

Christmas vacation and semester break were approaching which meant final exams. Chris, who only wanted to spend all his time accidently meeting Kyle was very busy. He was teaching anthropology, teaching computer science, working night and day on his own security research, trying to support his new friend Bill, and constantly talking to his mirror which he had named Kyle.

He had been requested by Dr. Roberts, his departmental chairman, to penetrate the security at Global Financial Transfer. He had been instructed to steal $100,000 as long as it was after the official announcement. On the evening after Mr. Manly's speech he was all set but had second thoughts.

It would be so easy exploiting the weaknesses that had been built into the system to accommodate Mr. Manly's ego and Mr. Manly's personal financial needs.

Chris had a standard. He would learn nothing useful by exploiting what he called the Manly paradox. He should save that one. Perhaps someday it might help Kyle. And besides, somebody at GFT might notice and fix the problem. The most honest approach was to find a non personal leak in the GFT security. He would hopefully find something that could be used in his doctorate thesis. It was better not to cheat and really look at the GFT problem without doing it through his knowledge of the family.

Instead, he created a program to probe the GFT defenses. Dr. Roberts should never have shared his personal password. Chris soon realized that even though it was changed regularly, it was changed on an easy mathematical progression. He used this knowledge to use Dr. Robert's computer as a link to every computer in the department. Since he was in on Roberts' password, he hoped that even if they realized that all probes were only being funnelled through different computers, all roads would lead to Roberts. He could have tried to route the probe through other universities but felt that was outside the rules he had been given. All probes could be traced back to Athené.

He tried a number of standard computer security probes. He started with SATAN (System Administrator Tool for Analyzing Networks). It had been developed and distributed free in the mid-1990's. It had caused a controversy. Did it help a system administrator look for weaknesses in his/her own system, or did it create an opportunity for network pirates? What he liked about SATAN, besides its name, was that it had become such a standard, that every system had automatic defenses in place. Chris wanted to see the defenses in action.

The next thing he did was look at the automatic clocks built into the system. And although quite a different thing, he analyzed the system for its clock speed. Then he had a long technical discussion with Bill about clock speed and whether it could be exploited. After some effort and a great deal of luck he was able to get his personal computer accepted by the system as just another processor on the main GFT system.

At this point he could have taken the money but there was a high risk of getting caught. They wouldn't know how it was taken but the theft would be visible. His goal was not only not to be caught as an individual but he wanted no one to even realize that the money had been taken. Rounding errors were too obvious. That one had even been done in a Superman movie.

Finally he decided to take a chance and actually, synchronizing with the clock and the clock speed at GFT, programmed his computer to take the money during the infintessimally small time interval when the accounting program rectified each day's results and the time the program was set up for the next day. He wasn't certain he could even measure the interval but he new it existed and it was all a matter of getting the GFT mainframe to steal its own money during this illusory gap.

Then there was the issue of where to hide the money. $80,000 would be moved into Dr. Roberts retirement account. Chris was impressed by how much Dr. Roberts had been able to put away for retirement but he figured when his boss got a statement showing an extra $80,000 received from GFT, he would know the theft had been carried out.

Chris would have put it all in the Roberts account if it wasn't for his intellectual curiosity. GFT had just begun to distribute what would become a revolution both in the ATM (automatic teller machine) industry, and in the history of money.

GFT had begun a campaign to replace cash with laser-based debit cards. Unlike a credit card, the consumer using a debit card puts the money up front and as it is spent it is debited on the spot. In the GFT version, the consumer gives up his/her money when he/she acquires the card. GFT kept the money until it was actually used in a retail sale. To use the new CASHcard ®, a consumer had to be registered with a digital photo at the bank (or chain of banks) from which he/she withdrew the money. If, for instance, one took a $1000 card, the information along with an embedded digital photo of the user was produced on a wallet-sized laser card. Then one could use the card wherever there was an appropriate laser reader. Conveniently these readers were produced by a subsidiary of GFT.

A supposed advantage of these cards was that whenever you used the card your picture appeared on the laser reader. Unlike real cash the owner could be identified at the time the money was used. On the other hand, you were allowed to sign a waiver, and get the card without a picture. If you elected not to use your picture, you could not take more than $10,000 in a single transaction. There was another supposed advantage. Because of GFT's international reach there was no exchange charge if you traveled out of the country. GFT made its money up front earning interest on the money during the interval between the time the card was created and the time the money was actually used.

This is how Chris disposed of the other $20,000. The local college bank was on an ATM network with GFT. Chris sent the bank his own digital picture. He authorized 20 cards each for $1000. Ten had his picture and ten were untraceable. At 1am he wandered into the bank lobby, punched a few keys, and walked out with $20,000. He then returned to his lab and erased his digital picture from the banks memory. He sealed the cards in an envelope and asked Dr. Black to put them in a safe deposit box.

All this happened just before Christmas vacation. Chris was sure he would receive complements from Dr. Roberts at the beginning of January when his boss received his monthly financial statements.

Chris knew he would be lonely over the holidays. The Blacks were going to visit their children. Bill was going to visit his parents. Kyle was going to the Cayman Islands to one of her family homes for the whole two weeks. Jennifer was going to Gotham and then flying to the Cayman's to spend her second week with Kyle. Chris had no pressing projects so he would just try to catch up with all the work he had to do in two departments. Maybe he would read a book.

Kyle flew by private jet directly to the Cayman's. She had to admit it was convenient. She was looking forward to seeing her mom. Her father would only be there the first week. Then Jennifer would join her. Jennifer's mom seemed to have plans and had apologized profusely.

Kyle hoped maybe she could begin relating to her father as an adult. She wanted to work at her relationship with her father for a lot of reasons. The most important was that she was a nice human being and wanted to relate to him. There were other reasons.

She was the second largest stockholder in GFT. She would soon have full control of her money. Someday she wanted control over her own security. She wanted him to respect her privacy. She didn't want him intruding into the lives of all her acquaintances.

The holidays were busy and she didn't really get to talk to him until just before he left. The evening before his departure only the three Manly's were at dinner. Her father took control.

"I am pleased with your progress at Athené. It was a good choice and they are doing fine work for us in their computer division. I am somewhat disappointed with your choice of anthropology but as long as you go to law school I don't care. Dr. Black is apparently highly regarded in his field and he is now your advisor. I have also arranged for you to meet Dr. Harris, the head of the law school. He will make an appointment with you as soon as you return. He teaches corporate law which you will need. You may choose another law school if you want but I am satisfied with Athené.

"While I think it is important to have Dr. Black as a reference, there is one drawback. I do not want you to spend so much time in the company of Chris Krail."

"WHAT?" interrupted his daughter.

"Sit back down. He's a nobody. He's inappropriate for you! He is not up to our standards. Not to mention that the money he receives from his grandparents seems to have an unsavory origin." I understand that he is your instructor but I want you to tell Dr. Black that the young man should move out. We will of course pay Dr. Black whatever the going rate is for his apartment." John Manly would never have understood that there was no rent. "Otherwise I approve of you dining with the Blacks on a regular basis."

Kyle was hot. She was on her feet. She knew the need to contain herself. She would never abandon Chris and certainly not because he was "inappropriate" – whatever that meant. What was this nonsense about grandparents? Chris didn't have any!

"Father, you will have to make a choice. I will not let you interfere with the happiness of others. The Blacks depend on Chris. He shovels their walk, he cuts their grass. He helps Mrs. Black with her shopping. These people are entitled to their lives. Do you want me to tell all the other students to go home until I graduate? Chris Krail has been one of my instructors. He might be the best teacher I ever had. He has never asked for anything from anyone. He's bright and he works and he helps his students."

"Make a choice, father. Stop interfering in the lives of innocent people or find yourself another daughter." She couldn't believe she had said that. She turned and went to her bedroom.

A couple of days before the end of vacation Bill appeared in Chris' lab. "Can I talk to you?

Chris offered lunch and they went to the bagel joint. "Chris, I have decided that I may be paranoid but I want to sweep the Black's home. Can you get me in there?"

At first his instinct was to dismiss Bill's concerns. Then Chris thought if Bill is reaching out, I have to encourage him. Maybe this is progress. "Sure, Bill, anytime you want. The Blacks are away for another four days. Why don't you come by for dinner tomorrow?"

The upsetting thing was that not only was there an audio pickup in the Black's dining room but it looked like it had just been installed. Bill took Chris outside. "Look Chris, I spent my whole vacation figuring out to deal with the bug in the girls' room. That solution is complicated because we don't have a lot of control. Kyle is right. Too much interference will make that situation worse. Here we have good control. Do you think the Black's will accept my suggestions?"

"Absolutely. They trust me and I trust you."

"I'm going to go back in and dismantle it. Then you and I are going to ask the Black's to be the test site for the Bill Marlin security theory. Basically, the intent is clear. Somebody wants to know what they say to their guests. I'm going to fix the bug so that anyone who tries to check why it suddenly stopped working will get an electric shock. I am a great believer in behavior modification."

"Bill, I think that's great and maybe it's time you met Dr. and Mrs. Black. I do have a serious question to ask you. You know we're friends and now we've worked together on a couple of things. Whether you know it or not, you were an immense help to me on a computer project I was doing before Christmas. So do know that when I ask you this, it is because I like you. Did you ever notice that whenever its more than just the two of us, you are terribly shy?"

"I know Chris. I just never had a friend before."

"I want you to do me a favor, Bill. I know you will find it hard. You know

I am nuts about Kyle. I have no business being interested in her. She's rich. She's beautiful. She could have anything she wants. I think she only likes me because I teach her anthropology course. But I need to spend some time talking to her. If I invited Kyle and Jennifer for coffee, do you think you could accidently wander in and distract Jennifer?"

"Jen-Jennifer? How can I help, Chris? I can't even look at her."

"I've noticed that you are terrific when you deal with the mysteries of electronics. How about if I set it up and you wander in and join us. You just happen to have the equipment they need to fool the bug in their room. We can't go back in there. Whatever you made, they are going to have to install by themselves. Also, if you would write a little instruction manual, you could just read it to Jennifer. What do you think?"

"Chris, you and Jennifer and Kyle are the only people who have made any effort to be nice to me since I started college. I'll try really hard. Somehow you'll have to get Jennifer to bring a relatively empty backpack. There is a lot of stuff. How long do I have to get ready?"

"One day next week. I'll let you know after they get back."

When Kyle awoke the next morning she was afraid to get out of bed. Her mother knocked and entered. "Your father left early. Get dressed. We'll take a walk on the beach." Then Mary Manly leaned forward and with a smile kissed her. "And I love my wonderful daughter."

They sat in the sand near the breaking surf. Mary Manly knew how upset Kyle must be. "You were wonderful last night. I have never seen your father back down before. After you left he said that he was glad you were tough. He said you were probably right. He only worries because Chris works on the GFT grant and he is always afraid someone will kidnap you for money. There is a fair chance Chris knows how much money you have. He said he will leave Chris alone but if anything happens to you he'll know where to look." She smiled and kissed her daughter again. "But you did it. He backed down. And more importantly, he doesn't have a clue that you are infatuated with Chris."

"Mom, Chris' major problem is that he doesn't know how much I like him. He probably knows better than I do how much I'm worth. He confessed that he had studied us before he knew I would be in his class. I almost started crying when he told me that I was far too nice to be Kyle Manly. He has used his knowledge of GFT to protect me. You remember how he inserted Jennifer into the dinner when father showed up without telling me."

"Actually, Kyle, you never quite told me that. You have been mysteriously indirect on the phone lately. I had no trouble understanding what you wanted to tell me but why are you being so obtuse."

"Father has his bodyguards following me. Jennifer and I call them the goons of Global. Remember when Chris came to set up my computer. He brought along this incredibly shy electronics freak who is into surveillance. He had all kind of gizmo's and unfortunately our room is bugged. And I'm even afraid to call you from a cell phone. Maybe every time I tell you I love you, twelve goons analyze it."

"Mom, will you come and visit me this spring. There is so much I want to show you. I want you to meet Chris. I want you to meet the Blacks. I want you to help me get away from the goons. But most of all I miss you."

As soon as Chris was in the limousine his new lawyer made him more comfortable. "Chris, I know how hard it is for you to trust strangers. I won't be able to prove my legitimacy to you until tomorrow night at dinner. I want to apologize for taking so long to get you out of jail. I had to remove Judge Branson and I had to do some serious research to do that. All I did was walk *into his office and describe his financial relationship to John Manly in less than glowing terms. We are very lucky with Judge Williams. She cannot be influenced. People have tried before."*

"I also know that you don't need to steal from Global Financial Transfer. Kyle would give you every penny she has if she thought it would make you happy. This trial is not about money or kidnapping. This trial is about a rich arrogant father who thinks he can manipulate the world. He sees you as a threat not only to his daughter but for reasons I can't understand you seem to be a direct threat to him. I hate to say it but I don't think he would go through this much trouble if it was just about Kyle."

Jennifer and Kyle returned to Athené in the private jet. They took a taxi directly to the home of Walter and Marcia Black. It was Sunday afternoon. They had called ahead from the plane and had received an enthusiastic invitation.

Mrs. Black read the look in their eyes as they entered. She hugged them both and calmed their fears. "Chris had his friend Bill look our house over. It's clean. No one can hear us."

"Where's Chris?"

"I think he's taking a nap. We weren't expecting you quite so early."

"Is there any way to get into his apartment without using the outside entrance?"

Marcia Black looked at Kyle and felt sorry for this poor child who so often had to pretend that she was someone else. "If you are half as desperate as you look, you can get there through the attic. I don't think anyone has been up there in 15 years." She called her husband. "Walter, Kyle wants to explore our attic. Have you got a flashlight?"

There was a pulldown stairway in the upstairs hallway. Dr. Black helped Kyle up. "Be really careful" he warned. "There is no stairway into the apartment, just a trap door. You will have to jump or get Chris to catch you. You sure you don't want us to call over there?" And as an afterthought said "Kyle, before you go can you see an old shotgun lying there. I used to hunt ducks as a youngster, but I think I ought to get rid of that gun before somebody gets hurt."

Chris awoke as Kyle crashed into his hallway. He tried to help her up but she pulled him down to the floor next to her. She clung to him and cried endlessly.

After half an hour she finally spoke. "Are you happy to see me? I promise not to cry every time I see you if you just tell me you missed me."

At first Chris was baffled. He loved holding her but this was the second time she had cried in his arms and he suspected he knew the cause, especially after her entrance. "I missed you, Kyle. I thought about you constantly. I was afraid to call. Bill says it is real hard to tell if an overseas call is being tapped. I was so happy when I heard you were coming for dinner. I missed you so badly. How did it go at home?"

"Well" Kyle smiled at him without letting him go "my mom still loves me." Someday, she thought, he'll have the courage to kiss me.

Kyle returned the way she came. Chris went by the door.

Jennifer and Kyle felt accepted and comfortable. Kyle knew that everyone in the room knew her secrets but liked her for who she really was. She had an announcement. "My mom is coming for two weeks before spring break and that means she'll be here for two or three weekends. Can she come to Sunday dinner?" And without waiting for the obvious answer she continued. "Jennifer's mom will be here for a long weekend in the middle."

Chris had prepared the girls for their next accidental meeting with Bill. Jennifer and Kyle were more interested in the problem of making Bill comfortable then they were in the problem of the bug in their room. It went better than they hoped. Not because of them. But because Bill worked at it and was determined to be as nice to the girls as they were to him.

Jennifer listened attentively for almost as hour as Bill went over the equipment and the instruction manual he had written. The basic plan was simple. The bug always had to choose between the two listening devices. It had been set up to always give preference to the bug closer to Kyle. Bill proposed taping the background noises in their dorm room. Then setting up a continuous tape of background noises. Whenever the girls wanted privacy they would just throw a switch. Both bugs would think the other one was the input source and transmit phony background noises for as long as the girls wanted. The 48 hour tape would run continuously (online or off) so the background would be appropriate no matter what time of day or night.

Bill was still concerned. He told Jennifer just to tape their room for 48 hours. Then Bill would take the tape and remove any voices or anything he felt wasn't part of the background. They could then start using the tape to wash their conversations and their phone calls. Bill's big concern was that if they used this trick too often, the listener would feel more information was needed and yet another bug might be put in place.

He had a lot of pride in his work and every piece of equipment was custom made. He actually made it easy for the girls by the simplest of connectors. While there was a large "black box" they girls would only have to make a single connection. There was also a warning light should the tape break or another malfunction occur.

Jennifer hardly said a word. She just indicated that she understood the directions. She was overwhelmed and thought that perhaps a written thank you note would be easier for Bill to handle.

Meanwhile Chris presented Kyle with a present. "This is a copy of a software program called Pretty Good Privacy. I set your computer up so you can send email to anyone on campus. That includes me. But I was concerned that if you ever needed me urgently it is possible to eavesdrop on basic email. This program will literally give us Pretty Good Privacy."

PGP had been written by a professor at MIT. It allowed electronic messages to be encrypted. It was written at a time when the government was proposing a device called the clipper chip which would allow authorized electronic eavesdropping on anyone. The government was so concerned that the average citizen would be able to have email privacy that they declared this program a munition. That made its export illegal as a risk to national security. The government also harassed the author of the program. Chris thought Kyle would have no problem with it.

"This program has great advantages. This extra disk is called my public key. If you want to write to me, you encrypt the message with my public key. Since I'm the only one with my private key I will be the only one who can read your message. On the other hand if I send you a message and encrypt it with my private key, my public key will give no doubt about its authenticity. You will know the message came from me. But you will need my public key to read it. When you get home, use the program to make private and public keys for yourself so I can have a copy of your public key. This will give us the best overall security for two way messages. I'm sorry I can't set it up for you but I don't think I should make any extra trips to your room. You'll do fine. If you have any doubts just bring the computer to class and I will fix it for you."

By the time they got back to their room the girls were convinced they were being brainwashed by two technofreaks. They were flattered by the concern. Jennifer told Kyle she thought she would send a written thank you note to Bill. Kyle had a better idea for Chris.

When Chris checked his email that night he smiled and used his private key. "Chris, how do I begin to thank you. One thing that I learned from Bill is sometimes it is easier to write than to speak. You have given me the means to connect, communicate, and respond. I will save the electronic version for the times I can't see you in person. I'd rather spend my time with you even if I never know what to say. Are you sure you're the only one who can read this?"

Kyle was truly afraid. And this time her reason to be afraid was very concrete. Kyle had not talked to anyone she knew in almost a week. Chris thought that by hiding she would be safe. She thought that by going into hiding she was helping Chris. She had chosen Chris over her father.

Kyle wanted her mom. The hardest part was that she had agreed to hide because somehow she knew it was not just Chris. Her mom could also get hurt. Mary Manly would protect her daughter at all costs. She wanted to believe that by hiding she would make it easier for her mom. And Kyle needed her mom!

They had not had very long to plan. Chris had returned from his mysterious trip in the middle of the night. His instructions were clear. Three different rendezvous on three different days in three different cities. All she had to do was make one of them. Travel only by bus or train; spend only real untraceable cash. Don't talk to anyone. She had already missed the first opportunity. She had been on time and then fled because she was afraid.

And the red wig. She was so tired of the wig. But Chris had said there were no pictures of her in the wig. All she had to do was to identify a van with the logo 'Bob's Electronic Service and Testing,' BEST for short. Get in the passenger seat and tell the driver her name was Bob. He would answer his name was Kyle before he started the engine. Trust him. Go with him.

Kyle had tried to be cool. She always rode a bus or train overnight so that she wouldn't have to worry about where she slept. Kyle knew every one of the few real friends that Chris had. He had even told her his darkest secret, not even the Blacks knew. Where had he found a man named Bob to whom he would trust the one person who truly mattered to him? Kyle started crying again. I can't do this she thought. Keep moving. Look inconspicuous.

In fifteen minutes she would get in the van. The last thing Chris had said was "Don't be afraid. No one would harm an angel like you." Then he had touched her cheek with his hand and had lifted her out through the bathroom window.

The second semester quickly settled into a routine. Chris and Kyle looked forward to every Sunday. Jennifer got to be a good cook. Kyle cleaned the attic, or so she said. No one else ever went up there.

Chris and Kyle would lay on his bed side by side and talk before they joined the Blacks and Jennifer for dinner. They were both amazed at how easy it was to become friends. He told her about Jason and his first computer. About the death of his parents right after his acceptance at Athené and how he almost decided to give up. He told her how lonely he had been before the Blacks found him.

Kyle told Chris how hard it had been to grow up as the trophy daughter of a powerful man who knew all the answers. She told him how much she loved her mom and how she thought that maybe the best thing about becoming an adult was that she and her mom could become buddies.

He was surprised by her laughter when he told her about his fictional grandparents. "What's so funny about my grandparents? I just did it so nobody could find out that before the Blacks I didn't even have a place to live. I did it to amuse myself and see if I could make something in my imagination into a reality that other people would believe."

"Oh they believe it all right" Kyle told him about how her father had investigated his grandparents. "My dad believes it but he thinks there is something undesirable about their source of income."

"Well" now Chris was amused "I kind of implied that my grandfather was a retired enforcer for an organized crime family in Europe. The idea was no one would get too close when they checked him out. It let me be very vague about his exact address."

"You are wonderful" Kyle glowed. Kyle told him how she was so happy that he had taken the time to notice that she cared. She was thrilled to be surrounded by friends who treated her like everyone else.

Chris told Kyle how he had investigated GFT for his security project and the Manly family as a role model for wealthy grandparents and that he was sorry he had invaded her privacy. He even told her that he had stolen to stay in school and how he had actually begun to pay it back. She looked at him and he was again amazed. She didn't offer money. He knew he could ask her for it but it was obvious that what interested her was his feelings. He was very touched.

Kyle told him how much she loved Jennifer and how she had struggled with the problem of her wealth. She had barely spent anything until she asked for a jet to buy Jennifer a dress. Chris told her he had found the joint checking account. She sat up and said "I can't believe my father never said anything about it. He must have seen it."

They talked, they made each other laugh, and finally on the second Sunday in February, Chris said he had spent weeks thinking about what to give her as a Valentine and he kissed her for the first time. On that same Sunday, Jennifer finally had to call Chris' phone. "So, you guys kinda missed dinner. It's getting late. I would be really afraid for both of you if we don't have a plan. Do you want me to stay over with the Blacks?"

"No Jennifer, that's too dangerous. I'll have Chris put me back in the attic. I'll apologize to the Blacks. Maybe the watchers will be pleased that for once Chris didn't join us for dinner." She kissed Chris and said "I love my Valentine. I'm going to use it every chance I get."

Bill wanted to meet the Blacks without the girls. He said he would do better in a smaller group. He would then love to come to a Sunday dinner but only if the Blacks liked him. So he came over one evening during the week. He discovered that no one could resist Marcia Black and he liked Dr. Black as well. Bill explained at great length what would happen if anyone tried to fix the audio pickup he had disabled. Essentially a low amperage but very high voltage shock would disable the intruder for a significant period of time. Since it might happen when no one was home, he had fashioned a switch which would then dial the phone and automatically summon the police. If the Blacks were home, there was a soft chime that would warn them to stay away from the dining room since the intruder might wake up and be dangerous. Bill felt strongly that if they embarrassed whoever had done this, then the bad guys would seek a less dangerous strategy which ideally meant staying out of the house. Also, he asked for permission to sweep the house once a week just in case.

Amazingly, only a day later Chris awoke in the middle of the night to the sound of police sirens. By the time he got to the dining room, the police had arrived, and Dr. Black was standing guard with an aging shotgun over a groggy intruder.

The intruder was an athletic male who appeared to be in his mid forties. He was dressed entirely in black including a mask which the police made him remove. He was wearing a utility belt with what appeared to be electronic tools. He was arrested. Dr. Black and Chris asked if they could go along to the police station to give statements and watch the process. An officer stayed with Mrs. Black.

Virtually as soon as physically possible he was bailed out by an attorney who appeared to be waiting at the police station when they got there. Before he was free, however, the police were able to identify the suspect as a former FBI agent. Chris would do a more thorough search.

Dr. Black met with his own lawyer and the police chief the next day. Since the suspect had literally been caught in the act inside a private home, there was little doubt about a conviction. Dr. Black told them his interest was maximum exposure and embarrassment. He said he would be willing to accept a plea bargain. But he wanted a four inch by five inch picture of the culprit on the front page of the local paper. He also wanted purchased space in the Gotham paper with the same size picture of the intruder. The accompanying text should say that this man could not be trusted. Dr. Black was an enthusiastic supporter of the Bill Marlin theory on behavior modification.

A week later Jennifer Martin called Bill. She knew he would be unprepared. "Hi, Bill. It's me, Jennifer. My mom is coming to visit the weekend after next. I wondered if you would come to Sunday dinner at the Black's. Mom will be there and so will Kyle's mom. They both want to meet the two young men who rescued us." That should give him plenty of time, she thought. And it will never occur to him that we looked up his birthday. "You don't even have to say yes or no. But I would be pleased if you came." She would let Chris make sure he was at the dinner.

The van was right on time. The driver appeared to be in his late forties or early fifties. Kyle was hidden in the shadows of a building. The van would wait only ten minutes and then leave. She bit her lip. She was desperate. She was afraid to get in the van but she was more afraid to be alone. She moved toward the van. She tried to appear as casual as possible. She took a deep breath.

Kyle opened the passenger door and climbed in. "Be brave" Kyle said to herself. She looked at the driver and said "Hi! I'm Bob." She smiled at the driver.

"I'm Kyle" he said. "Or maybe you're Kyle and I'm Bob. It's just the most incredible thing. Take off that silly wig and let me see if you look like your mom." He smiled at her as he started the van. He winked at her and said "I am

so happy to see you. Don't be afraid. Whatever happens, you are in for a couple of real surprises tonight." Bob pulled into traffic and headed for the highway.

Kyle was relieved to talk to someone. She sensed that she liked this man. She just had to know. "Who are you? How do you know Chris? Do you know my mom? Does she know where I am? You don't know how scared I've been. Am I talking too much? I only knew I was supposed to find you. I don't have a clue where we're going or what I'm supposed to do next."

Bob stopped for a red light and turned towards her, smiling again. "God knows how that boyfriend of yours ever found me. Your father thought he buried me long ago. But I would kill to help your mom and I danced with her at her wedding. I am your father's brother and your uncle. I have a great deal to tell you. I'm sure you're wondering why no one ever bothered to tell you of my existence." He headed for the expressway.

Dr. Black was grinning to himself. He had something to offer Chris. Dr. Black was going to use two full days to have a retreat with his entire department including his graduate students. He would have to cancel one of his lectures unless Chris would stand in for him. The department's own graduate students would be at the retreat. He thought it would be a great opportunity for Chris. He also knew that if Chris could keep it a secret, Jennifer and Kyle would be charmed when they turned up for a Friday lecture and found they had a guest speaker.

Chris looked at him and smiled. "What about the anthropology grad students or one of the other professors in your department? Shouldn't they really get a chance ahead of me?"

"They're all going to be at the retreat. It is mandatory for everyone. I can either cancel one lecture or ask you. I would love to see you do it."

"What would you like me to talk about?" Chris was worried about when he would find the time to prepare a lecture. He had never given a formal lecture to an auditorium full of students.

"Remember the paper you did at the end of your senior year? I think it would be a perfect topic. You've already done the work. All you have to do is turn it into a lecture. I'll be happy to help you prepare, but I remember my first lecture. Do it on your own. Don't even tell the girls. They'll drown you in support. On the other hand, you might tell Bill and invite him to attend. It might help him to see you struggling to speak in public."

Dr. Black couldn't resist just a little advice. "Plan carefully, Lead the students to your conclusions. Watch the time. It might help if you do a handout. Then your two girlfriends can pay attention instead of having to take notes."

Kyle's mom didn't arrive until Monday, three days later than she had planned. She wanted to stay at the same bed and breakfast the girls had found in the fall. Maureen Martin would join her Thursday night, and everyone would go to the Blacks on Sunday. Mary Manly would see the girls daily, attend some of their classes, have dinner with them each night, but spent some time alone so that the girls would get their work done.

On Wednesday morning, she called Marcia Black and introduced herself. With a minimum of bullying was able to persuade her to have lunch down by the lake. The two women spent the afternoon together. Mary Manly saw why all the children loved this woman. Mary, however, wanted to relate to her as a peer and not yet another daughter. Mary confided her latest idea for Kyle, received enthusiastic and supportive advice, and they both agreed Kyle would like the idea.

Anthropology met three times each week, lecture in the morning and section in the afternoon. Kyle had made her mom promise she would appear at the end of the afternoon class. Meeting Chris was a big priority.

Mrs. Manly and Mrs. Black appeared together and joined "their" children as the other students were leaving. All five then found a nearby coffee shop.

Mrs. Manly wanted to make it clear from the beginning that she approved of Chris. Fortunately they sat next to each other. "Chris, I really want to thank you for taking the time to get to know my daughter. She was just unbearable in the fall when she thought you didn't have any interest in her. Jennifer would tease her and tell her she was lucky to be infatuated with someone who didn't know anything about her. Then Kyle found out how much you really did know. She was actually relieved that you already knew and thrilled that you liked her for who she really is. I would like to get to know you better, too."

Chris liked Mary Manly, she had the same unpretentious way as her daughter. Maybe, he thought the problem is entirely Kyle's father. Kyle had told him that she was worried about her mom's secret. He looked at Mary Manly and thought "maybe she just loves her daughter." Then he answered Mrs. Manly. "Who could dislike Kyle. I knew about the grant and the Manly family before she even decided to study here. You wouldn't believe how surprised I was to discover that this wonderful human being was Kyle Manly. I actually had to apologize to her for being so prejudiced."

Continuing and trying to change the subject, Chris tried diplomacy. "You know, you and Kyle look so very much alike. Kyle thinks you are the greatest mom in the whole world. So I would like to get to know you better, too."

"Chris, Kyle is so grateful to you for identifying the bodyguards. She and I will try to work with her overly protective father. Please try to forgive him. He is an unusual and powerful man who has become accustomed to having whatever he wants. The only time I have ever seen him back down was when Kyle confronted him at Christmas." Chris remembered a crying Kyle clinging to him after Christmas break.

"My daughter has excellent judgement for a child her age. And Marcia Black tells me that she has managed to become friends with the nicest young man on campus. I will do everything I can to support your friendship, wherever it takes you."

Chris again tried to change the subject while hoping that he hadn't blushed. "You should attend one of Dr. Black's lectures. He's a great speaker and anthropology is a subject that is intrinsically fascinating. You have to be born with wires in your head to like computers, but Dr. Black makes you feel like you can understand the human race without even trying."

"Jennifer's mom and I are going to come to the lecture on Friday. We are really looking forward to it. Do you know the subject on Friday? On Kyle's schedule it just says 'to be announced.'"

Chris hesitated. He didn't want to tell her that he was the speaker on Friday but he hoped she would come anyway. He really didn't want to blow the surprise. Only Walter Black and Bill Marlin knew what was up. Bill was even coming to the lecture. On the other hand he didn't want her to miss the real master of anthropology so he selected his words carefully. "I can tell you it is on the schedule that way because it is going to be a little off the beaten path. I think the best thing would be if you would plan on coming both Friday and Monday. You'll get a better flavor of the course that way. The lectures are in the morning so hopefully, Jennifer's mom won't have to fly back to Gotham until after lunch on Monday."

"I guarantee that if Friday proves interesting, we'll both be there on Monday morning. The girls like it when we go to class with them." Mary Manly was rewarded with one of Chris' engaging smiles.

At Mary Manly's suggestion, Marcia Black made a foursome for dinner with the girls while Chris went off to have dinner with Walter Black. Chris knew she wanted to include Marcia in the group and was only too pleased to spend the evening with Walter. They both had work to do. Chris was pleased to see that Kyle's mom was just like Kyle. She had immediately sensed that even the warm ever mothering Marcia Black sometimes needed other people to make her feel special. The Manly women and their friend Jennifer were just the group to help Marcia Black really feel appreciated.

Mary Manly covered brilliantly. "Marcia, it's great that you'll come with us. We'll send Chris off to spend the evening with your husband. The best part is the four of us will be able to spend the whole evening talking about Chris. If we get bored with that, the three of us can always just tease Kyle about her boyfriend."

Chris wondered as he walked toward his Friday morning debut as a lecturer whether or not he could pull it off. He and his mirror had their first significant discussion that wasn't about Kyle. On the other hand, he thought, "everything is about Kyle!"

Bill caught up with him enroute to the lecture hall. Bill had carefully prepared to wish his best friend luck. Bill would sit inconspicuously in the back and root for Chris. Ever thoughtful of others, Chris reminded Bill that the moms would be there and that even if Bill didn't sit with them there was a chance he would get introduced. "Bill, if they want you to meet their moms just say 'it's nice to meet you.' You are going to meet them all Sunday at the Blacks, The girls want you to come to dinner. They are trying to thank you for all you have done for them. So just shake hands, look, at them and smile. If you can manage that, I'll try to get through the lecture."

Chris stood at the front of the hall. Bill was still hiding outside and would enter late. Chris took over the room. "Hi, everybody. We have a slight change in format today. Dr. Black is unavailable and asked me to fill in. For those of you who haven't met me, I am Chris Krail. I am one of the teaching assistants. Now I will be understanding if any of you fall asleep or have to leave early for the weekend. After all, I am not the head of the anthropology department. On the other hand, I will suggest to Dr. Black that the entire final exam be based on my talk. It is always possible that he might include as much as one question from this discussion. There is a handout."

Chris looked in Kyle's direction and was pleased to see her eyes telling him how happy this event made her. She was squeezing her mom's hand. He was going to talk about the subject of a paper he had written and a subject that interested him. He hoped it would go well. He hoped, more than anything else, that Kyle would like it. Maybe she would even read the original paper.

Chris spoke about the development of dichotomous categories as a model for societal development. While anyone could lump events or ideas into a category, the idea of categories as opposites allowed a heightened level of understanding. Opposites, Chris said, were the simplest groupings in society, not only for people but for concepts. For instance men and women are groups of people. Alive and dead are also opposite concepts. In each case the use of opposites helped to define the categories. The use of this critical dichotomy allowed people to understand themselves and their places in the universe. The problem was what happens when someone or something doesn't fit.

Suppose someone is neither a man or a woman and can't be classified. Someone is neither alive or dead. The borders become fuzzy. We respond in predictable ways. We want everyone and everything to fit. If a border becomes fuzzy we have predictable but not necessarily productive responses. Ambiguity is threatening and has a price. Fear and loathing is one response. If someone is a man but acts like a woman we may ostracize him or if we are threatened enough we may even kill him. Another response is to believe that the answer is magic. If someone is neither clearly dead nor alive, we may even invent a mythology to explain the phenomenon. In the most complex and difficult evolutionary step we may have to overcome our simple dichotomy and add new categories. This requires added effort and makes comprehension more difficult even while making the categories themselves more meaningful. A real downside to the way we categorize groups is our ability to hate when a group is too similar but not just like us.

Chris related the conceptual map he was creating to all the great accomplishments of society. He argued that the idea of using opposites could be looked as a basic model for many of our ideas and institutions and across many cultural lines. He discussed the structure of language, of religion, and in an effort to reach the one person who mattered most, he discussed his theory in terms of our legal system.

The Chris Krail guest lecture was very well received. He thanked everyone for their attention and then announced that the afternoon sessions had been canceled because all the other teaching assistants were unavailable for the day. His own section would also be canceled so that his students wouldn't have more classes than their colleagues.

Many of the students came up to him after class to offer their appreciation. Virtually every student in his section stopped personally. Kyle waited patiently until the crowd thinned out and then, before her mom could say anything, she hugged him, kissed him on the cheek, and whispered "you are wonderful."

Mrs. Manly introduced their friend Maureen Martin. "Chris, you are so sly. I will have to remember to listen very carefully to the words when you answer a question. What was it you said? Friday's lecture will be a little off the beaten path. You'll have to come Friday and Monday to get the full flavor. You were wonderful Chris. I can see why the girls say you are their favorite instructor. I hope Dr. Black will be as good."

Chris was becoming a master at modestly deflecting complements by trying to change the subject. "Aren't we missing someone?"

Maureen Martin answered him. "My daughter disappeared at the end of your lecture. She said she had to cut someone off at the door. She'll turn up. You should have seen her eyes. She loved your lecture."

They found Jennifer and Bill sitting on the steps outside the building. Bill was introduced to the moms and managed to smile and actually looked at each mom as he shook hands. Jennifer was happy. "Bill has done it again. It appears he knew about this in advance and recorded the whole lecture."

Bob told Kyle he would try to answer her questions. As they drove he gained her confidence but couldn't keep up with her questions and mentioned they would soon have dinner and then he would try to start over from the very beginning.

He was sad to say that Kyle's mom had no idea where her daughter was hiding. Unfortunately, he agreed with Chris, that while mother and daughter might have a hard time, it was safer for both of them. He told Kyle that if her mother knew where she was headed she would be happy and relieved.

"You do look a little like my father. I can't believe that I have always thought he was an only child. Do I look like my mom?

"Without the wig, you look just like I remember your mom. I haven't seen her since just before you were born."

Because of the crowd, the Blacks served their Sunday meal at two in the afternoon. Bill did come for the meal although he left in mid-afternoon. Considering the size of the crowd, he did very well. There were the Blacks, the girls, the moms, and Chris. Everyone else stayed until almost midnight.

They all told Dr. Black how well Chris had done with the lecture. Dr. Black said he was a little afraid to lecture on Monday. He was sure Chris was a hard act to follow. He was very anxious to borrow the recording Bill had made.

The almost always quiet Bill finally spoke. "I thought that you might want to hear the lecture. So actually I've already made copies and he produced six copies, one for each of the other guests and one for the Blacks."

Jennifer was always eager to support Bill's efforts. "Bill has this habit of rescuing us and solving our problems." She hesitated and put her hand on Bill's arm. "Bill, we actually have something for you, too." She waited until he looked up and her. She tried to tell him it was okay with her eyes. "Kyle and I have never been able to tell you adequately how grateful we are for your friendship. We wanted to give you something that meant a lot to us. We hope you'll like this as much as we do." She handed him a large envelope which contained a homemade certificate. "This is a gift certificate for six introductory rock climbing private lessons."

Bill was touched. He had no idea how to respond. But Jennifer had already planned his escape. "Come on in the living room. I'll tell you what you need to know to get your lessons." They left the rest of the guests at the table.

Mary Manly waited until they had left the room and then turned toward Dr. Black. "Kyle tells me there is an adult education program this summer in legal anthropology and she is going to apply. Do you think I could apply, too, and take it with her?" This seemingly innocent ploy got a lot of reaction from the group at the table.

Chris was ecstatic that Kyle might spend the summer at Athené. He was pleased that her mother might be there. He wanted to become friends with the person that Kyle loved the most.

Dr. Black was pleased. "Nothing would make me happier that having you both in the program. Actually, there will probably be more alumni and other older adults than there will be students. We've never done anything like this before. The faculty will be very diverse with lots of different speakers. I was even thinking of looking at the lecture Chris gave and seeing if it would fit with our agenda."

Mrs. Black had been prepared by her new friend. She already knew the answer and knew where the conversation was going but asked sincerely "Would you and Kyle like to live with us for the summer?"

Mary Manly looked at her daughter and answered. "We will spend as much time as we can with you but I have kind on an interesting plan for housing. Kyle, would you mind asking Bill and Jennifer if they could rejoin us for a minute."

When they all had regathered she outlined her plan. She had spent an afternoon house shopping in the areas that were walking distance from campus. She wanted to buy a house for Kyle and Jennifer. That way the girls could live off campus. It would make spying on them more difficult and perhaps make it easier for them to see their friends. Maybe they could even invite the Blacks to dinner. She had found three houses that interested her which she wanted to show to Kyle and Jennifer.

There was an interesting twist. "Bill, you are very important to my plan. All three houses I liked had a large attached two bedroom apartment."

"I hate to interrupt you, mom. But I think I see the beauty of this plan. Bill, Jennifer and I would never be safe without our friends. Would you consider renting the apartment from me? I would be happy to accept your being in charge of my electronic security in lieu of rent."

Bill saw that he needed to say something. "Would it be okay if Chris came by occasionally. If it got late he could even stay in the spare bedroom."

Mary Manly had something else to add. "Right now none of the apartments have any access to the main house. That will be very important because during the purchasing process I have a feeling there will be a few inspections we don't know about. Of course, I will be here for the summer and I was once a pretty fair carpenter, a little something my husband never knew."

"Also, every house I looked at has four bedrooms so Maureen and I might just get invited back. Oh, and I forgot to ask. Were you girls planning on living together next year?

"We cannot be separated. If Kyle likes this plan, I am her roommate." from Jennifer.

"We cannot be separated." Kyle turned and winked at Chris. "Even by Chris."

Kyle could not get over how different her uncle was from her father. He wanted to know how she felt. He was reassuring. He wanted her to feel comfortable. It was clear from the many questions that he asked that he cared about her mom.

"You are probably wondering about my business. I owe it to your father. He has a nasty habit of spying on folks. So my professional life has been devoted to protecting people like me from people like my brother. I even named my business BEST just to piss him off. He has quite an ego you know. I am the ideal person to hide you. Even though your father spies on me intermittently, I am way ahead of him. Chris and I got along great. We both love misinformation. In fact, he and I are going to start a little organization. We're going to call it the mothers of misinformation. Chris thinks we should call ourselves "mom" after you mom. It's also an acronym for our little group. Wanna join?"

Kyle loved the twinkle in his eyes. She was dying to hear the whole story. But she was loving his reassuring and friendly approach to her. It was also clear he was trying to comfort her and he would tell her everything if she gave him a chance.

Kyle and Jennifer talked about Mrs. Manly's housing plan. Their main concern was that they not be separated. The plan had great merit. They would have the control they needed to ensure their privacy. They would still visit the Blacks often. But they could return the favor without taking the Blacks to a restaurant. About half the undergraduates at Athené lived off campus so there was nothing conspicuous or snotty about the plan.

Kyle was pleased. "Can you get over that my mom knows how to cut a doorway? Next thing you know she'll be buying me a miner's hat with a light so I won't get hurt in the attic."

Jennifer had only one concern. "I wish I had time to prepare Bill. I'm going to look for him and make sure he's comfortable. I'll tell him how much safer we feel with him around. But you know how sensitive he can be. He has to know that it is up to him. He has to know that we will like him just as much even if he stays in his dorm room. Can you believe how fast he made us all copies of the CK lecture?"

"J, why don't you spend the summer with us. Even if you don't want to sign up for the course there will be other interesting things to do here."

"Well K, this morning my mom asked me if I would spend the summer with her in Italy. I was pretty surprised but she just said not to worry, we'd be fine. I don't think your mom did this, and I think she's keeping secrets again. Don't worry, I'll take my checkbook just in case."

"What did you tell your mom? Are you going to Italy?"

"Well, I told her I would go on two conditions. One, it had to be okay with my friend Kyle. Two, I want to be back here two weeks before school starts so I can spend some time just hanging out with you."

Chris was so pleased that Kyle, her mom, and the Blacks had all conspired so that he could be alone with his girl on Wednesday evening. They lay on the bed and talked. Kyle said her mom understood why she went to him through the attic. Her mom hoped the house they were buying would help them with their relationship. But Kyle knew at some point she would have to confront her father and she was afraid.

Kyle would be leaving on Friday for a week at Sun Valley. Jennifer was going but they were worried. Kyle's father had told her mom to bring both of them. It was a command performance. They were afraid he would use them as trophies with his business associates.

Chris tried to calm her. "Just go and have a good time. You both love the outdoors. Teach her to ski. Buy her something appropriate to wear. If your father treats you like part of his possessions just pretend he's part of your staff. I know you, you just want everyone to like you for who you are. What really upsets you is that you can't figure out how to be friends with your father. You are so lucky with your mom. If you have trouble with it all, remember that I'm your friend, too. I will miss you and I will be waiting for you when you get back."

Chris was trying to help but she started crying. "Last time I was home he told me I was spending too much time with you." She held him and said. "My father will never separate us. No matter what Chris, I will always come back to you. If he makes me chose. I will take you, Chris. What I want most is to be able to kiss you in the middle of the campus and not be afraid. I am so glad we're spending the summer together."

Kyle told Bob that she hadn't watched TV or looked at a newspaper since she had run away. "I've been afraid there would be something in the news that would make me even more afraid. I felt so alone and vulnerable, I didn't think I could deal with any bad news."

Bob looked at her as they drove and said. "Are you still afraid?"

Kyle looked at her uncle. "Somehow I feel like you will protect me. I am sure of it. But what about Chris?"

Bob pulled into a rest stop on the highway and parked the van. "Chris has been arrested. It is in all the newspapers because of the connection to Global. The incredible thing is that they have charged him with both grand larceny and kidnapping."

"Who did he kidnap?"

"You, Kyle. He has been charged with kidnapping you. So if you want to use the facilities and buy a paper, let's get you back in the wig." Bob hesitated when he saw the tears start. "Chris said they might try to use him to get to you. I think that the kidnapping charge means that you got away and the bad guys are very angry. Chris is right. If we can hide you, they can't touch him, they can't touch us."

"Uncle Bob, promise to tell me anytime you think I can help Chris by going back."

They bought a paper and returned to the van. The late addition of the paper had a note saying only that the young man accused of kidnapping the heiress Kyle Manly had been released from jail on $10 million bail.

"Where could Chris get $10 million?"

Chris borrowed the Black's car to pick the girls up at the airport when they returned from Sun Valley. He got a very public hug from both girls and he told them that he had missed them.

Kyle looked at Jennifer, then at Chris and said. "Well, my mom still loves me."

Bill was really happy to have a friend. He knew that he could trust Chris. He had, however, no concept about his relationship with the girls. Sometimes in his fantasy life, they were thanking him for rescuing them. The word had been used more than once. He didn't really believe that they considered him a real friend. He thought of himself more as a helper. He knew that Kyle and Chris were becoming more than friends so it was easy to think of Kyle in terms of Chris.

On the other hand, there was the problem of Jennifer. He tried not to think about her except when he thought he could do something for her. He was beginning to be okay about the fact that she stopped to talk whenever she saw him on campus. Except for the side effect. Actually he thought of it as the Jennifer effect.

Like the day after Chris' lecture. He had sat with her in front of the building for about 15 minutes waiting for the rest of the group to emerge. Since then at least five or six other students had approached him and wanted to know her name. It was like everyone wanted to be his friend because they might get introduced to Jennifer Martin. Bill saw his role as protecting Jennifer. Whatever the relationship, he realized that people wanted to talk to him every time he was seen with her. He had been thrilled to be included in the dinner with the moms even if he had felt awkward and had left early.

So when she called him and asked him to meet her for coffee, he was even more confused. It wasn't the first time she had contacted him. She had sent him that wonderful thank you note at the beginning of the semester after he had boxed the listening device in her room. He had saved it and he looked at it regularly. She had called him to invite him to dinner at the Blacks. And he was very sensitive to the fact that although Kyle and Jennifer used the generic "we" in all conversations, Jennifer would often use "I" when she was speaking directly to him. Last, he wondered if Jennifer was the one person behind the rock climbing lessons.

Bill rationalized that no male in his right mind could ever say no to a date with Jennifer no matter how trivial. It did make him feel a little special. He wondered if other guys had to stand in line to have coffee with the most beautiful woman on campus. So Bill practiced saying innocuous things so he could do it from memory.

They met off campus about four in the afternoon. Jennifer thanked him for meeting her. She told Bill it was great that she had a friend she could just call up and meet. Bill did his best to be in the conversation. Jennifer noticed and took her time and encouraged him. Two cups later she talked about the house Kyle would buy. Jennifer told Bill that she would be happy if he moved in with them. (Later, Bill would go over these words many times.) But she wanted him to know that she and Kyle would understand if he had other plans or he wanted to stay in the dorm. She, they would still be his friends and would like him just as much and would still want to spend time with him.

Jennifer was very anxious about this. She was so afraid that Bill would feel like he was being used. So she added "you are the only guy in this whole place who doesn't think of me in terms of being seen. Every other man I have met since I've been here, except Chris of course, just wants his friends to see me. You are a real friend. I don't have to feel like a trophy when I'm with you."

Bill was beginning to understand how sincere she was and how lucky he was that she actually cared about him. So he laughed. "I bet you didn't know I am a little bit shy. I actually have to struggle to take part in conversations. If it wasn't for Chris and you and Kyle, I wouldn't talk to anyone. I was only afraid that it was Chris that wanted me to take the apartment. Or Mrs. Manly trying to protect Kyle. If you guys really want me, I can't imagine where I would rather live."

Jennifer reassured him. "We all need friends, Bill. That includes girls who are incredibly rich and even girls who are a little bit pretty. I would be happy if you were my friend."

Bill told her about his Jennifer Effect Theory. He compared it to his homework effect theory. Like when everyone wanted to be your friend because you did good homework. He told her whenever anyone asked he now had a standard response. He would introduce himself to whoever was asking. Ask a lot of nosey questions about the person asking and then shrug his shoulders and say "Gosh, I wish I knew her name. I didn't realize she was that pretty."

Jennifer was pleased by this and Bill could see that she genuinely liked the story he told her. He said "But this time we've been here so long, no one is going to believe I don't know your name."

"Don't worry" Jennifer answered. "If anyone approaches you just say I'm that pain who is always trying to copy your homework. But you're right, it's late. Let's order a couple of hamburgers."

"It's me. I know I wasn't supposed to call unless it was an emergency. Chris made bail yesterday afternoon. We have to help him. Maybe the mothers could do a little work." Jennifer spoke to Bill over a Bill Marlin modified and scrambled cellular phone. Even with that she made only the most obscure reference to Bill's love for misinformation. Bill was the mother of all misinformation.

"Good, I'm tired of the bush and I've got some ideas. Can you bring me in."

Go to the northwest corner of the intersection in our first plan. A limousine will appear. Four terrible looking but well dressed men will appear out of the limo. Tell any one of them that you are looking for Mr. X, but use the name of the instructor you had with that certificate I gave you for your birthday." She really hoped this wasn't too cryptic. "You won't have any problem. They have all seen your picture."

"Clear. I can be there in 11 minutes. I'll wait ten. Call me if there is a problem" The line went dead.

Bill wasn't half as calm as he had been on the phone. He didn't mind being alone. He was good at that. But he wanted to help Chris. Also, the apartment where Jennifer was hiding him looked like some kind of professional safehouse. He had gone over it bit by bit. He really didn't have the right equipment with him. But the apartment was in perfect shape in a run down building in a run down neighborhood. If Jennifer was sending a limo he was not coming back. Someone would see them. He would be too obvious.

Where did Jennifer get access to professional muscle? Who was paying for all this? There was only one thing he knew for sure. This was not Manly muscle and this was not Manly money.

Kyle and her mom chose one of the houses shortly after they returned from Sun Valley. It was only a short walk from the Blacks. It had two big disadvantages. First, it needed renovation. Second the current owners did not want to move out until July first. But when they brought the group to look at it everyone agreed it was the best. The Blacks again invited Kyle and her mom to spend July with them and it was agreed that the Manly women would stay with the Blacks until the house was ready.

Meanwhile it was spring in Athené. Flowers bloomed. Kyle felt more and more sure that she was in love with Chris while he knew without thinking about it that he was very lucky and that whatever the risk he had to find a way. They both treasured the romance. It was only a matter of time before Kyle's father would try to stop them. They both wanted to avoid the conflict but they both really wanted to acknowledge each other publicly.

At the same time, Chris was becoming concerned because Dr. Roberts had never mentioned the money he had stolen from Global. He had written some preliminary papers on methods to protecting local area networks from outside computer pirates. He hoped these would lead toward his thesis, a doctorate, and perhaps a job. With a little luck he could repay all the money he owed without ever getting caught and without having to ask Kyle.

Chris received praise for what he was accomplishing as a first year graduate student from everyone in the department but he noticed that Dr. Roberts who had worked so hard to recruit him was growing a little distant. One day, he was called to Dr. Roberts' office. Chris thought perhaps he is embarrassed by where I hid the $80,000.

Chris was right that Dr. Roberts did want to talk about breaching the security at Global. "Chris, did you give up on stealing my $100,000 from Global Financial Transfer?"

"Gee, Dr. Roberts, I stole the money before Christmas. I was sure you would see all the extra computer activity and I hid most of the money in kind of an obvious place. I'd be happy to tell you what I did and where I put the money. I was just waiting to see if either you or the security at Global would see anything."

"Chris, I did see the activity and I thought it was cute that you did it with my password. But all you did was challenge them with standard security assessment techniques. It looked like you gave up. Global has so far not noticed anything wrong and I don't care where you put the money as long as you can give it back when the time comes."

A dark thought crossed the mind of Chris Krail but he kept it too himself. "Dr. Roberts, what I did was endlessly repeatable on their current system. If I wanted I could take a million dollars from them and they would probably never know. Actually, I thought what I did was so clever I am hoping to use it as a basis for my thesis. I was just waiting until you found the money before I revealed what I did."

"OK, Chris, I believe you. I'm going to let Global know that we have accomplished their goals. I will tell them the time frame and let them look for the theft and for the money. Can you give me a clue without giving it all away."

"Dr. Roberts, I stole the money during the last week of classes before Christmas. I moved the money in two parts. One lump of $80,000 and one of $20,000. Both were transfers directly from Global. Each aliquot of money was only moved once. I made no effort to launder it in any way." Chris could not believe the thought that kept recurring to him.

A week later Chris was again in Dr. Roberts office. "Chris, this is Mitchell Bierman, the head of security at Global Financial Transfer. He is in charge of all security including the computer system. We have talked it over. We aren't ready for you to tell us what you did. We haven't found the money but we believe you. I have convinced him that you are smart and that you are capable of moving the money. Last week you said you could do it again."

"It's nice to meet you, Mr. Bierman." Chris shook hands. "I did find a weakness in your security. I actually found a couple of places I thought I could get in. But my goal was not just to take the money. I didn't want to get caught. I will need direction from both of you. If I explain what I did and you change your system, I can no longer ethically use what I have learned as the basis for a doctoral thesis. On the other hand, if I don't help you, there might be someone else out there who is at least as clever as I am."

Chris waited. He hoped that they wouldn't want to know. He was sure that his information would make a great thesis. Maybe Dr. Roberts would let him submit a draft, grant a very early doctorate, and then repair Global. What worried him was the fact that Dr. Roberts had not found the $80,000.

Mitchell Bierman spoke. "If I ask you to steal a million dollars, how long would it take you?"

"It would take no more than two weeks unless you have substantially altered some basic aspects of your computer system in the last couple of months."

"Chris, take a million as soon as you can. Let Dr. Roberts know if it takes longer than the end of the month. Park the money where we have some chance of finding it. Give us another chance. We never thought you could have done it so quickly."

"No problem." Chris thought to himself that maybe Bill would like to watch him steal a million dollars.

He talked it over with Kyle. Did she think there were any ethical problems? "Chris, I don't think letting Bill watch you is a problem. The object here is to get caught. But listen to me, I have met Mr. Bierman. He has come to our house on several occasions. He makes my skin crawl. I have this overwhelmingly negative visceral reaction to that man. He and my father speak in whispers. I sense a very bad man. Be careful."

Bill was out of his league when he got into the limo. "This is serious muscle" he thought to himself. They were all very polite but they looked dangerous. They put body armor on him. Where did Jennifer find these guys?

The leader of the group introduced himself. "I'm Alex, and I would like to apologize if we seem a little abrupt. We take our job seriously. We were asked to bring you in alive and unharmed."

At ten in the morning he was taken into the back entrance of a private club. There he met the man he was sure was in charge. "Hi. I'm Tony Dragoni." He shook Bill's hand. "I need a favor. You will see Jennifer and Chris at dinner. They are too valuable and too much at risk to be out here in the streets. What I need you to do for me is to change your appearance. From what Chris and Jennifer tell me, you are going to be an important member of this team. I am going to need you to travel a little bit. So I would like you to agree to a little disguise. Think of it as a little misinformation."

An hour later, Bill had been measured by a tailor and was undergoing a professional haircut and manicure. It was the clothes that made him look so different. His shoes had slight lifts and some of his new clothes were cut to accommodate body armor. The clothes were also custom made and expensive. Money was not discussed but Bill could see that money was no object.

At one in the afternoon, Bill joined Tony Dragoni for a light lunch. Tony said "Always look right at people. Make them look away. If you stare at them they won't get a chance to get a good look. And never smile. I take that back. Jennifer and Chris deserve your best smile, but glare at the rest of us. And think about your body language. Don't be humble. Act like you own the world. Be aggressive. It's an act. It's a disguise. It's misinformation."

"Mr. Dragoni, I feel like a knight who has had his valet shine his armor and lift him on a horse. I will do my best."

"Good, now let me tell you what I have in mind. And don't worry, you'll get to see your friends in a couple of hours. But this afternoon we have to gather the equipment you'll need."

Bill loved the rock climbing wall. His lessons were set up once a week early in the morning when there were less climbers. He felt that the wall gave him confidence. He wasn't sure if he would ever be any good. He just liked doing it. And he had never had any friends who gave him presents, much less one that was thoughtful and personal.

Shortly after his sixth lesson he got a package in the mail. It contained two 8x10 photos of him high up on the wall. They had obviously been taken with a telephoto lens. There was a note from Jennifer. It read:

"Forgive me for spying on you. I came to your last session. I was pretty nervous about taking the photos but I am just thrilled with the way they came out. I hope you like them. Jennifer."

Bill wondered how she ever got two such flattering pictures. He guessed she had probably been there for the whole hour and taken hundreds of pictures. On an impulse he relabelled the mailer and sent the better of the two pictures back to Jennifer. He wrote right on the picture:

"Jennifer, I never had a friend like you. I could never have done this without you. Bill."

In the end Chris was glad that he had invited Bill to the theft of a million dollars. Bill made a significant contribution. They had met on campus and Chris outlined what he proposed to do and how he proposed to do it. He explained to Bill that their theoretical discussions several month earlier had helped him conceptually.

A key issue was that it would all be scripted in advance on his portable computer. They would download the script into the lab computer. Almost nothing would be visible except the confirmations including a log of what they had done. The log would have to be saved to confirm what had actually happened. Chris still had the log from the first theft. The original was in Dr. Black's safety deposit box. He had a copy. After this next theft he asked Bill if he would also keep copies.

Chris told Bill about Kyle's reaction to Mitchell Bierman. And there was more. "Bill, I have no secrets from Kyle. But I haven't told her yet that I am becoming very suspicious that I am being used in the GFT project. I hid $80,000 in Dr. Robert's retirement account. Either he never noticed or he doesn't want to notice. There was a lot of money in the account. Perhaps he has earned it consulting. Maybe he is a just not aware of how much money he has. The worst case scenario is that he has moved it and somehow washed his account so I can't tell."

"I am afraid to go back into his account because he is clever enough to have set some kind of trap for me. He might be able to set up some kind of handshaking data exchange that would tell him how I was slipping through the various layers of security. I had this really awful thought that perhaps Dr. Roberts has actually stolen the money and I am going to get left holding the proverbial bag. In retrospect it was probably a bad idea to hide the money where I didn't have control. At the time I thought it would be funny and everyone would get a laugh." As he said these things out loud for the first time, Chris realized his fears were justified.

"Chris, did you ever notice that I often start sentences with the phrase 'I know I'm paranoid, but.' A little paranoia is a very healthy thing. These people have proven that they play dirty. Kyle's father treats her like a criminal. His big mistake is that he forgot she can think for herself. Their big mistake is that we can think for ourselves and I bet that if you take my advice we can play at least as dirty as they do."

"Bill, when you first asked to sweep the Blacks' house, I thought you were nuts. I will never again doubt your judgement."

"First of all, Chris. Do you think there is any chance that Dr. Roberts or Mr. Bierman have been taping their conversations with you? That's what I would do. There is a fair chance they have you on tape talking about stealing a million dollars from GFT. Also, they have lots of your friends on tape. Suppose they want to frame you and Jennifer. No problem. Just use clips of what you said and create a conversation with your real voices. Not that I'm paranoid you understand."

So for a starter, Chris. I am going to set you up with a wire to record all your conversations with anyone related to GFT - except of course Kyle. I will give you a voice activated recorder. If you get caught just tell them sometimes it helps you to review conversations. Act innocent. I don't think they will ever suspect. They are way too sure of themselves. Even our little stunt with that high voltage shock at the Blacks. I bet you anything they still think it was a coincidence."

"Second, did you ever hear of taggants? The FBI has worked really hard to see that raw materials that can be used in the creation of explosives are tagged. Then if there is an illegal device used for terrorism, the FBI can examine the remnants of the materials and identify the source. Is there anyway that you can tag the money you move? The tag would have to stick even if the money were divided. And perhaps you could even devise a tag that would let you trace the money if the bad guys moved it."

"Third, there is nothing like a little misinformation. Chris, you are one of the nicest human beings I ever met. But you are so straightforward. I need to teach you to lie a little."

"If he only knew" thought Chris.

Bill continued. "Misinformation can be extraordinarily useful. If you are too straightforward you can be outflanked. What we need to do is provide a few false clues that lead the enemy astray. Perhaps if we're clever we can use a little misinformation to let them lead themselves into a trap. Chris, you and I have worked together before. I think we need a little private organization. Let's call it 'mom' - the mothers of misinformation."

Chris was gratified that he had asked Bill to watch the theft. In the process Bill had probably made some incredible suggestions. He wasn't wild about the recorder, but the idea of tagging the money and providing a little misinformation was wonderful. "Bill, can the girls join our organization?"

Based on his conversation with Bill, Chris had another idea. If he could successfully tag the stolen money he didn't need to have control of where he parked it. If he was right that he was being used to really steal some money, then tagging it was a brilliant scheme. Tracer dollars he called them, like tracer bullets, you can see where they are going.

Chris also wondered if Mr. Bierman had set up any new traps for him. First he ran all the same standard probes he had run the first time. He didn't need to do this to steal the money. He needed to run the standard probes to take advantage of Bill's suggestion that he provide a little misinformation. Chris assumed that if GFT was ready for the standard probes, they would be trying to learn about Chris by trying to extract information from the probes.

Chris ran the probes off a brand new portable computer. The computer had nothing on it accept an operating system, the standard probes, and a few lines of code specifically written to look like a program for transferring money from a Global Financial Transfer account to Chris' personal checking account. If GFT could counterattack and use his probes to access his computer they would find what appeared to be a program built to steal money and move it to Chris' account.

Then Chris used a different computer to access the local bank. If anyone from outside were to check his credit electronically it would reflect a million dollar account. On the other hand, if the bank were legally asked for a credit report, they would report that the account had never had more than $3000. If someone questioned the bank about the electronic credit report, the bank would report an error.

Then Chris, with Bill watching, used his original technique to move a million dollars into the personal checking account of Mitchell Bierman. He also created a track record by using the Global payroll to make the direct deposit into Bierman's account. The money was also tagged and as long as Mitchell Bierman didn't transfer it in amounts less than one dollar, he would be able to follow most of the transactions. Since he was actually moving the money within the Global organization, it would be harder to accuse him of stealing.

If all went as planned, the computer security team at GFT would think the money had been by some unknown means been moved into Chris' personal account. Meanwhile the money would actually be parked with Bierman. If Dr. Roberts was actually stealing he and Mitchell Bierman would undoubtedly come up with a way to make the million dollars disappear. Chris wasn't sure yet if Dr. Roberts was just not paying attention or actively stealing but he was confident that Mr. Bierman knew how to launder money. He just hoped his tagging scheme worked.

Bill told him not to worry. They would be so confident that they had him that they wouldn't bother to actually pick up the phone and confirm with Chris' bank. It would be in the best interest of Mr. Bierman for GFT security to believe the misinformation about where the money went. Whatever happened, Chris would know where everyone stood within a few days.

Kyle and Chris came to the conclusion that it was impossible to hide the fact that they were friends and that it would be counterproductive to try. They agreed that there would be no public displays of affection that might be seen by the goons. Jennifer and sometimes even Bill would help cover. Bill saw it as providing distractors for the watchers. Misinformation soon became a theme in Bill's life. He began working on a scheme to record his friends voices so he could even provide phony phone calls. An occasional suggestive rendezvous that never took place.

Kyle and Chris, like any young lovers were able to overcome the obstacles that they had to work with. But they did take chances. Like picnics at Kyle's favorite waterfall. Or occasional visits to her dorm room with appropriate business-like conversations provided by Bill for the listening device.

While Kyle and Chris began to hope that perhaps her father had better things to do, their friends Jennifer and Bill began meeting regularly to provide them with cover. Jennifer had become increasingly worried after Kyle had told her about some of her father's remarks in the Caymans. The trip to Sun Valley made her very uncomfortable. Kyle saw her father as rigid and aloof. Jennifer saw Mr. Manly as calculating and potentially dangerous is he were crossed.

One afternoon in the spring, the four met under a tree ostensibly to discuss dinner plans. Bill who usually had the least to say had an agenda and was anxious to express himself. "Could we consider the next five or ten minutes an official meeting of the mothers. Mom does not meet often and, of course, we don't keep minutes, but we all know while we're here."

"I believe there is some chance that Kyle's father just loves his daughter and wants to keep her away from bad influences like me. However, there is also some chance that he is capable of using his power to protect Kyle without considering whether or not she wants to be protected. It occurs to me that all this nonsense with the GFT grant is being done to set up Chris. The question of motive has great importance. It is possible that Kyle's father wants to control Kyle by threatening her friends. We all know that Chris is an obvious target but, Jennifer, I want you to be careful also."

"Chris and I have tried to manage his role in the GFT project so that we can defend him if there is ever trouble. It is clear now that Roberts and Bierman have kept the money that Chris was asked to steal. Someday Chris will be asked to give it back and they will claim they never saw it. What worries me is whether they are doing this on their own or whether a very rich and powerful John Manly is manipulating all these events from behind the scenes.

"Unfortunately, this is one time we need more than just a little misinformation and I wonder in any of you have any suggestions?"

Kyle had never met Dr. Roberts but responded badly every time anyone mentioned Mitchell Bierman. "If they are stealing now, they have probably stolen before. I wouldn't be surprised if there isn't something in their pasts."

"Great idea" from Jennifer. "Chris, you are the only one who can do this. Can you peek into the past and lives of Roberts and Bierman?"

Kyle and Chris wanted to spend more and more time together. They were looking forward to the summer. Jennifer was going to Italy with her mom. Bill was going to Gotham where he had a summer job with an electronics firm that designed high tech optical surveillance equipment. Kyle's mom was going to join them for the summer but there was no doubt that she supported her daughter's relationship.

The spring semester ended. Jennifer and Kyle spent a week together biking in Vermont. Chris went to Gotham with Bill to help him find a place to live for the summer. They ended up staying with Maureen Martin who finally convinced Bill he should just stay in her home for the summer while she was gone. Chris suspected it wasn't that it was free that convinced Bill. It wasn't that Mrs. Martin protested that it would be a help if someone would stay in their apartment while they were away. Bill finally agreed to live there after Mrs. Martin told Bill that she and Jennifer had talked it over and Jennifer would like Bill to stay in her room.

Jennifer and Kyle spent one night in the city but Kyle stayed with her parents. The next day the Martins flew first class to Florence. Bill stayed in Gotham and Chris, who had actually never been in an airplane before, traveled with Mary Manly and Kyle in a private jet back to Athené.

Mary Manly and Kyle indicated to Chris that no secrets should be shared on the flight so the conversation was mostly about the legal anthropology month. Chris apologized and said they would have to hear a revised version of his lecture which they had already attended. He had been invited by Dr. Black to deliver his lecture on the primal dichotomy as it applied to good and bad, right and wrong, legal and illegal. Mrs. Manly responded for both of them. "Chris, your talk is the reason we are so excited about the course!"

Mother and daughter moved in with the Blacks several days before the July program was due to begin. Mary Manly was given a guest room upstairs, and it was suggested that perhaps Kyle would like the guest room that was downstairs and off the den. Kyle smiled to herself that her mom and the Blacks were so anxious to aid and abet her romance with Chris. She immediately saw that the downstairs guest room had the advantage of being separate from the older adults.

On one of her first nights in town, Mary Manly took the Blacks to dinner, leaving Chris and Kyle by themselves. Chris tried to impress her with his skills on the grill. She laughed at him and told him that she loved him because he just kept trying all the time. After dinner they lay on her bed to talk. They were careful to leave the light on and the door open so that no one would be embarrassed when the Blacks and her mom returned.

Kyle loved cuddling in Chris' arms and kept trying to get closer and closer. Her conversation turned to murmuring and she fell asleep. Chris lay holding her and listening to her breathe. Eventually Chris also fell asleep.

An hour later Mary Manly looked at the two of them wrapped around each other and sound asleep. She smiled to herself and hoped fervently that she would be able to protect these two young lovers. She shut off the light, closed the door, and went upstairs to bed.

When the sun came up Kyle awoke and kissed Chris. "I love you, Chris." She wondered if he had heard her but she would tell him again soon enough.

"I love sleeping in your arms" Chris told Kyle. They fell back asleep for an hour. When they awoke again they could smell coffee. They agreed it would be better to do this together and with rumpled clothes and hair they sheepishly appeared in the kitchen where the other three were having coffee.

"You two look a little bit crumpled" volunteered Marcia Black.

Kyle and her Uncle Bob drove for several hours. They told each other small

vignettes about their respective lives. They both tried really hard to become friends. They liked each other. Bob sensed Kyle wasn't ready for the whole dark story. It could wait until they were home and out of the van. Kyle could not get over the fact that she had an uncle. Why had no one told her? How had Chris found him?

Kyle began to relax a little. She was comforted by his presence. And he seemed to understand her fears and issues about her mom and Chris. "Don't worry" he told her "if you are safe, your mom is safe." But they both knew someone would have to reach her. Of all the players, her mom was now the most alone, and presumably the most terrified.

"We are going to a ranch. It is a large piece of property and easy to defend against snoopers. Interestingly, so are buildings in a city. It's the suburbs you have to avoid. We'll be approaching in a couple of minutes. Just in case slip into the back so if anyone is watching you won't be seen."

They passed through a gate, down a long drive, and entered a large garage with an automatic door. Once the door was back down, Bob and Kyle entered through a door directly into the house. Bob kissed an older woman and said "Hi, mom. Where's dad? Kyle, I want you to meet your grandmother." Kyle was speechless.

The older woman crossed the room and hugged Kyle. "You look so much like your mom."

Kyle wondered how she could possibly have a more amazing month. She was spending time with her mom. She was spending more and more time with Chris because of the living arrangements. And she loved the Blacks. The course, which was even better than she had hoped, met five mornings each week but only for three hours. Kyle was deliriously happy.

Mary Manly loved her daughter and was quickly becoming friends with

Chris. She couldn't imagine a nicer young man. And he went to great lengths to make her feel included in everything they did. She deliberately postponed moving to the house they were buying in order to make it easier for her daughter to sleep with her boyfriend. She hired workmen to fix the house and solved the problem of the separate apartment by putting in a laundry room which had access from both living areas. Both Chris and Kyle would have just stayed at the Blacks if given their choice.

One day when she was alone with Chris, Mary Manly said "Chris I wish there was an easy solution. My husband can be cruel and dangerous. I don't think he would deliberately hurt Kyle. But he thinks he knows what she should want and he definitely wants to control her. Sometimes I think you should just move in with Kyle and take your chances. Sometimes I think that you should grab a backpack and run. I am so afraid you will get hurt."

"Mrs. Manly, I have no doubt that my relationship to the GFT grant is how someone will try to separate me from Kyle. Do you know Mitchell Bierman?"

Mary Manly cringed and Chris continued. "He and the professor who advises me keep asking me to steal large amounts of money from Global. There is no way to say no. They claim it is part of the security improvement effort and that I am the star of computer security. Thanks to our friend Bill and to Kyle and Jennifer, I have been able to keep them guessing. The current game is that I find a weakness in their computers and exploit it and they try to figure out what I did. One day they will have learned everything they can from me and I have no doubt that they will claim I stole the money on my own. There is no proof of any kind that I was doing this as part of my graduate studies."

"Chris, I wish I could just give you two your happiness. I will do whatever I can to help you."

Two or three evening each week Chris would be in charge of the grill. Whenever it was nice enough to eat outside in the evening. He would do everything himself. He insisted that if we waited on everyone then maybe the goons would think he was part of the servant class.

One night Kyle woke Chris in the middle of the night. She was shaking and upset. "What's the matter, darling?" he asked.

"I'm afraid, Chris." He stroked her hair and tried to calm her. "I must have been dreaming," she said. Kyle kissed him, looked at him in the dark, and kissed him again. "No matter what happens, Chris, Even if we get separated, I will always come back to you. Always."

The month passed too fast for everyone involved. Even the Blacks were sad to see the month end. Kyle and Mary Manly moved into the new house for a couple of days. Then they returned to Gotham. Kyle told Chris that she would be back in mid-August to 'meet Jennifer.' Chris and Dr. Black rented a small boat and spent several days fishing and talking about life. Chris missed Kyle but loved the Blacks and was happy to spend a couple of weeks with them.

John Manly confronted his wife. "You went to the courthouse today." It was not a question. "Did you talk to Chris Krail?"

Tears appeared in Mary Manly's eyes. "I need to find my daughter." She looked right at her husband and said "I will do anything to find her. I want my daughter."

"Did he talk to you?"

"Yes he did."

"What did he say?"

"He said that she asked for me. He said that she needs me."

"Did he tell you where she is?"

"No, he did not."

"If you went back again, could you get him to tell you where she is?"

Mary Manly looked at her husband. She wanted her daughter but didn't want to be used to hurt either Kyle or Chris. "I would try but the judge told me he would make bail this afternoon."

"What!" John Manly lost his composure for a moment. He grabbed a phone, punched the speed dial and said "Get me Bierman!"

Kyle and Jennifer loved their new home. They spent a lot of time discussing how Chris and Bill would fit in. All they could decide was that Chris should come and go through Bill's apartment. They were pretty sure that would be okay with Bill.

Jennifer wanted to know about the romance with Chris. Kyle wanted to know about the summer in Europe.

Kyle told Jennifer about her month where everything went perfectly. She even told her roommate the episode where her mom had first found her sleeping with Chris and had shut off the lights and left them overnight. She also told Jennifer that she was more and more sure that the world would come crashing down around Chris. She, Kyle, would kill to protect him.

Jennifer's story was actually a lot more interesting. The two girls sat up the entire night. Jennifer said. "I know you have no secrets from Chris but please tell him these are my secrets and I would like to tell him myself. Where do I start? Did you notice that we flew first class? It would seem my mother has a friend and he provided the tickets. He must be in love with my mom. You wouldn't believe the effort he made to win me. He tried as hard for me as that crazy Chris does for you. Yet they insist they are just old friends who ran into each other after many years. Apparently he knew her before she married my dad."

"It was like when I first met you Kyle, he wanted very badly for me to know him, yet I don't know a lot about his background. It is clear he is wealthy, and as best I can tell he is a lawyer. I don't think he lives in Italy. What he wanted was to be sure that my mom and I had a wonderful summer. And she helped him keep his secrets. She is still there. I flew straight back here." She blushed and looked at her friend. "I wasn't sure if I should stop in Gotham. Bill is staying at our place in the Gotham. He is alone in our apartment. Do you think I should go by there for a couple of days? I'd like to but he freaks so easily."

"Call him first and ask if you could stop by for a day or two. Go, it'll work."

Jennifer spent a week with Kyle and then over everyone's protests took a bus to the city. She stayed for five days. Bill then went to see his parents and would rejoin them just before classes. Chris, Kyle and Jennifer got his apartment ready. The construction crew had put in enough electrical circuits to run the department of defense command center.

Classes started. Chris' worry level increased as he was given yet another problem by Dr. Roberts. He sensed it was a set up. He was to regularly take funds from every leak in the GFT system. This time he was directed to park the money in an account within the Division of Computer Sciences. He agreed to do it. But he told himself he would never use the one GFT problem created by John Manly's incredible ego. John Manly had made that problem, Chris was not about to fix it for him, and someday he might be able to exploit it to help Kyle.

Chris knew that Kyle had no secrets and it worried him that she never mentioned any of the things about her father that Chris had learned. Chris often thought he should raise the subject but felt he should understand the issues before he opened what might be wounds. He even considered discussing it with Kyle's mom. Finally he told himself he should not invade their privacy any more than he already had.

Chris pretended that he had moved in with Bill. He entered and left the house through the apartment. He spent all his time with Kyle. On Wednesdays they had ladies night and it was expected that he would stay away until bedtime so the girls could just hang out together. He never missed a Sunday with the Blacks and he never came without Kyle. Jennifer almost always came and sometimes Bill. The Blacks were frequent guests at the commune, so named by Kyle because she thought it would be antithetical to her father's wishes.

There was one other problem besides the GFT cloud over Chris. Jennifer was trying to figure out her relationship with Bill. She had gone from rescue to friendship but she saw things in him that no one else could understand. Chris and Kyle were amused. It had been so easy for them.

Bill listened to the tape twice. "Chris, Dr. Roberts and this jerk Bierman talked to you for almost two hours. They never said anything new. They just kept getting you to say that you have stolen millions of dollars from Global Financial. I'm sure I am right. They are taping this. They want samples of your voice saying you stole money from Global."

"I know Bill. But I still can't imagine that they can really hurt me. If there is ever a fight, they will have their evidence but I know where the money went. Your suggestion to tag the money was great. My big fear is that Kyle's father just wants a way to separate us. But he doesn't know his daughter like I do.

Dr. Black studied the letter. He even tried to be funny by looking at it upside down. "Chris, this is so wrong I don't know where to start. I have never seen anything like it. I would suggest that we make copies and put the original in my safety deposit box. Keeping this letter as a hedge against your future is only a start. We need to talk about what this means."

"The Board of Trustees of Athené is assuring you that your work is so valuable in the field of computer security that they are taking an unprecedented step. They guarantee that applying your discoveries before your doctorate is complete will in no way keep you from receiving your degree or be allowed as a challenge to your thesis if you chose to use your current work as a basis for that thesis."

"I have said it before. No one should have this much influence with the board. I am sure that this is not a spontaneous outflowing of affection for your greatness. This was bought. You were bought and sold so you could solve some of Global Financial Transfer's security problems. They even have the nerve to add that you cannot profit privately from your discoveries. Since they were financed by the grant they are technically the property of GFT. This is outrageous. Chris, whatever happens, once you are safe and feel secure, I would like your permission to show this to the faculty legal counsel. I will do nothing as long as you are in danger but this compromises the whole university as well as you."

"Another way to look at this, Chris, is that the board is saying that since GFT gave us a grant they have the right to ask you first to explain exactly what you are doing, and second, the implication is they have the right to determine what you study. This document on the surface tells you the university believes your work has incredible stature. Underneath it says that academics can be bought. Most importantly you no longer have any excuse to say you are still working on the details. They are entitled to constantly view your progress."

"Dr. Black, I really do love Athené and if you see this as a threat to the university maybe we should consider a strategy that doesn't wait three years until I get my doctorate. I agree with you this letter is supposed to look like it is for me but it is really to give GFT the right to push me around. Basically, I am being threatened by GFT and the university is telling me they won't stand behind me because they don't want to lose the money. Hardly seems like something that is in keeping with academic freedom. Maybe I had better tell you my suspicions about Dr. Roberts."

Chris then related that he had accidently blundered on the fact that Dr. Roberts seemed not to be surprised that he would directly receive large amounts of money from GFT that were outside the grant. He told Dr. Black how Kyle felt about Mitchell Bierman. Chris wondered if it were possible that someone besides Dr. Roberts was being bought.

"I can start investigating peoples finances but someone might notice." My plan had been to wait. If I am accused of stealing I will go on a witch hunt into people's finances but with witnesses so that money doesn't start getting laundered."

"Chris, I will start putting together a list of university officials you ought to look at."

Chris hesitated. "Dr. Black I have a very risky plan. I can't stand feeling like at any minute they will try to take Kyle from me. I think I know how to force their hand. But my plan involves you and I want to talk about it with Kyle. Please don't tell anyone about our discussion but think about whether you would accept me as a graduate student in anthropology at the end of this semester. Don't even bring this up at dinner. I want to think for a week or so before I even tell Kyle."

"Also," Chris continued "I have given this a lot of thought. While I like to work with computers, you know how much I am interested in your field. And at least it would seem that anthropologists don't put themselves up for sale. If I transfer to your department I would like to get a Masters degree as opposed to a doctorate. When Bill graduates he and I may go into business making special needs devices."

Chris was very anxious to see Jennifer. He had called the apartment but no one was there. He always knew where to find Kyle but occasionally Jennifer was not with her. Fortunately, Kyle knew where she was and she shared Chris' concern.

"Bill just came to me out of the blue and asked if I thought the Blacks would let him use my apartment over the garage for a couple of weeks. He had a backpack. At first he wouldn't talk about it at all and then just said he's upset and needs to be by himself for awhile. So I walked him over there. He went straight up to the apartment. I talked to Marcia Black. I tried again. He just says he needs some space and needs to be alone. He just wouldn't talk to me. The only positive thing that happened was when I was finally leaving. He asked me if I could take care of the two of you by myself for a couple of weeks."

They sat with Jennifer behind the library on the hill that overlooked the lake. Jennifer was clearly also upset and they remembered that she hadn't been at breakfast. They had not worried because both Bill and Jennifer were gone. Jennifer looked at them both and just said "give me a minute."

Kyle rocked her friend. Chris didn't know whether to leave or stay until he looked at Kyle. He stayed and sat on the other side of their friend. Jennifer voice was firm. "I am glad Chris that he asked you to take care of me, I sure he never had any doubt about Kyle."

"You guys know that once all I cared about was convincing Bill that he was just as good as the rest of us. When I finally got him to talk, I worked really hard at being his friend. I even figured we were both alike. We both like to rescue people. I have never pushed him and I have worked at never forgetting how sensitive he can be. This summer I asked my mom to have him stay in my bedroom while we were away. When I went down there before classes, he actually told me that it was sweet that I wanted him in my bedroom."

"So I have been thinking about this for months. I go rock climbing with him. You know I don't date anyone else. We all spend so much time together. Last night you guys kind of faded and we were watching TV. I finally just asked him if I could kiss him. You know how he gets. He said he'd have to think it over. Then he just got up and went to his apartment. I went down and knocked after fifteen minutes. I was going to apologize. He wasn't there. I have no idea where he spent the night."

Chris took Jennifer from Kyle and hugged her. He kissed her on the forehead. "He didn't say no, Jennifer."

Maureen Martin looked at Mary Manly over lunch and lied. She hoped that Mary understood the lie. "Jennifer called me about two weeks ago, just before she disappeared. She said she had to go and find Kyle. She couldn't stand all the questions from the police. Next thing I know she and their friend Bill have both vanished off the face of the earth. I have no idea where they went."

Mary looked at her friend across the table. Maureen was not at all upset. This was an act. "Do you think Kyle is with them?"

Maureen took Mary's hand. "Mary, I wish I could help you find Kyle. I think everyone is right. Chris has hidden Kyle. No one will be able to find her until Chris is ready. You can be sure she's safe. I don't believe that Chris would harm her. And I'm sure he has her with someone he trusts. I'm sure he wouldn't let her be all alone." Maureen had been told that she must tell Mary that Kyle was not alone but Maureen knew nothing else.

Mary thought about her courthouse conversation with Chris. She knew how important it was to listen to his words. Chris had also told her that Kyle was not alone. She could see from looking at Maureen that her friend knew where to find Jennifer. She could see from Maureen's concern that her friend did not know where to find Kyle. Then Mary thought she understood. It is a message from Chris. Chris is telling me that Maureen knows where to find him.

Mary looked at her friend and thought carefully. She didn't have to fake the emotions and she was on the verge of tears. "My husband always said Kyle would be held for ransom. I have always tried to protect my daughter. I always wished that if there were a kidnapping it would be me and not my daughter."

Maureen looked at her and smiled. Every word was on tape and Maureen would be able to listen to them over and over to help her understand the conversation. She was sure that Mary understood the basics. The accidental meeting just before lunch conveniently near a good restaurant had been choreographed. Mary understood that Maureen was there to deliver a message. Now Maureen had to do one more thing. She had to set up a way for Mary to get her a message if Mary wanted another meeting.

"Mary, I've taken a part-time job. I am not at home very much. I guess you know I have been seeing someone. But you can leave me a message at work. I'll write down the address for you. If I'm not there you can leave a message with the manager." Maureen wrote an address but no phone number on a piece of paper. She showed it to Mary and said "do you know where this is?"

It had been chosen to be an easy address for Mary. Mary smiled. "Yes, I know exactly where that would be." Maureen pretended to hand her the paper but palmed it.

The girls invited the Blacks to dinner leaving Chris, the grillmeister, to lure Bill out of hiding with his ever improving cooking. Chris had thought about this a lot. He decided that they were all making it worse by constantly apologizing to Bill as if he needed to be protected. So he took a different tact.

"You know, you really hurt Jennifer. She has been crying a lot and skipping a lot of classes. Kyle and I are doing our best. But you really made her feel inadequate." Then he lied. "She won't tell us what happened but I don't think the details matter." Then he told the truth again. "I think she feels that she has lost you as a friend and she is someone who really needs her friends."

"Chris, I like Jennifer so much. I just withdraw whenever she is near me. I feel safe when we're all together. I am getting better at rock climbing. But I don't know what to do when I am alone with her."

"Think about how much she likes you. Didn't she ask her mother to put you in her room last summer? Doesn't she keep doing little silent favors for you? Did you ever notice that our laundry, our shopping, and even our cooking sometimes magically get done? Did you ever notice that she never complains or whines? It's not that we don't do things for them, too. We're friends. And think about this. Basically, Kyle and I are just really close friends. Stop thinking of Jennifer as a beauty queen and ask yourself who are your best friends."

"If she pushes you Bill, just tell her to give you a little slack, but don't run away. She is lost without you. Just find some way to tell her how important she is in your life. There is something else. All her life men have just followed her around without knowing anything about her. What she wants is to be rescued from the wolf pack. What she wants is a friend who wants her as a friend. She needs to be rescued, and she wants you to rescue her."

Chris talked over his plan with Kyle. Kyle's initial reaction was that she wanted to postpone what she called the day of the crash as long as she could. But she understood why Chris wanted to do it this way. And Kyle, almost as much as Dr. Black, resented her father's interference with the university.

Chris hesitated and then told her the things he needed to prepare. "Kyle, would you mind if I took $60,000 from one of your accounts. I want to repay all the money I had to borrow from the university before I am arrested. I want to be free of all real thefts before that happens."

"Why don't I just give it to you Chris? Why do you have to take it out yourself? You know you can have as much as you want."

"If you give me the money, darling, it will be very visible. I need to make it disappear from one of your accounts and reappear in the university accounts. No one except you should know about this. Trust me if one of your larger accounts shows a little less growth one month, no one will care. The university doesn't know the money is missing so I have to sneak it into their account."

"Chris, if this is all I have to do to help you, I will feel that I am not doing my share. Take the money and tell me what you really need."

"Kyle, when the crash comes, I would like you to disappear. I think both your mom and I, not to mention you, will all be much safer if you are hidden. I will need to hide you where no one you know will be able to find you. I need to hide you beyond the reach of your father. Your father and that charming Mitchell Bierman appear to be suspicious by nature. If we can hide you, they will think I am using you as a bargaining chip. Hopefully, they will miss the real point and think that I am just looking for a plea bargain or negotiated settlement."

"Chris, I see three major problems. First, I cannot imagine where I can go where my father's security forces can't track me. Second, what will we tell my mom? And last, I don't want to be separated from you."

"I can see no way to tell your mom where you are hiding. Somehow we will tell her you are safe. Your mom is my major worry in this. I thought about asking your mom to hide with you but one reason for hiding you is to make your father think that there is a possibility I am holding you against your will. I can only promise that after your safety my next major concern will be trying to protect your mom."

"I think I have always known where to hide you. I have never kept any secrets from you but just this once I am asking you to trust me a little longer with this one. After Thanksgiving I am going to disappear for a week. You and Jennifer, Bill and the Blacks, along with a host of phony tape recordings will make it look like I am out with a terrible case of the flu. You can help in another way. I will need at least five thousand dollars in real cash for the week. You will need that much for yourself when you run. So slowly and inconspicuously start accumulating cash."

Chris left out one important conclusion. He and Bill had begun to believe that for reasons they couldn't understand, Mitchell Bierman and the goons were a threat to Kyle. Maybe it was all the stock she owned. Maybe her father wanted to be sure he would never lose control of her stock. He had to get Kyle away safely. He could not protect her on the open campus.

Jennifer and Bill had gotten in the habit of climbing twice each week. Thursday afternoon was a regular time and the other was unscheduled. Jennifer spent an hour looking in her mirror trying to decide if she should try to look more pretty or more plain. Finally she did nothing and went the way she was. She really hoped he'd show. It was something they both liked. And it was non-verbal and non-threatening.

Bill was at the wall half an hour before Jennifer. He was ready. "Hi, Jennifer. I'm glad you're here. I could never climb without you." Then he leaned forward, held her with the one arm that wasn't full of rope. Bill kissed a very surprised Jennifer on the cheek and whispered "next time I'll ask before I run away, I promise."

They climbed for an hour. When they got back to the commune Bill went to his own apartment to change for dinner. Jennifer looked at Kyle and smiled.

"So? You haven't smiled in days. Does this mean that Bill will be joining us for dinner?

"Kyle, he asked me if I would go home with him this weekend and meet his parents."

Chris slipped out of bed and turned on his laptop. He went over his entire file on the Manly family and reviewed everything he knew about John Manly and the early years of Global Financial Transfer.

Then he set up macros. Scripts that would allow him to investigate Mitchell Bierman and the list of questionable university officials that Dr. Black had given him. He didn't think he would get caught. But just in case. He would show both Bill and Dr. Black how the macros worked in case someone got to him first. He would wait until the last possible moment, download everything he could get his hands on, and then make his big announcement.

He turned off the computer. It was after 5AM. He slipped back into bed. Kyle rolled toward him, put her arms around him, and kissed him. She never woke up. He didn't think she had even been aware that he was gone.

mom, the mothers of misinformation, held a pre-Thanksgiving meeting. Chris spoke. "I just want you all when you go home at Thanksgiving to think about the risk I am asking you to take. We all agree that I am going to be arrested. If you help me, you may all be in trouble."

All three of his friends tried to stop him but he continued. "I wouldn't even be the first graduate student from my department to go to jail. Years ago, one of the graduate students tried to insert a "worm" in the national computer network. The idea of his worm was that there would be a notice on everyone's computer. A message like 'Kilroy was here.' Well somehow he screwed up and actually infected some critical computers with a virus. He clogged 6000 computers on the old ARPAnet in 1988. There is a precedent for computer graduate students to do time."

"Then there is our little organization. We have an image of ourselves that we are doing no harm. Look at me - the hacker , the anti-hero of the information age. I'm a rebel with a modem. But I am certainly not the first. In 1993, five young men from Gotham were caught slipping through cyberspace. Several did time. The most notorious, *Phiber**Optik* was sentenced to a year in jail. These five high school kids just played with phone circuits, just to see what they could do."

"Want to know what these five cyberpunks called themselves? They were MOD, the masters of deception. They were MOD, we're MOM. Lots of difference."

"I just want you to know that you are all taking a risk. Even Kyle. When I think about this, I bet her father might want to punish her for siding with us."

"Chris" Kyle finally interrupted. "What you say is true. But I am a part of this. I have chosen sides. If my father and henchman Bierman back off there is no issue. If they don't, you didn't do anything wrong. You have committed no crimes. The worst thing you ever did was think you knew about me before you met me."

"Chris" Jennifer wanted to talk. "Kyle's right. There is no crime here. Mr.

Manly just likes to have things his way. And you are in his way. Good thing, too. There is nobody else I would ever pick for my buddy Kyle."

"Chris" Bill asserted himself. "Even the best computer whiz occasionally needs technical support. I have unusual technical expertise, but I am the support you need."

John Manly and Mitchell Bierman met in a secure room. They knew each other really well and they both knew they needed each other. John Manly listened as Bierman filled him in.

"There is not a lot of good news. First, Judge Branson removes himself. I told him that if his relationship with us was challenged in court we would win, no sweat. You know what he says to me? He says we use money as muscle but the other guys use real muscle. He says he doesn't even want to think about the guys who pay this attorney that took the kid's case. Branson looks me in the eye and says that we can threaten him but the other guys never threaten, they just make people disappear."

"So I look into the attorney. Anthony Dragoni. Nobody will tell me the names of his clients. All you ever hear is stuff like 'you don't want to know.' He has corporate offices that we can't touch. He transfers money through GFT but mostly it moves from one numbered account to another. We can't tell the source or where it goes. I approached a couple of banks. I keep being told that there are some secrets that aren't for sale. They are guaranteed in blood."

"There's another side to this lawyer. About once a year he emerges to handle a pro bono case. Usually some destitute slob accused of a serious crime. He has never lost a case in court. At first I thought he took Chris Krail as a pro bono client. Then I remembered the grandparents. I am sure there is a connection. And the reason I am sure is that we were able to find out that he only met with the kid for ten minutes. An hour later Dragoni posts a $10 million cash

bond. You better believe this lawyer isn't risking his own money. This has got to be family money."

"Dragoni takes the kid out of court in a bulletproof vest with bodyguards. He is whisked away. We think he is in the lawyer's offices. The down side is the kid now has access to a computer. We can try anything we want but I bet the kid can still get into our stuff. Would you believe the new judge made him promise not to steal if he were released on bail?"

"Then there is the new judge. Unapproachable. The last three guys who tried are in jail. On the other hand, the prosecutors still think the kid stole the money. Most importantly, they see him as a rogue hacker, a threat to society. They also think he's dangerous because he absolutely refuses to discuss your daughter. The judge let him out because there is no ransom note. We should have thought of that."

"Then there is Kyle. We have no clue. She hasn't accessed a single asset since she disappeared. She has not called anyone that we know of. She has not used her phone. We have been watching the Blacks. I tell you what I hope. I hope she disappeared because she found out what a schmuck the kid really is. I hope she's hiding out because she's too embarrassed to come home. If she turns up we got to get to her first and make her say she escaped from being kidnapped. But I still think it is a real kidnapping and the kid wants her as his ace. If the kidnapping is not real, we can still control Kyle through her mother."

John Manly thought this might be Mitchell Bierman's most diplomatic presentation in the thirty five years they had known each other. "So Mitch, basically you think the kid will go down because the prosecutors believe our evidence. We have lost some control over events. We have a defense lawyer that has to be considered dangerous and our best guess is that the kidnapping is real."

"Just don't lose sight of two facts, Mitch. We have to regain control over Kyle and Kyle owns a lot of stock. Let's be very clear that we are out of time with Kyle. Originally, we were going to isolate her over Christmas and then make our choices. She is getting too close to her twenty-first birthday. The fact that

Kyle is missing, and then everyone believes that Chris is responsible for her disappearance may actually work in our favor. But lay a tight net. We gotta get to her first. Either she signs over her stock or she never sees the boyfriend again. One way or the other. Have a look at the contingency plans. We may have to move on Kyle faster than I thought."

Thanksgiving arrived. Kyle and Jennifer wanted to stay together. But Maureen Martin asked Jennifer to come home alone. She had something important to tell her daughter. Kyle was a little more comfortable when her mom told her that the two of them might be alone for the holiday since her father had important business. The two girls would meet Sunday morning and return to school early.

Bill went home to his parents and Chris moved back to the Blacks.

All the way back to Athené it was clear that Jennifer had something to say to Kyle. As soon as they landed they rented a car and went to a nearby park. Kyle waited patiently. Her friend was happy but clearly didn't know where to begin.

"Kyle, did I ever tell you that you're the best friend I ever had? I have something just incredible to tell you and I don't know where to start. I have to ask you again not to tell Chris. I would like to tell him myself. If he asks you what's wrong with me, just tell him to ask me himself. But I have to start. We told the Blacks we're coming for dinner. We only have four hours and I have a lot to tell you."

"You know that my mom has this friend. I told you about Europe this summer. Well, they finally stopped pretending they were just friends. I can't tell you what an incredible weekend I had."

Anthony Dragoni knew it would be an interesting dinner. Chris was one day out of jail. The two had already begun to work with each other. Chris had fortunately trusted him enough that the two already had a working outline of the court case. He laughed to himself when he thought about what a great case this would be.

Jennifer's suggestions about the young man Bill were right on target. He now looked quite different. Jennifer was turning out to be calm under fire. She was going to be the key to his credibility at dinner and he had agreed to let it be her dinner. The dinner would be in the private dining room of his law firm. He knew that by the end of dinner, neither Chris nor Bill would have any serious doubts about the choice of legal counsel.

Jennifer had always liked the entrances she and Kyle had made. She decided to be the last one at dinner. She would enter with her mom instead of the absent Kyle. So Chris and Bill were reunited by Chris' new attorney. Bill had never met Mr. Dragoni until that morning but surprised Chris by telling him that the meeting had been arranged by Jennifer.

The ladies entered. Jennifer went directly to Bill and just looked at him. Finally she said "Wow!" After quietly asking "may I?" she kissed him. Then she went to Chris and hugged him. "Thanks Chris for accepting my suggestion as your attorney."

When they were all seated Jennifer asked to speak. "We're here this evening to celebrate the fact that Chris is out of jail and safe. Also, things got a little hectic after Thanksgiving so I didn't get a chance to tell either of you two something of some consequence."

"It all comes together. I chose the attorney to represent Chris. I chose him because he is my dad. Take a look at us. There is no denying it."

The second week in December Chris was gone for eight days. He left after dark with this backpack which contained a change of clothes and his laptop. He had convinced his friends that if they would worry about covering him at school, he would worry about the rest.

Bill had worked out a tape of Chris' voice. He had altered the frequency slightly to make Chris sound sick. The tapes were carefully played into Dr. Roberts' voicemail. No one went to the Blacks on either Sunday that Chris was gone. But on Tuesday, Marcia Black showed up at the apartment, allegedly shared by Chris and Bill, with her homemade chicken soup. Dr. Black himself filled in for the three sections Chris was unable to teach in his course.

When Chris returned he smiled at everyone, lay down on the couch and slept for fourteen hours.

"It would be better if no one knew where I am going to hide Kyle. You all know how I feel about Kyle. I have done my best to see that she will be safe and secure. She will be as happy as anyone could be under the circumstances." Chris was at the Blacks for Sunday dinner. The following week final exams would begin and then Christmas vacation would follow. "I haven't even told Kyle where she is going."

"I am going to make my announcement on Wednesday. I will just say that I have decided not to continue graduate studies in computer science and that I have been accepted in the anthropology department. I will do this by leaving a letter for Dr. Roberts on his email and following up with a hard copy which I will put in his hand on Thursday while I am wearing a wire. The timing is deliberately contrived to let everyone complete their exams for the semester. Kyle and Jennifer may or may not be able to finish their anthropology final which is the last one scheduled. Not surprisingly, their advisor and teacher thinks if there is a crisis, he will allow them to complete the final when things return to normal."

"Kyle will ask her mom to send a jet for her. She will never make the plane. A lot depends on how fast Bierman and his boys respond. They can't just come after me. They have to file a complaint with the police. I suspect the police will respond quickly. I would be very surprised if I am not in jail by Christmas. This may be our last dinner together for a while. If events move slowly we may still be here next Sunday but I doubt it."

Everyone looked at Kyle. "I don't feel that there are any other real choices. My father will never willingly accept my choices in life. I don't think that it has ever occurred to him that I am a person that he cannot control. What's that Dylan line: 'Your sons and your daughters are beyond your command.' Command is the key here. He thinks of me and even the university as events that can be controlled. Once I heard him on the phone to Bierman. You know what he said. He said ' money is muscle.' "

Kyle continued her rationalization. "The thing I feel most badly about is what is going to happen to Chris. He was in the wrong place at the wrong time. He had the right skills but the wrong attitude. He believes in right and wrong which makes him unacceptable to the goons. On the other hand" she smiled "maybe he was in the right place at the right time. He got lucky. He got me."

"The other thing that truly worries me is my mom. I need her. She needs me. I would like all of you to reassure her if you get the opportunity. I have written her a Christmas card. It just says that I love her and that I miss her. Could someone mail it a day or two after I disappear? She will be alone in what I have come to consider the enemy camp. If any of you can do anything for my mom I will be forever grateful."

After dinner they were all quiet. There was a lot of unspoken emotion. Finally Kyle and Jennifer and Bill left. Chris stayed behind to go over his hit list with Dr. Black. Just before turning in his resignation he would be accessing lots of private data on a few selected university officials as well as Mitchell Bierman. He hoped that no one would notice but he wanted to wait until the last minute just in case.

Mary Manly thought about her lunch with Maureen Martin. It had helped her a great deal. Jennifer and Bill were hiding but probably helping Chris. Maureen knew where to find Jennifer and Chris but not Kyle. She had repeated Chris' statement that her daughter was not alone. She had been given a means of getting in touch in an emergency. For her part she had tried to tell Maureen that they should consider kidnapping her.

But what she kept going over in her mind was the rest of her conversation with Chris. What else had he been trying to tell her? She looked at the Christmas card from Kyle.

Dinner at the commune on Wednesday was quiet. After dinner Jennifer wrapped sandwiches for Kyle. She took the opportunity to put a little note in with the sandwiches. It just reminded her that Jennifer would go with her in her thoughts. She hoped the note would give her friend courage when she found it. She wrapped everything in a brown paper bag and put it Kyle's backpack.

Chris sent his email resignation and said he would be in the next afternoon to discuss it in person.

It was a dark and stormy night. They shut all the lights off at ten. At eleven Kyle left through the bathroom window.

On Friday Chris spent his whole day being questioned by officials from various state agencies. Bill wasn't sure when Chris would be arrested so he switched Chris from a tape recorder to a hidden transmitter which could be recorded remotely. As the day wore on Chris tried to assert himself. In the end it was agreed that if he were to be arrested and charged with any crime, he would surrender voluntarily.

The following Monday morning, after spending the night in a hotel, Chris turned himself in at the Gotham state courthouse. It was clear that the trial had state, possibly wider implications, so everyone was pleased when Chris agreed to be tried in Gotham. He would not fight the move and would surrender voluntarily, all in return for not being taken away in handcuffs.

By the time it was noticed that Kyle was missing, Chris had already left for Gotham. The kidnapping charge was added at the time he surrendered. He was glad it hadn't happened earlier. Things might not have gone so politely.

By this time Jennifer and Bill were being questioned intensively about the disappearance of Kyle Manly. Jennifer was suddenly grateful for the new resources that life had unexpectedly brought her. She had been waiting to tell Bill that she had learned that the man who had raised her was not her biological parent. It would have to wait. Meanwhile she suddenly had the means to make both Bill and herself disappear. She simply asked Bill if he would let her hide him in Gotham.

Anthony Dragoni thought it would be easier for him to talk about some of the details. Once Jennifer had made her announcement proclaiming her newly found parent he thought perhaps he should tell the boys the story. There were parts Jennifer had not yet heard. But he had a lot of respect for his new daughter and knew he could safely tell the story to the group. Maureen had heard it all before.

Twenty years ago, Anthony Dragoni had met Maureen and had been swept away. At the time he was poor, right out of law school and working as a legal aide lawyer. He was young and had trained to be a lawyer, but he had not trained to be a lover. Whenever he wasn't sure what to say to Maureen, he would go home and work on being a lawyer. He loved Maureen but didn't know how to tell her and retreated every time she tried to tell him. Nevertheless, they had once spent the night together. He awoke in the morning next to Maureen. Totally confused he had fled. Jennifer had been conceived.

The young attorney ran from his feelings. He became immersed in the case of a young girl who had killed a man. The girl, a runaway, had killed a man in a hotel. Like many runaways she was easily identified by the vultures when she arrived in the big city. This young girl whose name was Nicoletta, Nicole for short, was different from most runaways. She had several thousand dollars in cash but no identification of any kind. She took a room in a cheap hotel. The wrong one it would seem.

The manager of the hotel knew the look and conspired with a friend to try to entrap Nicole and make her into a prostitute. She was young and pretty. She didn't appear to be on drugs. And she was alone and clearly using a phony name. The manager pretended to go out of his way to help her get a job with a friend. At first the girl was taken in. She wanted to believe that these men were just being nice to her. One night the friend was given a key to her room and he tried to rape her. There was steel in the soul of this lonely child. There was a stiletto under her pillow. He died in her bed.

When the police arrived she was still holding the knife. She was wearing a nightgown and covered in blood. The police treated her like a prostitute. Nicole made it worse by refusing to be identified. She told the truth about the attempted rape. But the police thought she was just another prostitute whose john didn't pay up.

She had been in jail for days when Anthony Dragoni was assigned to the case. He thought Nicole was a runaway unhappy child. He thought a woman attorney should be assigned to work with her. The court said no. He asked about counseling. The court said no. He asked for a psychiatric evaluation. The psychiatrist agreed with the police, just a street punk. The psychiatrist said she understood the difference between right and wrong and could stand trial. Anthony Dragoni made a decision.

In retrospect, he thought, some of what he did was because he cared. Some of what he did was so he could hide from his feelings about Maureen. He was busy. He would save a life. After, then he could talk to Maureen. Anthony Dragoni discussed the case with his widowed mother. Their only financial assets were her home and about $10,000 that they had left from his father's life insurance. They mortgaged the home and bailed Nicole out of jail. It was his mother who probably saved Nicole from herself.

The pre-case went on for several months. Nicole's new attorney spent everything he had and every bit of time defending his young client. He even staked out the hotel and was later able to prove that this was not the manager's only attempt to hurt a runaway. The case was made very difficult by Nicole. She would not tell anyone her real name or from where she came or even how she had arrived in Gotham.

One bit of progress came through keeping her at his mom's house. His mom liked the girl. She pointed out that Nicole's English was excellent and that she was apparently well educated. One day she guessed correctly. She spoke to Nicole in Italian. Nicole responded in fluent Italian. When she realized she had been caught, Nicole continued in Italian. She asked if she were acquitted if she could live with the Dragoni's for a while until she sorted out who she was.

The district attorney offered Nicole a plea bargain. Nicole would have turned it down even if her attorney felt differently. As it was, she had an attorney who fervently believed in her innocence. Anthony Dragoni would never plea bargain an innocent just to get a disposition.

After about five months the case went to trial. Nicole and her attorney wanted a jury trial. The trial finally started and made the papers. The prosecution was limp and Anthony Dragoni put the girl on the stand. She described in vivid detail what had happened. She gave her name as Antonia Dragoni. She said she wanted to take the name of the only person who believed in her. She had no trouble with the district attorney. She even volunteered that she was a virgin and was willing to be examined. It turned out the dead man had a long criminal record. The jury deliberated for forty-five minutes. She was acquitted. Self-defense.

Nicole continued to live with the Dragoni's and became friends with the older woman. Gradually she opened up. She told the Mrs. Dragoni that she had run away just to find out about herself. She wanted to go to school and meet people without the shadow of her family. She still wouldn't tell them her real name.

Meanwhile, Anthony Dragoni, thought only about Maureen and how he had abandoned her. He tracked her down but was afraid to call. He followed her and saw that she was pregnant. When he learned that she was about to be married to an older man named Martin, he thought the best thing he could do was to vanish from her life. He hoped that she was happy and vowed to always be there if she needed him. He never married and occasionally would check on how the Martins were doing. When Jennifer grew into adolescence he had a few pictures taken by telephoto lens and wondered if it were possible that this was his child.

When Mr. Martin died, Anthony struggled with his conscience. He finally waited until Jennifer entered college. He then called Maureen and asked if he could see her. Jennifer was indeed his child. His biggest regret was not being together with Maureen and helping to raise Jennifer. He was grateful for the kindness of the stepfather who had treated the child as his own.

Bill sat through this story and wondered about how close he had come to running away from Jennifer. He felt sorry for a man who had lost twenty years of his life because he couldn't tell a woman he loved her. He was happy that he was finally able to talk to Jennifer.

Meanwhile Jennifer's dad continued his story. It seemed that Nicole just needed a little space to think. She read incessantly. She helped around the house. She got Tony's mom to teach her to cook. And one day a man came to see Tony Dragoni in his office. The man invited Tony to lunch. He claimed to be Nicole's father. He had been frantic when Nicole disappeared. He had found her because the trial had made the newspapers. He had been watching ever since.

Nicole's father said that he was a powerful man in an obscure business and that he was wealthy. Nicole's mother had died in an accident when the child was twelve and that had obviously not helped. He wanted to give his daughter the time she needed. He felt that eventually she would call him. Nicole's father expressed effusive gratitude for all that the Dragoni's had done. He apologized for spying. He went on to say that he wanted to repay the Dragoni's for their kindness. Would Anthony Dragoni consider being his private counsel? He would give him a million dollars as a retainer in advance.

This was a dilemma for the young idealistic attorney. The two spent the afternoon together. Anthony Dragoni was very firm that he would not do anything illegal. Nicole's father explained that he came from a background where muscles and brutality often mattered as much as brains. He had succeeded when he realized that planning and organization were more important than the old ways. He had turned a series of once dubious enterprises into a legitimate international business. He admitted that old reputations, and sometimes old habits, died hard. That explained the well dressed bodyguards that hovered politely in the distance.

What Nicole's father wanted from Tony Dragoni was an honest lawyer. If anything smelled rotten he wanted to know. He wanted to move into a future where one out thought ones adversaries. He would like to see his enemies politely kill themselves with stupidity. The other reason that the young attorney was so attractive was his background wasn't enmeshed in complicated histories of family loyalties. It was Nicole's father who owed the young attorney. Not the other way around.

Nicole's father asked Tony to tell his daughter that they had met. He asked her to tell Nicole that he would not interfere in any manner but he was a phone call away and would love to be invited for dinner.

Tony had over the years come to see that many businesses were built on ruthless and cutthroat tactics. He even alluded to the days when the government financed privateers on the high seas. He felt that he had made real contributions to corporate battles being fought with words instead of weapons. Nicole's father was actually refreshing in his honesty about his past. He might even be able to make a few contributions to the Krail case. Tony Dragoni never once mentioned the last name or business of Nicole's father.

Chris had to agree with Jennifer that she had chosen well. His lawyer was the right man for the job. They sat all the next morning and discussed strategy. Chris told him about Bill and the recordings. He told him about how he suspected Dr. Roberts was taking money. He told him how he and Dr. Black and compiled a list of others to check out. He talked about Mitchell Bierman.

Then Chris went through his computer based research. He showed his attorney the mass of background data. He showed him all the records of the money stolen from GFT. And he explained as best he could how on Bill's suggestion he had tried to create a tag system so the money trail could be followed.

Tony Dragoni was impressed. "This is the first time I ever had a client who was better prepared than I am. You have an incredible mass of information. I have no doubt that your friend Mitchell Bierman will end up in jail. We need to scour the data. I have never met Kyle but I don't want to hurt her. I will do nothing against the wishes of you and Jennifer. What we need is to find something illegal here that can be traced back to John Manly."

Chris looked at his attorney. There were a few moments of silence. The thought occurred to Chris that trapping John Manly might mean freeing Kyle Manly. "That may not be too difficult, Mr. Dragoni." Chris then proceeded to tell his attorney everything he knew about the Manly paradox. "The only problem I have with using this data is that Kyle must be protected at all costs. I would like to protect her mom as well. Before we send her father to jail. I will need to know their wishes."

The attorney was in awe. "You are the most amazing researcher I have ever met. It is my experience that everyone has done something that can come back to haunt them. John Manly has made this an easy legal case. It is all a matter of what is best for you, Kyle, and I won't forget her mom."

"Having told you about the Manly paradox, I'm sure you'll be the first to understand how I was able to hide Kyle so completely."

"You're kidding. You sent her to her grandparents?"

"Yup."

"Who else knows?"

"No one but you. Kyle went on blind faith. I am sure she never even knew she had grandparents until she walked through the door and they introduced themselves."

"How do you know they can be trusted?"

Chris explained how he had vanished for a week and tracked down the uncle and the grandparents. He had stayed with them for four days. Not only could they be trusted but they all liked Mary Manly and a child they had never met far more that they liked John. In fact, they all felt guilty for making a deal with John and abandoning Mary.

"There are two possibilities that would help. We need to reach Mary Manly and let her know that Kyle is okay. I would like to offer Kyle's mom some kind of sanctuary but her disappearance might really provoke her husband. The second, I am sure you have guessed. I am desperate to reach Kyle. I want her to know that her father may need to go to jail. Unless she agrees I am not willing to testify to all I know."

"Reaching Kyle will be relatively easier. I have a partner who has been on business in Italy for the last two months. We'll speak in Italian on a scrambled phone line. I will give half the instructions. They will make no sense without the other half which will be delivered on an encrypted computer disk by personal courier. I have done this kind of thing before. Trust me. Would you like to include a note? Your girl will appreciate something tangible."

"Reaching Mary Manly will be far more difficult. It will have to be in public. It will probably be overheard. Jennifer and I have talked about an emergency plan. We track Mary. We can have Maureen accidently bump into her and take her to lunch. Delivering any message of substance will be a problem."

Kyle's uncle Bob made every appearance that nothing had changed. He went to work. Kyle was kept indoors but indoors on a large ranch included an indoor pool. And she wanted to be with her grandparents as much as possible. The grandparents maintained all their social engagements. Chris had guessed correctly. Protecting Kyle was the opportunity of a lifetime for this family.

Bob was walking back to his office in mid-afternoon on Friday when an attractive well dressed woman in her late thirties tripped and smashed into him. She landed squarely in his arms. She thanked him and brushed herself off. "Now that we're acquainted why don't you buy me a drink?" she asked. She caught Bob's wariness and his glances up and down the street. "If a restaurant doesn't look natural, how about your office?"

They discussed possible ways to get her to the house to see Kyle. Once Bob believed that she was authentic it was only a question of the best route. He picked up the phone. He knew it was secure but he was in the habit of being cryptic. "Hi, mom. I think I just met the woman of my dreams.

Nothing would make me happier than if I could bring her home for dinner tonight so she can meet the whole family."

When they entered through the garage Bob looked at his mom and said "Kyle, too."

As soon as his niece appeared Bob said he would let the guest introduce herself.

"My name is Nicoletta Milocellio. I am an attorney. I am one of two partners in the law firm known as Dragoni Law. I am here at the request of our client, Chris Krail. First, I have something for you, Kyle, and she handed over a small sealed note which was instantly opened. Next I am here to bring you up to date. Before I leave I need to carry back your wishes for what we can and cannot use with respect to John Manly. I especially want everyone to think about whether or not we should kidnap Kyle's mom."

"One of the reasons I was sent is to look at the trust that Kyle's father set up. Of key importance to our options with respect to John is the question of whether or not Kyle can vote her stock at this point or whether John still retains the power to vote her shares."

Bob answered. "I will get the trust for you to look at but my memory of the way it was set up was that at age 18 she only got complete control of only 5 percent of her money. She has to wait for age 21 for another 45%. When she reaches age 25 she has absolute control. But we forced John to agree that if he were convicted of any crime at any time full control would go to Kyle immediately unless she was less than 18. In that case full control would have gone to me. I will pull out all the papers after dinner."

It was a long dinner and Kyle finally agreed she was ready to hear the details that had been kept from her all her life.

John Manly had been a problem even as a young child. He was just mean. As a small child he would do terrible things to pets. He once wrapped a gasoline soaked rag around the tail of a dog and set it on fire. He had once tried almost successfully to kill his brother by poisoning Bob's food after a disagreement. All his childhood pranks were aimed at causing pain, not laughter.

By the time John was a teenager he was better organized and knew he could push people around. Before each birthday he not only had a list of demands for what he wanted as presents but threatened the relatives if he didn't get what he wanted. Usually the threats were in the form of blackmail.

In his early teens, John also got in trouble with the law. Mostly for burglary, once for attempted rape. He was treated as a juvenile. The records were sealed. He had served time in juvenile detention. On one of these enforced vacations from his family he met Mitchell Bierman, also in juvenile detention. They had become friends. They both liked to hurt people.

As best anyone could tell John cleaned up his act. But his parents and his brother thought that all he had done was shine up the surface. John learned to be polite. He convinced his new friend Mitchell that not getting caught was more important that anything else. The family had no doubt that the two were committing crimes. They just didn't need the notoriety of getting caught. They needed the pleasure of the act. Eventually, Bierman joined the marines. He told everyone that he wanted to learn to be a trained killer. People laughed but John's family took him seriously.

John was sent to college. His parents told him that if he were arrested, they would stop all payments to him. For six years during which he finished college and got an MBA in finance, no one caught John doing anything illegal. On the other hand he drove an expensive car for which his parents had not given him the money. When they challenged him, he said he was keeping his end of the bargain and that he hadn't even been accused of a crime. At college he was considered a model citizen. Once his college reported that someone had deliberately killed 25 monkeys that were part of a psychology experiment. No one was ever caught. John's family thought it might have been John wanting to show them that he could still get away with it.

Meanwhile Bob had learned computer programming and had been working on money transfers. The parents were able to help him go into business for himself and he found a niche in selling software to banks and financial houses to help them move money from one place to another. Bob's business grew. Bob bought a small mainframe and began handling transfers for clients that were too small to manage without a middle man. Originally called Confidential Financial Transfer, it was the beginning of Global Financial Transfer.

Mitchell Bierman returned. No one knew where he had been but they all assumed jail. He and John regained their friendship and shared a rented house. John was working for a bank and looked like Mr. Right. He was too nice to his family but everyone was polite and they might have believed him if he didn't always have his friend hanging around. He encouraged his brother Bob to take his company public. He even offered to help put the stock offering together since he had the skills and had done it for other clients at the bank.

Bob knew it was the right thing to do. The timing for growth in his business was good. The overall climate for IPO's, initial public offerings of stock, was looking good. But he delayed. Bob and his parents debated whether or not they should use John. There were pluses and minuses. He was capable, there was no doubt. He could not be trusted, there was no doubt. If they didn't use him, he could be cruelly vindictive.

Meanwhile, John had met a charming young woman named Mary. He swept her off her feet. She didn't see the bad side. John kept her away from his roommate. Mary liked Bob and John's parents. She was open and unsuspecting.

The family thought if he is actually going to get married, let's support him. So John put together a public offering. Just before it happened he went to Bob and demanded one percent of the stock as a wedding present. Reluctantly Bob agreed so long as it was everything John wanted from himself and their parents. John was pissed but agreed.

Over the next year, several events quickly followed one another. The public offering was a big success. The influx of capital was superbly timed and Bob's company quadrupled its revenues in a single year and added dramatically to its transfer division. The company began to sell software as a link to their own transfer business. Bob was successful beyond his wildest dreams. John increasingly wanted the credit.

Quietly and without the knowledge of the family, John added to his stock and soon owned 4.5 percent of the outstanding stock. It had never been clear where he got the financing. John's marriage looked happy and on the surface it continued to look as if John had reformed.

Bob was a technician and liked to play with this software and his hardware. John wanted to take over management of the business. Bob knew that for once he had to say no. There was risk in denying his brother but it was unacceptable to turn over the business to John.

Kyle's grandmother interrupted. "Kyle, the next part of the story is about you and your mom. While it is the reason that you have been kept in the dark, it is a terrible story of anger and cruelty on the part of your father. Do you want us to stop?"

Kyle thought, then spoke. "I have already chosen sides. My loyalty is to my mom, to Chris, and to my new grandparents, and to my uncle. Chris once told me that my problem about my father was that I wanted everyone to like me and that I might have to accept that if my father didn't like me it was his problem, not mine. Even if it hurts, I have to understand him. I'll manage but I am glad you're all here. I don't know what I would do without my new family. Chris was so right to send me here."

"Kyle, we all love you and if you want us to stop just say so. Your father is like having an alcoholic family member whose uncontrollable urges constantly put the family in turmoil. But thanks to Chris we are strong enough to deal with him now."

The story continued. Right after Bob turned his brother down, Bob's dog disappeared. John, of course, had an alibi. A few days later the dog was found dead and mutilated staked to the lawn in front of the house. John had an alibi.

John had an attorney call Bob. He was initiating a hostile takeover of the company. He already owned almost five percent of the stock. The sources of his financing were not clear and we didn't know if he could put it together and take over. But one night in the early morning hours John's terrified bride turned up at the home of her in-laws.

She was pregnant. When she had told her husband his thin veneer cracked and she got a good look inside. He told her to get rid of the child. He didn't want it. If she didn't get rid of it he would have his friend Mitchell help her get rid of it. Later when he calmed down, he said he was sorry. He said they were just too young to have a child. He was sorry he yelled, he was sorry he hit her, he was sorry he threatened her, it would never happen again. As soon as he fell asleep, Mary had slipped out the door and run to his parents.

What followed was extremely ugly. Bob agreed to the takeover. Mary agreed to go back to her husband. There were terms. John didn't get quite everything he wanted. In the end all the stock held by the family was split in thirds. John got one third. His parents and his brother would split one third. The unborn child would also get a third. In addition, the one percent wedding present would be put in Mary's name. There were a couple of conditions. In addition to the voting issues that had already been described, the family wanted to protect Mary and the child.

John insisted that he would only agree to the deal if his wife "forgave" him and returned. The family thought that John wanted Mary literally as a trophy wife and that she would make him look legitimate. Mary confided to Bob that John had offered her continuing marriage and a good life for herself and her child. If she failed to agree, John would tell Bierman that the child should not enjoy its life. Bob had been concerned for Mary. Mary had said repeatedly that the only thing that mattered was her unborn child.

Bob had done his best to protect Mary and the child. In the event of the accidental or untimely death or disability for either, Bob would gain complete control of their shares. It was better protection for Kyle than her mom because Kyle had an immense amount of stock. Of course, back when all this happened, it hadn't been worth nearly as much. And, of course, the agreement was that if John went to jail, he wouldn't be able to keep the voting rights to Kyle's stock.

In many ways it was John's control of his daughter's stock that gave him control of the company. One of John's biggest mistakes was the belief that he would always be able to control his daughter. One had to consider the threat to Chris was an attempt to influence Kyle.

Everyone looked at Kyle. She had tears but was composed. "Does Chris know the whole story?"

"Chris knew most of this story before he ever met you. He told us that it took him the longest time to realize that you had never been told." Her grandfather spoke. "He is such a nice young man. Initially he felt guilty for invading your privacy. He said that once you had become friends he told you all his secrets. He thought maybe you were just too ashamed of this part of the story to tell him. Then one day he just knew."

"Part of the bargain was that John wanted nothing to do with any of us. We had our stock and our dividend income. But he told us never to contact him ever again. He would consider that a breach of our agreement. He wanted to deny our existence and his history. Chris said it was only by wondering why we had so much stock in GFT that he had any curiosity about us. Your mom had to agree never to speak to us ever again. He was punishing her for running to us for protection."

The thought on Kyle's mind was pretty obvious. "Is my mother safe? Will he hurt her?"

Bob picked up this answer. "Chris feels that if your father doesn't know where you are, there will be too many unknowns. Your mom could be his last bargaining chip. Nicole has asked us to consider kidnapping her. She also brought the tape of a conversation your mom had with Jennifer's mom. We think your mom is asking us to kidnap her."

Nicole pulled took out the tape and a small recorder. They listened to it twice. Then they listened a third time to just three sentences. Kyle listened intently as her mom said "My husband always said Kyle would be held for ransom. I have always tried to protect my daughter. I always wished that if there were a kidnapping it would be me and not my daughter."

Kyle knew that the others would wait to hear her thoughts. "I would feel so much better if my mom was here with me. I would have to vote for getting her away from my father. I think that's what she wants. But there is so much to think about. Can it be done without risk to her? I am sure he's watching every word she says and everything she does. Are we waiting for her to try to contact Mrs. Martin? Will kidnapping her affect the trial? Is there any chance that Chris will have to go back to jail?"

Nicole knew some but not all the answers. "We have figured out how to get to your mom without endangering Chris. We would follow the standard advice of leaving a little misinformation. Your mom would have to write a note to your father. It would basically say that she has gone in search of her daughter. The note would say she can't look for her daughter when she is being followed night and day by goons and bodyguards. We would ask her to do two other things. She will send him updates mailed from around the country. She will also occasionally access funds in her own name ideally from obscure ATM's during non-business hours. We could provide a trail. He wouldn't find her but at least it would look like she was doing this on her own. It might be transparent to your father but it will keep Chris out of jail."

Nicole looked at Kyle. "I have listened to this tape a hundred times. I have spoken to Maureen for hours. I think your mom wants us to help her. But you are right. There is risk. There is risk to your mom, there is risk to

Chris, and there is also the risk that your father will think he has lost his last safety valve and may become unpredictable. It is possible that John Manly sees his wife as his last bargaining chip."

"My brother and his pal Bierman are more than capable of violence. They may have become a lot more subtle. But they still have their spots."

Nicole looked at the ceiling and made her decision. "Unfortunately, my family has a history that is far more violent than anything John Manly could ever imagine. Over time we have become very reluctant to use violence but we are not afraid. Kyle, you know that Jennifer has found out the truth about her conception. Jennifer's dad, Tony Dragoni, has helped my family immensely in their conversion from brawn to brains. I am an attorney today because he rescued me from a world of violence. But even Tony knows that if necessary violence is the last alternative in self-defense."

Kyle looked at Nicole and didn't quite get the message. "Everyone is afraid of my father. I have always sensed the menace but never understood until today that he could actually be so brutal. Do you really think you can stand up to him?"

Nicole didn't want to talk about the exact nature of her father's resources. It made her shiver just to think about them. John Manly was an amateur. She tried to help Kyle by being honest. "Kyle, twenty years ago I killed a man. I put a knife through his heart. If it wasn't for Tony Dragoni I would still be in jail or dead. I detest the thought that I still own that knife. But believe me, I am not afraid."

The next morning at the ranch was quiet. Kyle swam before breakfast as did Nicole. Bob talked quietly with his parents in the other room. Kyle was reflective. She didn't know where to start with all the new information. She was so happy that Chris was safe and that Jennifer and Bill were with him. Kyle was frantic about her mom. She was sure Nicole was right. In a few minutes at breakfast she would ask that her mom be rescued. She liked Nicole and she loved her family.

"Nicole, did anyone tell you that I want to go to law school even though that's what my father wants me to do?"

"You could do a lot worse. Sometimes the law is a great thing. But be warned. When it is bad, it can be very bad."

"I'm interested in the way the law holds society together and provides a framework. It let's everybody play by the same rules. I am majoring in anthropology and I can see how the law should evolve from the needs of a society to develop and preserve its advances."

"Kyle, if you like, I'll talk to my partner. I am sure he would join me in inviting you to work with us next summer - or any summer while you are in school."

"Nicole, can I ask you a question?"

"Of course."

"Did you really kill a man with knife?"

Nicole hesitated and smiled. Kyle would hear the whole story eventually anyway. "Yes, Kyle, I did. It was necessary. Fortunately, there was someone to rescue me. I have never been able to repay Tony. I hope to help him rescue you."

Jennifer and Bill floated ashore with the four commandos. They all wore black from head to toe. They all wore black ski masks. Jennifer and Bill had been very insistent that they be allowed to go along. The climbing gear was in waterproof bags. The extraction team was a half mile off shore in two fast but beachable boats. They had practiced for three days with the commandos. Only one of them spoke English. None smoked. None joked. They were serious.

Jennifer and Bill pointed out that they had been climbing two days per week for a year. They were sure they were up to this job and they wanted to go. Jennifer added that as a young woman she would be far less threatening than the professionals. It was finally agreed that if the commandos thought the two friends could make a contribution without endangering the mission they would be allowed to go. After only one day the commandos had given a favorable report on both of them.

Unlike their comrades Jennifer and Bill carried no weapons. They had watched in awe as the commandos loaded numerous weapons and protected them for the swim ashore. Bill was confident that the silencers were not exactly legal. Now the commandos quietly rechecked their weapons in the dark. Jennifer and Bill assembled the climbing gear. After watching her climb for only two hours, the commandos had asked her to climb lead.

Lead climb was the most taxing and the most dangerous. If she screwed up she would fall. Perhaps only ten feet, perhaps more. But a fall might put the whole group in danger. Jennifer was glad she had been given three days to practice. She had never before climbed in the dark.

At breakfast Saturday Kyle and Nicole looked relaxed. They had made their decisions. They thought Mary should be pulled out of the equation. But Bob looked serious and spoke for his parents as well as himself.

"We have talked it over. We all hate to admit that we still have emotional ties to John. Nevertheless, all three of us would feel relieved if he goes to prison, the longer the better. We remember the time we were actually most hopeful for him was when he left for juvenile detention. Jail may be the only solution. We know that means that we regain control of Global, but that is not our motivation. The problems that he creates hurt too many people. Kyle, we hope you will understand our feelings about your father and that you will come to support our position that jail is the only answer."

"When I think about the horrible story you told last night and I think about what he has done to you, and to me by keeping you from me, I don't know what to think. It is still hard to hate him. He is my father. But last night I made my decision. There is no other way to rescue my mom. Let's kidnap mom. If he committed a crime, then he will have to live with the consequences of his actions. I am okay if he goes to jail as long as I get my mom back."

Bob still looked worried. "There is one other problem. We talked it over this morning. Kyle I bet there is one other part of your life that your father forced your mom to hide." He hesitated and looked at his equally worried parents. "Have you ever met your other grandparents?"

The climb went flawlessly. Jennifer had been told time was not an issue. Slow and careful. The commandos just thought she was smooth. Good instincts. Strong arms for a girl. They reached the top of the cliff about a hundred yards from the house that was their primary target. One commando stayed behind on guard as Jennifer and Bill set up their escape ropes. Getting an elderly couple down and unhurt would be a challenge. The other three moved toward the house. Their job was to neutralize the opposition. Jennifer fervently hoped that neutralize did not mean kill.

Twenty-five minutes passed. Their guard was calm. Jennifer and Bill were pumped and ready to go convince an elderly couple who had never heard of them that they were all leaving my sea.

Kyle apologized that at every surprise she started crying. "My poor mom. How could he do this?"

Her grandmother put her arm around Kyle. "Your mom apparently promised not to tell you but she has been in contact with them. We see them once or twice a year. That's how it is that we have pictures of you. Your mom told them that she had to make a terrible choice. She had chosen you as the most important person in her life. She asked for her parents support and got it. They are also afraid of my son and have done their best to support her. They love your mom. Maybe when this is all done you will get to meet them."

Kyle composed herself. "Are they safe? Does my father know where they are?"

Bob looked very concerned. "Your father checks on all of us intermittently. But you can bet that once you escaped, the way to control your mom is to threaten her parents."

Nicole was thoughtful. "Don't worry. I have the resources. Kidnapping the grandparents will be relatively easy. They can just leave a note saying they went on a road trip. The day before they disappear a recreational vehicle will be bought and registered in their name. The problem is snatching Mary in broad daylight in the middle of a big city. We have to find a way to let Mary know what will happen. She has to leave a note saying she left to look for you."

It was two in the morning when the commandos cut into the phone line. Mary Manly's mom answered, still not fully awake. "Hi" Jennifer said. "I know this sounds strange but this is Jennifer Martin. I am your granddaughter's roommate at Athené. I am going to knock on your back door in about two minutes. Would you let me in? Please don't turn on any lights. I don't want anyone to see me."

Jennifer and Bill slipped into the kitchen without their ski masks. They carried a bag containing black jumpsuits for the elderly couple. The suits had been fitted with rescue harnesses. Jennifer talked. She quickly told them that Kyle was safe. She showed the grandparents several pictures of herself with Kyle at Athené. Jennifer didn't want to take Kyle's grandparents by force. The commandos had given her only thirty minutes to convince them. Thirty minutes had been a fight. Originally the commandos said ten minutes and we go. Jennifer said they were too old to act that quickly.

Jennifer talked rapidly. It was necessary for them to disappear so that their daughter could be rescued. She had no proof to offer them that she clearly came from Kyle and not from their son in-law. After fifteen minutes of silently listening the couple asked for two minutes alone. They returned.

Kyle's grandfather spoke. "Not only do you fit the description of Kyle's roommate but our daughter already showed us one of the pictures you are carrying. Mary told us she didn't know where Kyle was hiding. Do you know?"

"No one will tell me where to find Kyle." Jennifer voice filled but she regained control. "I was told to tell you that if we can get you and your daughter away safely that Kyle wants to meet you. I want to see her as badly as anyone but I want her to be safe."

Five minutes later they were helping the grandparents to the edge of the cliff. The rescue was uneventful.

Nicole took an instant photograph of Kyle. Kyle stood in front of a white sheet. In front of her she held the daily paper from Hong Kong. It was two days old. All that was visible was Kyle's face and hands. On the back Kyle wrote: "I love you mom. I miss you. Kyle."

Nicole told her it would be postmarked in Melbourne, Australia within

48 hours. Then Nicole took Bob aside and talked to him at great length. They talked for hours.

Bob spoke to his parents and everyone was relatively serious. Finally Kyle said "It can't be that bad. Tell me."

Bob did. "Nicole has an interesting thought. The minute my brother knows that your other grandparents are missing, it will be impossible to get to your mom. The minute your mom disappears, her parents are in grave danger. And furthermore, if my brother is half as smart as he thinks he is, he will eventually realize that his own parents now constitute a threat. He is not above trying to threaten any of us."

"What Nicole is suggesting is that we, too, have to change our hiding place. The Dragoni law offices in Gotham are already hiding the kids including Chris. So far there is no one there that would make it look like a conspiracy. We don't think it would be a good place for the rest of us. Nicole suggest her father's estate as a safe haven. I think it is a good idea. We will create a little misinformation about where we are really going. We will all be transported in small groups by private boat to avoid crossing too many international borders and being seen in too many airports."

"While John is not dumb, Nicole's father is not someone who can be threatened by John. With any luck the trial will be over before John figures out where we went."

"I would suggest that Kyle leave with Nicole. Kyle, you will have to go back in your wig. Mom and Dad and I will time our move so that we are visible until the last moment."

Nicole used the same combination of encrypted disk by courier and scrambled phone conversations to relay her information back to Dragoni Law. The kidnapping of Mary Manly's parents did not seem to be a problem although at first everyone resisted Jennifer and Bill who wanted to participate. When the commandos reported that they were useful and capable, Tony Dragoni relaxed, a little.

Nicole had set up a code to communicate with Bob. All he really needed to know was the date. Bob and his parents would leave a day or two early and head initially for Hawaii. They had a small house on the big island.

The real dilemma was extracting Mary Manly in the same timeframe. First, someone had to reach Mary and be sure she wanted to escape. Then, timing was everything. There was the minor problem that Mary would have a squad of goons following her everywhere.

The movements and habits of Mary Manly had been intensely studied. Opportunities for contact were analyzed. The problem was the need to communicate large amounts of detailed information and to get her consent. It was clear that Mary was making an effort to leave her house at least once per day. She went everywhere by limousine. She had approached the address given her by Maureen three or four times but then seemed to be uncertain and left. A plan evolved.

Tony Dragoni's mom who had once committed her home to help a young girl was more than willing to help another. She was living on the west coast of Florida and hopefully invisible to those studying the moves of Dragoni Law. Mrs. Dragoni was registered at a midtown hotel under a phony name. She was daily given a phony copy of the Gotham Times. The headlines and photos looked like the real edition but the entire front page had the text altered.

Mrs. Dragoni was stationed in a limo and on call. When Mary Manly entered an exclusive beauty salon for her hair and nails, an elegant elderly woman materialized apparently on the same errand. She managed to get close to Mary as Mary was waiting for the manager. "It's all right here in the fine print, Mary." She slipped her the paper without looking directly at her.

Two hours later as they were leaving the newspaper was handed back with the comment "all the news is good news."

After that Mary Manly bought a paper every day and very carefully read the personal ads. If asked she would have said there might be a message from her daughter. She was relieved when she finally saw the message which was not from Kyle.

Several hours after her parents were abducted, Mary Manly left a sealed note for her husband. She confided in the maid that she was going to look for her daughter. She 'accidentally' left the picture of her daughter with its Australian postmark where the maid would find it. She put on a bright red overcoat that was visible from miles away.

Her first stop was for breakfast. She had a cup of coffee and a toasted bagel. She returned to the waiting limo but then seemed to change her mind. She told her driver. "I'm just going in the department store to look for a scarf."

As Mary entered the store she loosened her coat. She stopped at the cosmetics counter where a polite young woman offered her some blush. Amazingly quickly the outlines of her face were changed. She rose shielding her face with her arm, turned the corner disposing of her red coat behind a bush as a young man helped her slip into a grey London Fog. She was not surprised to find someone holding the elevator door for her. As soon as the door closed she was changed to a black wool cape and fitted with a wig. She was also given a large pair of sunglasses.

Another woman with a similar build took the grey coat and was wearing a wig and make-up to look like Mary. The woman got off on the next floor and took the escalator down. Two other women who looked like Mary were wearing red coats on the ground floor. Mary was taken to the top floor and to a back stairway that led to an alley entrance. She squeezed into a delivery truck whose next stop was another department store fifteen blocks away.

Mary was whisked from the delivery truck and into the main store. She walked out the front entrance and hailed a cab. She directed the taxi to the airport. At the airport she used her credit card to buy a first class ticket to Melbourne. She handed it to another woman made up to look like her and who was now wearing a bright red coat. The woman handed her back a coach ticket for a domestic flight to Florida and a small tape recorder.

Mary's domestic flight left first. Five minutes before the Australian departure a man who had been handed the recorder called the Manly home and left a message using Mary's voice. It said she was going to Australia to look for her daughter.

John Manly was angry. John Manly did not like losing control and he did not like the way the events were going. The sudden disappearance of both his own parents and his wife's parents within hours of each other was upsetting. His wife and daughter could no longer be played against each other. He knew that including Kyle his family owned more voting stock than he did. But he still had a couple of things going for him. He met with Mitchell Bierman.

"Mitch, I am upset. How did we lose control of both Mary and her family? I thought we were watching them?"

"John, I had eight men watching Mary but you said she wasn't to see them. She clearly must have had a lot of help. If it weren't for the disappearance of her parents I might actually think she is in Australia looking for Kyle. We lost her before she went to the airport. But we know she bought a round trip first class ticket to Melbourne. It was her signature. There's another thing. The security cameras caught the transaction. She was wearing a disguise. This was a deliberate attempt to get away. Someone sat in her seat but Mary did not get off the plane in Australia."

"Her family is another story. They live in a isolated area. We had a team of six men around the clock. When they didn't check in, I sent an emergency backup team. The first team was taken out by professionals. All six were neutralized. They all survived. Five of them saw nothing. The one who sensed there was a problem said he was taken down by three men who didn't say a word. Unfortunately we missed Mary's escape by about an hour."

"I have to conclude that Mary and her parents had a coordinated disappearance and they had help. Real help."

"Alright, Mitch, let's concentrate on what we have left and how we can use it. First, I still have control of Global's board of directors. I own them. I can still vote 95% of Kyle's stock and even when that gets reduced to 50% in a couple of years, I will still control enough stock to do anything I want. There is no threat unless I lose control of all of Kyle's stock. What other assets do we have?"

"I still think the Krail kid is going down. We might be able to manipulate your family by offering to ask for leniency at the last moment. In the meantime, we own that guy Roberts up at Athené and we own some the board. You were right to let your daughter get attached to that jerk. We might be able to use him to lure her out of hiding."

"So the worst case scenario is that I lose control of my wife and daughter. I used to think I could train Kyle to work in the legal department. At this point I can only say who cares. We have wasted an incredible amount of time and resources on my family. Let's just get Kyle's stock and then good riddance. But I would like to send the kid to jail just to teach them a lesson. I want my daughter to come to me and beg for help. What about this attorney for the kid?

"You're right, John. I need to find a way to have a private conversation with Mr. Dragoni."

Pre-trial events had been moving forward. Mitchell Bierman had met with the DA on several occasions but John Manly stayed discreetly out of the picture. Tony Dragoni introduced all the usual maneuvers to try and get the charges dropped. He refused a plea bargain twice. The plea bargain was based on return of Kyle and the stolen money with a minimum of ten years in jail. The prosecution thought they had a hard case.

Tony and Bill had set a trap for the goons from Global. Mitchell Bierman fell right into it. Bill had managed to get a video camera into the ceiling of the men's restroom at the courthouse. He also had a hidden video camera with a transmitter inside Tony's tie. They hoped that at best the goons would find one but not the other. Bill had also hidden a third camera outside where the restroom door could be filmed. All had date and time encoded. Tony made a point of using the restroom twice every time he went to court. He thought that it would only appear natural not to have his bodyguard follow him into the restroom.

In retrospect, they would have never predicted that Bierman himself would approach Tony. They thought it would be some nameless and faceless goon wearing sunglasses. It was too good to be true. Bierman stationed a goon outside the door while he and another man followed Tony into the restroom. They never looked for a camera. Bierman was not only direct and threatening but he actually hit Tony and broke his glasses. Tony was not hurt but they had two great tapes with Bierman being very clear and very specific about this threats.

The group in the Dragoni office watched both video several times and made copies. Bill and a bodyguard were on a plane to Europe the next morning carrying copies.

A date was set for jury selection. Tony Dragoni appeared in court with an oversize bandage on the side of his head. The reasons for the bandage were not discussed. He asked each juror if they knew about computers. He asked each juror if he/she was presented with two versions of the truth would they be able to decide for themselves which was real. He really wasn't too concerned about the individual jurors. He was much more concerned about jury tampering. He argued that each juror should have to do a financial disclosure before and after the trial. The prosecutor thought that was preposterous. Judge Williams would not allow that. Chris said not to worry. It could all be done in retrospect.

As the trial was set to begin Tony Dragoni consulted a neurologist. He said he had been having dizzy spells and trouble speaking since inadvertently walking into a door in the restroom at the courthouse. He told the neurologist that he was having so much trouble he might actually ask his partner to take over the case.

The case began.

The prosecution asked that bail be revoked since the kidnapping remained unresolved and there was no clue as to the whereabouts of the missing child. (The prosecution always called Kyle a child to invoke sympathy.) Judge Williams refused to revoke bail.

The prosecution then pointed out that a witness they hoped to call, Mary Manly, the mother of the missing child, was herself missing. They were planning to show that Kyle would never voluntarily not tell her mother where she had gone. They felt that the disappearance of Mary Manly added a new and dark turn to the kidnapping.

Judge Williams looked at the prosecutor. "So, let's hear your case. Are you saying that Mary Manly went to join her daughter in hiding? Or are you saying that Mary Manly was also kidnapped?

Tony Dragoni asked to be heard. "Is it possible that the Manly's are all involved in a conspiracy to send Chris to prison? Maybe they are both in hiding to make Chris look like a criminal. I want to subpoena them both as hostile witnesses."

Judge Williams wondered to herself. "What is this case really about?" To the group she made a different statement. "Mr. Krail will remain free on the existing $10 million bail. Mr. Dragoni, I look forward to your subpoenas. At least then we will know the whereabouts of the missing women."

John Manly was not only the chief executive officer of GFT but he was also the chairman of the board of directors. Not an unusual arrangement for a powerful executive especially one who had a part in establishing the original organization. It never occurred to him that he could be threatened or even approached from within his own organization.

Late one afternoon one of the members of the board of directors came to see him in his office. Larry Albright was thinking that being a board member was supposed to be a perk for well connected businessmen. It was not supposed to turn out like this.

There were eighteen members of the board in addition to the chairman. All were very senior executives. Most of them were retired from within the financial industry. They had the experience and the knowledge to provide guidance to the leadership of a world class organization. In return for being on the board each member received $100,000 dollars per year plus expenses. They each had to attend four meetings each year at which they discussed crucial issues but almost always supported the position of management. Altogether they earned their money in about six days of total involvement. Many sat on multiple boards. It was an interesting job. It was supposed to be benign.

It was highly unusual for a board member to ever have an unscheduled meeting with the CEO. Larry Albright screwed up his courage. "John, I have to ask you for a very important favor. I have been asked to arrange for you to meet with a gentleman. He would like to meet you at your home at 7:30 tomorrow morning. He wants to meet with you alone. I was specifically asked to tell you that Mitchell Bierman is not to be anywhere in the vicinity. His name is Mr. Sarducci. He only wants fifteen minutes of your time."

"Larry, come on. Why should I meet with this guy? What's going on?"

"I can only tell you that if you don't meet with him I will be resigning from the board before noon tomorrow. This gentleman is an emissary from someone who represents important financial interests."

Larry Albright had barely left when the one female on the board called. She was calling from Hawaii. "Hi John, it's Susan Smith. How's everything?"

"Fine Susan. I am surprised to hear from you."

"John, I have to ask you for a very important favor. I have been asked to arrange for you to meet with a gentleman. He would like to meet you at your home at 7:30 tomorrow morning. He wants to meet with you alone. I was specifically asked to tell you that Mitchell Bierman is not to be anywhere in the vicinity. His name is Mr. Sarducci. He only wants fifteen minutes of your time."

John Manly was concerned that someone had used two board members to set up a meeting. "Thanks Susan, I'll do my best. My schedule is kind of hectic but I will try."

"John, you have to do this. I'm afraid if you don't I will have to resign from the board."

John Manly put the phone down. Before he could think it through, there was another board member on the phone with the same request. In all, six board members asked for the same favor.

He calmed himself. He knew this was not the time to let his temper get out of control. No one should have this kind of influence with the board. Who could have gotten to six board members? It was clear he would have to meet with the mysterious Mr. Sarducci. It occurred to him that maybe the board just wanted him to replace the sometimes unpleasant Mitchell Bierman. But then why didn't they just tell him.

He was resigned to the meeting but kept wondering what it had to do with Bierman. John Manly and Mitchell Bierman knew more about each other than was healthy. Either could put the other in jail for life. He was always careful to treat his old comrade as if they were partners. Underneath he had nothing but contempt for Mitchell's lack of subtlety and his lack of education. He tolerated Mitchell like a dangerous pet. You admired a cobra but you didn't let it lose. If possible you found a way to remove its venom. A cobra was more useful as a threat than as a killer.

Kyle liked Nicole. She found her to be confident and competent. Kyle admired her fluency in English, Italian, Spanish, and Greek. Most of all she believed Nicole when Nicole had said that she was not afraid.

They traveled together by a circuitous route. Nicole treated it as a vacation. They even traveled one afternoon on a fishing boat and were then picked up by a yacht that took them to a waterfront estate. Along the way a real friendship developed and Kyle shared the details of her life.

Nicole had talked about her father. "Like your father, mine is rich and powerful. Like your father, my father can be ruthless. But there is a real difference. My father wants to be much more. He wants to find a way to bring peace and prosperity without resorting to the violence which established his reputation when he was young. He sees himself as some kind of feudal baron who is responsible for the lives and happiness of all those who acknowledge him as their leader."

"I once ran away from my father. It broke his heart. He responded by letting me have as much space as I needed and then in the end approached the Dragoni's with whom I was living as asked them to see if I would let him come for dinner. I only wanted to be treated like everyone else. He was only concerned that I be happy. He would have let me become a fisherman or fisherwoman if that's what I wanted. He was just being a father and I was a little rebel. I love my dad."

"Kyle, the question we are all going to have to face is whether we want to come to peace with your father or line up against him. Much depends on you and your mom. My father believes that your father is not only dangerous but randomly destructive. He believes that we cannot come to terms with John Manly. My father believes that the best choice we have is to contain him. It will be much less painful that an all out confrontation. I hope I haven't lost you with all my euphemisms."

Nicole hoped that there was some alternative to destroying Kyle's father but she didn't see how.

When the yacht landed, they were greeted by Nicole's father who kissed Kyle on both cheeks and made her feel welcome. It was clear he loved his daughter.

Bill arrived in time for dinner. He was whisked in by helicopter. He told Nicole, Kyle and Nicole's father everything he knew and then handed an encrypted disk to Nicole.

They all sat and watched the video of Mitchell Bierman threatening Tony Dragoni. Everyone was apprehensive until Nicole's father laughed. "Kyle, I am sorry to laugh at your father. It is such bad manners. But they are such amateurs. And they have no sense. This is like a grade B movie from the 1940's."

"I know Tony well. He is the smartest and bravest attorney, except of course, for my daughter. He is a great actor. How did he keep from laughing at this creep? Never threaten like you are a street punk. You approach someone carefully, assume you will be recorded. Then you ask for the help of your opponent. Could they do you a favor? He should have told Tony it was a great pleasure to meet him. Perhaps an off color joke about being alone together in the mens room. Never bring a witness. He should have told Tony he would be grateful if Tony would not forget the missing child. That her father loves her and wants her back. He would be forever grateful if the child could be found. Look what he does. He has set himself up. He is no longer a player in this case and he will be out of Global by the end of the week."

Kyle liked Nicole's father. He was so warm and charming. It was hard to believe that the allusions Nicole had made were even related to this man. "Mr. Milocellio, I think it would help a lot if more people laughed at my father. What would help the most would be if he would laugh. My new grandparents tell me that my father and Mitchell Bierman are true partners in crime. How could you ever separate them?"

Artruro Milocellio had intimate knowledge of how to change people's minds. He detested threats of violence. He was certainly neither afraid of violence or afraid to use it. He looked forward to a day when he would only think of self-defense as its justification. He and his only daughter had had lengthy discussions. She had wanted him to move away from his past. He had wanted her to know that sometimes killing a man is necessary. He didn't want her past to haunt her. He had done a good job.

Artruro Milocellio had turned the smile and request into an art form. In many places in the world quiet, well-dressed and well-spoken young men would make a request on the part of their leader without ever mentioning his name.

"Kyle, what was the name of that priest on that old TV show. Ah yes, we will invent a Mr. Sarducci to meet with your father. We will put a little pressure on his board of directors. The meeting will take place. Mitchell Bierman will be looking for a job."

John Manly watched his front door from the second floor of his townhouse. He wanted to see how Mr. Sarducci would arrive. Ten minutes before the appointment he saw four young men appear on his street and take up positions where they could watch his front door. Since Bierman didn't know about the meeting these were not his men.

Two minutes before the appointment a limousine arrived. Nothing unusual for his neighborhood. Four more young men climbed out and looked at the original four. When everything appeared alright, a gentleman stepped from the limo and was accompanied to the door.

The door was opened by the butler who led Mr. Sarducci into a sitting room. John Manly joined him and introduced himself.

"Mr. Manly, it is such a pleasure to meet with you. I have heard so much about you. I am so sorry to ask for this meeting on such short notice. I will try to take up as little of your time as possible."

"I have come to ask for a favor. Like you, my employer has only one child. He is very concerned for the well-being of that daughter. She is his life. That daughter is now an attorney. I understand that your daughter also wishes to go to law school, is this true?"

John Manly nodded assent. He wondered what this was about.

"My employer's daughter has a partner here in Gotham. You know of Anthony Dragoni? It seems that Mr. Dragoni has not been feeling well after a recent head injury and has asked my employer's daughter to take over as defense counsel for the young man accused of kidnapping your daughter. My employer was very concerned. He did not want his daughter defending someone who would kidnap a young girl. But my employer and his daughter owe a debt of honor to Mr. Dragoni and feel compelled to pay that debt."

"My employer has sent me to ask you for a small favor. We would like you to make every effort to see that his daughter never comes face to face with Mitchell Bierman. She is a delicate child and we are led to believe that your associate can be unsophisticated at times. Do you think you could do this for us?"

John Manly did not have to be told that eight bodyguards were not a game. Nor were six board members who threatened to resign if he did not meet with this mysterious Mr. Sarducci who doubtless had other names as well. There was also the disappearance of Mary and her parents. There was serious money and professional labor involved. Mitchell Bierman always bragged he hired the most capable men available. It looked like someone had access to even more capable men.

And then it dawned on him. He was not being threatened. Someone was asking for his help. This was all polite conversation. Perhaps he should just say of course he would help another father with his daughter. But John Manly was in love with the trappings of power. He wanted to know where it was coming from and who could wield it so effectively.

"Mr. Sarducci, you and your employer seem to have the advantage. I know that sometimes my security chief can seem a little gruff but he's really okay. Is there something I should know? And I confess, I am somewhat at a loss, as I am not sure who you represent."

"Mr. Manly, it is with the utmost reluctance that we came to you for this favor. In case you asked the reason, I have brought this." Mr. Sarducci put a single glove on this left hand and reached into a small valise. He handed a DVD to Mr. Manly, then removed his glove. The gesture with the glove was not lost on John Manly who knew that there would be nothing about the disk that could be used to trace the source.

"Mr. Manly, my employer suggests that you watch the video by yourself. I have been instructed to offer to stay while you watch it. This offer is only to make you feel more secure. With your permission I won't stay. The video contains three segments of the same time period taken from three different video inputs. Please watch them all."

"Mr. Sarducci, if the video explains your request adequately, I will be happy to honor it. I still don't know who sent you."

Mr. Sarducci looked around the room apprehensively. "The name of my employer is usually never mentioned. It is considered very bad luck. Fortunately, I can tell you the name of his only daughter who still carries the family name. Her name is Nicoletta Milocellio. Her father asks only that she does not come in contact with Mitchell Bierman. She is a delicate child."

John Manly watched the surveillance video of his primary ally physically threatening an attorney at the courthouse. He had no problem accepting it as real. But he had a problem. Mitchell Bierman had become a problem.

He had other sources. He had no trouble discovering that Nicoletta Milocellio, a delicate child, had once put a knife through a man's heart. Her father, he thought, has high standards of delicacy.

John Manly had been told. Someone had evidence that could send Bierman to jail. John Manly could not afford a plea bargain if anyone chose to use this video. He would be only too pleased to keep his friend away from this delicate child.

Nicole and Bill returned to Gotham although they deliberately separated so they would not arrive together. Jennifer was happy to see Bill and both Chris and Jennifer wanted to hear about Kyle. Nicole had let Kyle type encrypted messages for both friends. She handed a disk to each of them.

The strategy was that Tony would tell the judge that Nicole was replacing him for medical reasons which he hoped would be short. Nicole would cross examine the prosecution witnesses and reserve the right to recall them during the defense. They would all act as if Chris would not testify but he, in fact, would be the star defense witness. The other defense witnesses would be recalled prosecution witnesses mostly being recalled to establish perjury. Depending how things went, Tony would or would not recover from his supposed neurologic difficulties.

After watching the opening arguments, Chris smiled to himself. Tony Dragoni might be the best but he had never seen anyone as capable as Nicole. He believed in teaching as a method of communication. Nicole had been incredible.

The prosecution said it would show that Chris Krail had used his position of authority as a teacher to take advantage of a freshman, an innocent and sheltered young woman who Chris just happened to know was rich beyond anyone's imagination. He knew about her because he was assigned as a graduate student to the GFT grant. At the same time he was an acknowledged expert in computer security and had used his access to steal millions of dollars from the world's largest financial firm. He had then kidnapped the girl to use as a bargaining chip.

Nicole seemed to have Tony Dragoni's brilliance matched by her father's smiling charm. The defense would show that it was Kyle who established a relationship with Chris. Chris was an orphan. He had been used and manipulated by both the university and GFT. The defense would show that there was a conspiracy within Global Financial Transfer. Chris was the scapegoat. Plus the true criminal was inside the GFT organization itself.

If someone were holding Kyle Manly, it was not Chris Krail, but rather someone much more sinister. Nicole did not say whether or not Chris would testify in his own defense.

The prosecution had a long line of witnesses. They were divided into two parts. First, the kidnapping charge. Two of Kyle's bodyguards testified. It was fortunate for them that Kyle was not there. They told incredible stories of how they had warned Kyle that her teacher was trying to get too close and had a hidden agenda. They told how Chris had spied on Kyle and followed her. They had telephoto pictures which showed the two together. Notice how trusting Kyle looks. Both bodyguards knew they were risking perjury if Kyle appeared and couldn't be controlled. They thought the risk was low, they were being well compensated, and were confident that they would have the best defense that money could buy.

It was pointed out that as an orphan (the prosecution was being proactive) Chris grew up early and was a very worldly 21 compared to the sweet, innocent, protected 18 year old Kyle Manly who had never been away from home. Dr. Roberts made his first appearance and testified that Chris had begun doing research on Global a year before Kyle showed up on campus. Any halfway decent researcher would have quickly learned that Kyle was Global's second largest shareholder. Further, Dr. Roberts believed that Chris was capable of manipulating the campus computer and might have scheduled Kyle into his anthropology section deliberately. Chris and Nicole exchanged a glance and did not object to this speculation. Judge Williams could not imagine why they would not object.

Dr. Black was subpoenaed. He couldn't believe that he was asked to testify for the prosecution. He was asked directly whether he thought that Chris had ever taken advantage of Kyle during all the time they had spent together at his house. Dr. Black answered that Chris had clearly never taken advantage of Kyle. The prosecution rephrased the question. Did Dr.

Black believe that there was an opportunity for a sexual relationship to have occurred.

Dr. Black almost brought down the house when he answered. "Well, Marcia and I gave them every opportunity."

The prosecutor calmly asked. "Were you aware that they were alone together with enough time and privacy to have a sexual relationship? Just answer yes or no."

Dr. Black smiled and said "Oh yes, it was possible, you know kids."

Chris wasn't sure what Nicole would do on cross examination. He had told her how much he liked and admired Dr. Black. Chris didn't know about a week long transoceanic cruise Nicole had taken with Kyle.

"Dr. Black" asked Nicole "do you have an attic in your house?" It was all Chris could do to keep a straight face.

The next day Dr. Black was still on the witness stand. Nicole took advantage of the situation by letting Dr. Black talk for almost an hour about Chris, his wonderful qualities, his fine teaching skills, and his intellectual integrity. She also let him explain the random, non-computerized process by which students were selected for the different teaching sections in his course. Dr. Black added that Kyle had deliberately sought him out to make sure that during her second semester she would continue to have Chris as a teacher.

Then Nicole took a chance based on Chris' analysis of Dr. Black. "Dr. Black, were Chris and Kyle involved in an improper relationship?" Now Judge Williams was amazed that the prosecution didn't object.

"Well," Dr. Black wondered why Chris would let her ask him that, "they smiled at each other a lot. However, I am not aware of anything improper in their relationship."

"Dr. Black, do you think that Chris and Kyle are good friends?"

The prosecution finally objected that this was speculation. If Dr. Black was aware of a current friendship between the two then he was obstructing justice in a kidnapping case. Nicole rephrased the question.

"During the time that Kyle and Chris were frequent visitors to your home, did you think they were good friends?"

"They were best friends."

Dr. Black and Chris exchanged a few glances. They had agreed to have no direct communication throughout the trial. Chris wanted to protect the Blacks. He couldn't believe the prosecution called him as a witness.

Since Dr. Black did not prove to be a useful witness for the prosecution, no one could believe it when the prosecution subpoenaed Jennifer Martin. There had been a long discussion whether Dragoni law should admit to knowing the whereabouts of Jennifer but Jennifer wanted to testify.

"Ms. Martin," asked the prosecutor "would you lie to protect Chris?"

"Of course, I would lie to protect either Chris or Kyle."

The prosecutor asked the judge to direct Jennifer to confine her answers to just yes or no. "Ms. Martin, was your friend Kyle Manly involved in a sexual relationship with Chris Krail?"

Jennifer thought about her answer. She had discussed it with her father and Nicole. The words were true. "I never saw anything that would confirm that suspicion."

"Ms. Martin, young women often share secrets with their best friends. Are you telling me that Kyle didn't tell you, her confidant, the nature of her relationship with Chris?"

"She told me she adored Chris. She told me that she was incredibly happy that she and Chris had become such good friends."

"Are you telling me that you and Kyle, two freshmen women, never discussed sex?"

Jennifer hesitated. "The last time I ever discussed sex with Kyle she said she was a virgin."

"When was that?"

"Our freshmen year."

Nicole stood. "Your honor, could we get to the point. I am beginning to think that the prosecutor just wants to talk about the sex lives of young women. How is it relevant whether or not a sexual relationship existed or didn't exist?"

Judge Williams looked at the prosecutor. "I have to agree. Make your case. Why are you interested in whether or not there was a sexual relationship? It does not seem relevant to me."

The prosecutor was confident. "This is very important, your honor. The state will show that Chris seduced this young woman, took advantage of her knowledge to steal millions from an organization that is critical to the world's flow of cash, and then kidnapped her to use her as a bargaining chip. By seducing her and making her think that he was in love with her, he broke down her judgement so that he was able to steal the secrets he needed about GFT."

Judge Williams looked over her half glasses at the prosecutor in disbelief. "Would you two please step into my chambers?"

In her office, Judge Williams told the prosecutor what she thought. "You have a very low opinion of women. If you think that sex disconnects the brains of women, you have a major malfunction. Unless you can find a compelling reason, I don't want to hear another word about Kyle's sex life. I see no relevance and I am personally offended by your approach."

Back in the courtroom, the prosecutor tried again. "Ms. Martin, do you believe that Kyle trusted Chris unconditionally?"

Judge Williams quickly realized why the defense didn't object to another speculation. "It's a fact, both Kyle and I trust Chris unconditionally. And we aren't the only ones."

"Ms. Martin, do you know where I could find Kyle Manly?"

For once, Jennifer was happy that no one would tell her where they were hiding Kyle. She told the prosecutor that she had no idea where to find Kyle and then was led through Kyle's disappearance. She told the court it had been a dark and stormy night. She had gone to bed early, around ten. In the morning, Kyle was gone but Jennifer thought she had just gone to campus early, perhaps to have breakfast with Chris. She had no idea that Kyle was missing and had never believed that Chris would kidnap her. She had seen no evidence of a fight or of a forcible entry into their house."

Nicole then led Jennifer through the part of the story where she and Marcia Black had conspired to help Chris and Kyle become friends. Jennifer confirmed that Chris was an exceptional teacher and a wonderful human being.

"How do you feel about Chris, knowing he has been accused of kidnapping your best friend?"

"I love Chris. I would do anything for him."

Somewhere on a island in the Mediterranean, a large extended family worked through their pasts. Kyle never stopped thinking about Chris. She was reassured daily by reports from Gotham. In the meantime, she had to get to know two sets of grandparents. She wanted to show them and her uncle how much she liked them all and how this was the part of the family to which she wanted to belong. In the end, the one thought that always intruded was her compassion for her mom.

"Kyle, you always wanted to know the secret I was keeping from you." Mother and daughter sat near the water. "How could I tell you all this? How could I tell you the horrible choices I had to make to protect you? How could I tell you how hard this has been on me and my parents? Now that it is in the open, I can allow myself some self pity. I feel such release. You must know that I can never go back to your father. He has taken so much from me in return for giving you a life."

"Mom, I always knew how much you cared for me. I can't believe that you gave up almost twenty years of your life for me."

"Don't feel badly, dear. You have been more than worth it. I made a mistake that was costly, but having you as my daughter and friend more than makes up for it."

"Do you think if I had gone away to private school, you could have left him sooner?"

"No, I don't. I can only thank you again for staying at home with me. Let's put this behind us. I want you to enjoy all your new family. Maybe together we can all find a solution to your father. He is very vindictive and dangerous. He can be cruel for no reason at all. We are all afraid that we must find a way to control him. Even when you turn twenty-five and have control of your stock he will still be dangerous. We need to deal with him now. We are all so lucky to have found a hiding place beyond his reach but we can't stay here forever."

In Gotham, the prosecutors and John Manly were the only people who felt a kidnapping case was being made. No one else believed the suggested motive. The prosecution was unable to demonstrate that Chris had the resources to kidnap Kyle. They might have made a better case for murder and a hidden corpse. It would have been more believable if they had said she caught him stealing so he disposed of her. The prosecutors thought of that, too. They pointed out that they were looking into the possibility and were scouring the university and its surrounding environment. If they found a body, Chris would hang. They had even checked all the rentals of wood chippers in the surrounding area.

The prosecution turned to the theft of money from Global Financial Transfer. Dr. Roberts returned to the stand.

"Dr. Roberts, tell us about how you recruited Chris."

"When Chris was an undergraduate, the entire computer faculty felt there had never been anyone like him. Words like brilliant and unbelievable were used constantly. He spent all his time cruising his computer. He was so good that as a junior we gave him his own small office and access to virtually anything he wanted. When Chris was a senior and we knew we would eventually get the grant, we started grooming him to work on the grant."

"Was there anything special about Chris that made him the ideal candidate for the grant?"

"Yes, Chris was essentially interested in computer security. He was an expert in spoofing. He could make any computer think he had legitimate access. He wasn't interested in money transfers at first but he quickly saw it as a really challenging area related to his own security interests. By the time he finished his undergraduate studies he not only knew more about computer security than any faculty member, but I would venture that he probably knew as much as anyone in the world."

Nicole stood. Judge Williams thought that finally she would make an objection to this speculation. "Your honor, the defense would like to speculate as well. We agree with Dr. Roberts." Judge Williams would talk to Nicole later and tell her that she shouldn't try to make the judge laugh.

"Dr. Roberts, how did you become aware that Chris was stealing money?"

Now Nicole, did object and was sustained.

"Dr. Roberts, what led you to believe that Chris might be stealing money?"

"Originally, I asked Chris to use a typical university computer and probe Global to see if there were any obvious weaknesses. I told him just to let me know if he could see any glaring holes that needed to be fixed. I was hoping to be able to give a plum to our benefactors."

"Then what happened?"

"Chris came back to me several weeks later. He told me that while he didn't see any obvious security breaches. He was sure that he, Chris, could steal limitless amounts of money from Global. More importantly, he thought he could do it in a way which would be undetected. Global would never even know they were missing any money. Records could be altered so that under standard accounting practices everything would balance."

Dr. Roberts continued. "Fortunately, Global has world class security. It was standard practice for critical Global initiatives to be tape recorded. Mitchell Bierman, the head of Global security, had set up a voice activated tape recorder in my office." Chris smiled to himself as his professor continued. "On that first occasion and numerous others I have time dated tape of Chris bragging about how he had stolen millions and would never be caught. Of course, I brought this to the attention of Global. They wanted a chance to find the leaks with their own people before we went to the police."

"Did they ever find the leaks?"

"They didn't find them all. But because Chris had bragged about two specific dates, they were able to document two times that Chris stole one million dollars."

The prosecutor introduced the tapes and played them for the court. Then Dr. Roberts was asked to walk the jury through an exercise to show how the computer theft had been perpetrated.

Nicole objected. She wanted to challenge the credentials of Dr. Roberts. He had not been shown to be an expert witness in computer security. He had only been brought as a witness to testify about Chris' role in the department. The prosecutor walked Dr. Roberts through the necessary steps and then Nicole was allowed to question his credentials.

"Your credentials are very impressive, Dr. Roberts."

"Thank you."

"I am concerned about only one thing. A few minutes ago you ventured that Chris knew more about computer security than anyone else in the world. Is that true?"

The prosecution objected. Nicole offered to accept a read back of the previous testimony in lieu of a direct answer from the Dr. Roberts. Judge Williams let her continue.

"Is it true, Dr. Roberts, that you think Chris knows more about computer security than anyone else in the world?"

Dr. Roberts wondered how he had gotten trapped. "Yes, Chris is absolutely brilliant."

"So, Dr. Roberts, do you think that Chris knows more about computer security than you do?" Judge Williams wondered what she would do with this lawyer. No wonder Tony Dragoni had allowed her to cross examine.

Nicole turned to the judge. "The defense finds Dr. Roberts to be an acceptable expert in computer security."

Dr. Roberts then tried to lead the jury through how Chris had stolen the money and how he had tried to cover it up. It was only by painstaking detective work and massive calculations that Global's computer team was able to identify the missing millions. He concluded that Chris was unbelievable and would never have been caught if he hadn't bragged that he could take money whenever he wanted."

Nicole reserved the right to recall Dr. Roberts.

The next witness to be called was Mitchell Bierman. It was late in the day so court was recessed until the morning since Mitchell Bierman was not in the courtroom. Back at Dragoni headquarters the mood was buoyant. The prosecution wasn't reading the tea leaves. A call was received from the police.

Mitchell Bierman was dead. The prosecution had tried to confirm his appearance for the next day. When he couldn't be found they had gone to his residence. They had found him with a silenced nine millimeter in his hand and the back of his head on the wall. There would be no court session the next day, but Judge Williams wanted to meet in her chambers with both sides to discuss the events.

Everyone was stunned. The game plan had been to force the head of Global security to perjure himself. During the defense portion of the trial they were going to paint him as the bad guy. They could demonstrate that he was taking huge amounts of money. He had physically threatened the lead defense attorney. While they could still do this his death was not in their best interest, at least not in the short run. Nicole was silent. She left the room.

Tony Dragoni guessed why Nicole left. He opened a discussion with Chris, Jennifer, and Bill. "Anyone have any thoughts about this? What could possibly make this man kill himself?"

Chris spoke first. "Bierman had nothing to gain by killing himself." He laughed. "I guess that's obvious. If he had helped convict me, he could have continuously ripped off Global. If I were acquitted, then he might be facing a long time in jail. When I get acquitted, it will be because we have shown his criminal side. Then it would make sense. I wish I knew what he was thinking. Do you think he knew he was going down and just gave up? That's not the Bierman I knew."

"One interesting turn," Tony thought of all the wasted theatrics, "is that I can now rejoin the defense table. We will have to decide what to do with the video. I think we should all review it again after dinner. Maybe I should consider showing it to the prosecution and the judge tomorrow. Maybe that would shorten the trial. If I don't show it to them soon, they may accuse me of improper behavior.

Nicole returned. Everyone looked at her. "We didn't kill him." She looked relieved.

Jennifer asked "You think he was murdered?"

"We asked my dad to intervene. We wanted John Manly to know he was playing in the big leagues. We also wanted to create a rift between him and Bierman. I didn't know the details. Manly was forced to meet with a mysterious stranger who gave him a copy of the tape. Manly was told that an important man of influence and wealth would appreciate it if thugs like Mitchell Bierman were kept away from the delicate child of that influential wealthy man. I, of course, am that delicate child. I just wanted to be sure we didn't go a little too far."

"Do you really think he was murdered?" Bill had some interesting thoughts he would reserve until more was known.

"Does your father have an opinion, Nicole?" Tony had grown to respect

Nicole's father. On the one hand he was moving away from violence as fast as he could. On the other, he was an expert and would have valuable commentary.

"Yes, he doubts suicide. He thinks both Bierman and Manly probably have escape scenarios if they see jail in their futures. This is his suggestion. We went to Manly and showed him that someone had evidence of Bierman breaking the law. Bierman has a bigger fish to trade for his freedom. My dad thinks John Manly looked at his options. Mitchell Bierman was just too big a liability. He had to die before he testified and got cross examined. We put the handwriting on the wall and John Manly read it."

"I'm sure your dad is right. I've known him for twenty years and he has never been wrong about the motivations that drive men to kill each other. I think we all wait for the police to figure it out. While I'm sure that John Manly had him killed we can't prove it so we won't suggest it. I'll show the judge and the prosecutor the tape tomorrow. I'll claim I was afraid to come to court so I sent Nicole. When they see the tape maybe they, too, will wonder if someone saw Bierman as a liability. And don't worry Chris, I'll just sit there. Nicole is winning this case. I'll just help her.

The following morning was predictable. The Bierman suicide made all the papers. Even the journalists questioned the suspicious timing of the suicide. An autopsy would be performed. Because his job involved the national and international transfer of enough currency to affect the stability of governments, the crime scene was sealed immediately and the FBI was asked to participate.

Tony Dragoni showed the tape to the prosecutor and the judge. He said he had been too intimidated to proceed. "As I'm sure you both know, no one would have the courage to threaten Nicole." There was no answer. He said he thought perhaps Mitchell Bierman had made one threat too many.

In any case, Tony Dragoni was ready to resume his participation. Both attorneys would now defend Chris.

The prosecution said that Bierman would be replaced as a witness by one of the senior computer security experts from Global.

While the day was predictable, the afternoon and evening were not. Both Bill and Chris each approached Nicole alone and each asked if he could speak privately with her father. Nicole arranged both phone calls on the encrypted phone which even satisfied Bill's more than cursory inspection. She knew that many people treated an audience with her father as the confessional, a path to the secret truth and purity. She was flattered that both these capable young men sought her father's counsel. She placed a preliminary call, spoke to her father in Greek, and told him both Chris and Bill would be worth his time.

Bill Marlin was pleased. He had met Nicole's father briefly at the estate. He was charmed and impressed but knew far too much to ever underestimate such a powerful man. His call was simple. Bill told him that Bierman was into surveillance games. Bill had some ideas he wanted to discuss with the FBI. Bill could not think of a better source to know who was the most honest and approachable agent. Who at the FBI could not be bought?

Bill Marlin wore the new persona that Tony Dragoni had constructed. In an expensive suit and with confidence in his eyes, Bill appeared in the Gotham office of the FBI. His appointment had been made by Nicole. He as amazed that whenever she used her last name she got through to anyone she wanted. No one would even speak her father's name except Nicole.

Bill was ushered into an office where he met with three senior agents. He was impressed that they were taking him seriously. Bill carried an old Gotham newspaper showing a picture of the former FBI agent who had been knocked cold by his home built bugging deterrent. He told the agent of his association with Mitchell Bierman generated surveillance. He told them that he and Chris Krail were friends. He said simply that if the FBI could learn anything about the death of Mitchell Bierman it would doubtless help his friend's case.

If the FBI could find the former FBI agent on the Bierman payroll, perhaps he would know what arrangements the deceased had made to record any threats he might received. Bill further suggested that if they took the walls and ceilings of the Bierman residence apart, they would certainly find fiberoptic cameras with transmitters. He would bet that the death of Mitchell Bierman had been recorded on both audio and video. The problem was that it was certainly transmitted to a remote location. The key was finding the former agent who did Bierman's surveillance.

Chris had been impressed when the Milocellio analysis revealed that John Manly probably had an escape scenario. His call to Nicole's father was considerably longer. Chris was, after all, the person who knew more about John Manly than anyone except perhaps Mitchell Bierman. Chris wanted to know if Nicole's father thought that there was a reasonable chance of finding the Manly escape route, and if John Manly could be forced into running.

Nicole's father was intrigued by the access Chris had to hard information. Together they made a list of all the things that Chris should look to find. Property registered in the Manly name was relatively useless. Property in Bierman's name would also probably be a waste of time, but Chris had some ideas of where to look. Assuming there was a refuge out of the country, Nicole's father would provide the footwork to confirm the situation.

There was one other thing the crafty and experienced older member of this conversation told Chris. If you run and your enemy knows where you will go, you are doomed. He suggested to Chris, that with only a little assistance, John Manly would walk into a box that he himself had constructed. There was an art to letting someone trap himself.

The trial resumed. Mitchell Bierman was replaced by a security team from Global led by Mark Allen. The prosecution apologized for the last minute change in the witness list but felt everyone would understand under the circumstances. The prosecution had asked Mr. Allen to come and tell the court that by using the tapes where Chris bragged about exact dates and amounts they were able to identify that money was missing.

Chris had discussed Mark Allen with Tony and Nicole. They had considered him as a possible defense witness. However, because of Chris' concern that Mitchell Bierman might be a threat to Mr. Allen, they had left him off their original witness list. They had planned to use him only if they couldn't prove their case any other way.

Mark Allen looked like a logical prosecution witness. At Global he had responsibility for the computer system and its security. It was an extremely senior and important position at Global. He had been chosen for technical skill and experience. Since John Manly was not a technician he underrated Mark Allen and thought of him as a geek. Geeks made the business work but real security problems were handled by Bierman.

Mark Allen was accompanied to court by his two most trusted aides, the White brothers. Joshua and Jeremy White were twins. They were also mute. Neither had ever spoken from birth. No neurologist could ever explain the cause. In all other ways they were normal and extremely smart. While they could both sign, but they often chose to use text to speech technology which was more easily understood by the rest of the world. They would type messages into their computers. The computer would translate into speech.

The White brothers also used scripted macros to speed up the speech of their computers. Phrases like 'We're Josh and Jeremy White, it's nice to meet you' could be generated with one or two keystrokes. They chose a voice with two speakers. To the Whites it meant that they always spoke in unison. It also gave their chosen speech vehicle an out of this world quality.

The prosecution asked predictable questions. Had money been removed from Global accounts? Had they been able to find the transfers based on the tapes provided by Mitchell Bierman and Dr. Roberts? The prosecutor was careful not to let Mr. Allen go off on any tangents.

Nicole stood up. "So, Mr. Allen, there is money missing at Global Financial Transfer?"

"Yes."

"Where did it go?"

"I have no idea."

"So you don't know who took it?"

"That's correct." Nicole suddenly was fearful that this was too easy. She had known in advance that Global's security expert would not even try to accuse Chris."

"Had you ever heard of Chris Krail before this incident?"

"Yes."

"How did you know the defendant?"

"Chris spoke to our group several times. The first time he did a general review of known ways to breach corporate security systems, the second time he talked specifically about financial transfers, and the last time we met, he led a discussion group on imaginative and novel approaches to computer security. He called it 'Are we feeling a little too secure about security?'"

"What did you think of Chris Krail?"

The prosecutor objected. Nicole tried again.

"The professor who taught the defendant thought that he was a world class computer guru. Do you agree?"

"Chris is the best there is."

"Is he capable of getting past Global's security?" How could the prosecutor object?

"Absolutely."

Nicole continued. She wanted to rub it in. "Do you think that if Chris wanted he could steal millions of dollars from Global and get away with it?" Judge Williams knew why the prosecution didn't object. She just couldn't understand why the question was asked. Judge Williams was looking forward to Nicole when the defense took over.

"Chris could definitely steal any amount he wanted."

"Were you concerned that Chris had access to your computer through the grant?"

"No."

"Why not? If he were such a threat why wouldn't you be concerned?"

"We actually discussed the issue before the grant was given to the university. The purpose of the grant was to learn our weaknesses and build better systems. We wanted outsiders to probe our systems. We wanted the best and the brightest to work with us."

"But what about the defendant? Once you realized how good he could be, why didn't you ask to have him removed from the grant."

"Chris was just what we wanted. And Chris with a portable computer and a modem anywhere in the world could probably breach almost any security system. He doesn't need the university or his professors to help him."

"How long would it take for Chris to steal a million dollars?" Judge Williams was feeling sorry for the prosecution. She almost intervened on their behalf.

"Chris ran a demonstration for us. It took him twenty minutes to get our system to accept him. He calls it spoofing. Then it took him less than a minute to remove $20 million from John Manly's personal cash account?"

"What happened to the $20 million, Mr. Allen?"

Mr. Allen blushed. "He put it my personal savings account."

"Do you still have it? Did you steal $20 million from Mr. Manly?"

"I gave it back as fast as I could. Chris had to help me erase the logs that showed the two way transfer."

Nicole turned to the judge. Assuming its true that Mr. Allen gave back the $20 million I have no further questions at this time. I reserve the right to recall him.

Chris excused himself after dinner. At three in the morning Nicole got up for a glass of water. She saw the lights and interrupted him. "Chris, the judge made you promise you wouldn't steal? Are you being good?"

"I'm just doing a little homework for your dad.."

The next day was almost anti-climatic. No one was really surprised when the medical examiner announced that the death of Mitchell Bierman was murder not suicide. An X-ray of what remained of his head had made him suspicious. There was something wrong with the pattern generated by the bullet fragments.

A large caliber, powerful weapon like the nine millimeter does leave bullet fragments. Traces of lead, even though in this case most of the slug was mixed with bone and blood in the wall, mark the path taken by the bullet. Sometimes the slug will deform and/or break up. It depends on the design. The X-ray was not consistent with death by a single bullet.

When a small caliber bullet enters the skull it may not have the power to exit. It depends on the load. Small caliber bullets may ricochet within the skull. In the case of Mitchell Bierman, a .25 caliber slug was seen on X-ray in the frontal lobe.

The medical examiner felt that someone had put a small gun in Mitchell Bierman's mouth and pulled the trigger. The small caliber missile had entered his brain, hit the back of his skull, and bounced forward. The victim was probably still alive when the assailant wrapped the victim's hand around his own handgun and finished the job. Presumably the murderer thought the second bullet would hide any other evidence. The medical examiner ruled homicide. The FBI was notified.

The prosecution finally rested. They knew the kidnapping case remained weak. They had intensified the hunt for a body in the university area with no results. On the other hand, the prosecution believed they had clearly shown that Chris was guilty of the grand larceny charge.

Tony continued to have Nicole run the case. He sat at the defense table every day and admired her performance. He thought of the strange young girl he had first met in a jail cell.

Dr. Roberts was recalled to the stand. Nicole asked the judge to remind him he was under oath.

"Dr. Roberts do you understand that if you don't tell the truth you can be charged with a crime?"

"Of course."

"Dr. Roberts, all your previous testimony is true?"

"Of course."

"You testified that you asked Chris to test Global security?"

"That is correct."

"Did you ask Chris to steal money to demonstrate that it could be done?"

"Absolutely not!"

Nicole turned toward the judge. "Like the prosecution, we have tapes of conversations between Chris and Professor Roberts. We also have tapes in which Mitchell Bierman takes part in the conversation. While our tapes have some similarities to those submitted by the prosecution, there are some remarkable, glaring differences. We have submitted our originals to the FBI and the FBI lab is prepared to testify that ours have not been altered in any way."

While Dr. Roberts sat on the witness stand, the defense tapes were played and compared to the prosecution tapes. Nicole asked the prosecution if their tapes could be examined by the FBI. The prosecution was forced to say yes.

Nicole returned to Dr. Roberts. "There seem to be two versions of the conversations you had with Chris. Do you have any thoughts about why there could be such a large disparity?"

"I have never had any tapes in my possession. If they were altered it was either by Mitchell Bierman or Chris Krail."

"Dr. Roberts, after listening to our tapes, certified by the FBI, do you remember ever asking the defendant to actually take money from Global?"

"No."

Dr. Roberts, do you recognize your voice asking the defendant to just put the money somewhere he could give it back?"

"I think these tapes have been altered."

Nicole turned to the judge. "I have no further questions at this time. The defense will need to recall Dr. Roberts after the testimony of Mr. Allen. I would advise Dr. Roberts to retain an attorney."

Nicole recalled Mark Allen from Global computer security. "Mr. Allen, thank you for returning. I'm sure you remember your previous testimony. Just to review for the court, you have testified that Chris is capable of bypassing any security you put in his way. You have testified that by reviewing tapes in which Chris can be heard giving the dates, times, and amounts you were able to confirm that indeed money was missing. Then you testified that you do not know who took the money or where it went. Is this all correct?

"Yes."

"While this was in progress, did Chris offer any solutions or did he just poke holes in your security."

"Chris had what I consider a brilliant idea to control theft."

"Will you tell the court what he suggested."

"Yes I will. But first I have to ask a question. Chris spoke to me alone about his suggestion. Only two other members of my staff, the White brothers, were involved. I believe that Chris was going to use this idea as a basis for his Ph.D thesis. If I explain what he was doing, will I prevent Chris from graduating?"

Nicole asked to approach the bench. The defendant wished to keep no secrets. Clearly his doctorate is not as important as his innocence. Furthermore, because of Mitchell Bierman and Dr. Roberts he had resigned. He is no longer a candidate for his doctorate. The defense was more concerned whether this discussion would compromise Global. The prosecutor felt protecting Global was a cheap trick to make Chris look good. Judge Williams said the discussion would go forward if it were okay with the representatives from Global.

"Mr. Allen, the defendant has no problem if you wish to discuss his ideas publically. He is grateful that you are giving him the credit. He is concerned that you may compromise Global if you make public your tactics. You may discuss Chris' plan to control theft if you feel it won't hurt Global."

"One of the great things about the plan is that it is meant to eventually be public knowledge as a deterrent. Chris invented a method to tag electronic transfers so that even if you lose the trail, you can find the money again. Only if the money is removed from the electronic world can you lose the trail. Money laundering usually involves such large amounts that cash is not an issue. Even then you know the last owner. He said the system was modeled on the taggants used in the fertilizer and explosives industry."

"Mr. Allen, I'm afraid I need more help with that."

"Chris gave us a method to tag money. All money that is the property of Global even for a brief interval will soon be tagged. If a legitimate transfer takes place the tag is removed. If the money is stolen, it can be identified by its tag. Also, if a legitimate government agency asked us to, we could leave the tag on and the money could be followed."

"Mr. Allen, at the time you identified the theft of $2 million were you using tags?"

"Yes, we had an experimental system that Chris and I set up with the help of two of my managers. I have brought them with me in case I need help."

"Earlier in the trial you testified that you didn't know who stole the money. If you were tagging the money, why can't you find it?"

"Chris Krail felt that either he or I might be accused of stealing the money. So he set up a fail safe program. In order to find the stolen money, both Chris and myself must authorize the search. The software is set up to need encrypted authorization from both of us. While I have no doubt that Chris can bypass my authorization, I would not even try to get past his."

"Mr. Allen, are you saying that if you and the defendant work together the stolen money can be recovered?"

"Absolutely."

"Why didn't you come forward with this information earlier?"

"For two reasons. First, and most important Mitchell Bierman made it clear to me that if I valued my job, not to mention my life, I would deny all knowledge of the details and say they were being handled by him. I was physically threatened in no uncertain terms. I would not be here today if he were still alive."

"Was Mitchell Bierman your boss?"

"He was everyone's boss. All senior level people knew he was not to be questioned."

"You mentioned a second reason you didn't come forward."

"Chris Krail didn't steal from Global."

The prosecutor was on his feet objecting. The judge told the jury to disregard Mr. Allen's last remark. The judge called a recess and spoke with the attorneys. It was agreed that the prosecutor would be given time to submit all original tapes to the FBI for their opinion. Judge Williams asked where the defense was going. She was told that they were considering having the defendant testify on his own behalf. The judge asked if they were going to refute the kidnapping charge after the theft charges. Tony Dragoni smiled and told her that they thought the prosecution case was so weak that they weren't going to bother. If they put the defendant on the stand the prosecution was welcome to cross examine him about Kyle even though there were no direct questions. However, the defense would not tolerate a discussion of the sex lives of college students.

The FBI would not allow Bill to participate in their investigation. They thanked him for his help and the leads they had given him. Bill also provided them with a list of the usual frequencies used by the Bierman surveillance team.

It took the FBI less than a week to track down the former agent who had been caught in the Blacks' dining room. He readily admitted that he might have gone a little too far for his employers. He was extremely surprised to find that he had been knocked unconscious by a trap. But he was gratified to know that it was not his error in electronic skills that caused his capture.

And yes. He had helped Mitchell Bierman set up his personal surveillance systems. At first when he had heard that Mitchell Bierman was considered a suicide, he had gone to ground to consider his options. As soon as the papers announced the findings of the medical examiner he knew he could help his former boss get revenge. He had waited a day and then called a former colleague at the FBI and was pleased to hear they were looking for him.

That evening Bill Marlin received a call from the FBI. They had an announcement to make at nine the next morning. They thought he might like to be there or watch it live on television.

Nicole received a call from her father. They spoke in Greek. Nicole and Tony went into a office to speak in private. When they returned they asked the others to join them.

Tony Dragoni spoke. "Nicole appears to know what the FBI will announce tomorrow morning. Her father seems to have unusually informative sources. We debated keeping you all in the dark until court tomorrow. We thought it might be fun but we actually could use your advice."

"Tomorrow morning at nine the FBI will announce that they have executed a warrant for the arrest of John Manly. They say he is wanted for questioning in the death of Mitchell Bierman. It would seem that no one can find John Manly. That is all that Nicole's father told her. However, it would seem likely that if he is missing and if there is a warrant for his arrest, that he is implicated in the murder."

Maureen Martin was worried about Mary Manly. "Tony, do you think you should get me to wherever Mary is hiding. She might need my support." Maureen had never been told the details of how much support Mary really had.

"I wouldn't worry about your passport. You'll see her soon enough. There is a plane on standby. As soon as we're sure its safe, we're going to fly Mary and Kyle right into Gotham. Jennifer, you always said Kyle could make an entrance. Wait until she walks into court."

"Oh, and Chris, Nicole's father wants you to call him tonight. He says he needs to discuss some of the details of Operation Robinson Crusoe. What are you two up to?"

The next day the prosecutor met with the judge and the defense attorneys. He had been told as a courtesy about the announcement. He seemed a little unsure of himself. He wanted the trial to continue. He said the strange death of Mitchell Bierman and the disappearance and subsequent arrest warrant for John Manly did not alter the fact that Chris had committed crimes. He wanted to know if Chris would take the stand in his own defense. Nicole asked him again if he just wanted to ask about the sex lives of young adults. The judge had to intervene. Sex would not be discussed. Chris would take the stand. But they were not through with the other witnesses.

Nicole asked for a 24 hour recess to prepare Chris for his testimony. She told the judge and the prosecutors that after Chris testified or possibly between areas of testimony, they might ask Dr. Roberts or Mr. Allen back for clarification or corroboration. Also, they hoped to find one more witness who might shed some light on the alleged crimes. She would know in the morning.

The FBI made their announcement. The papers had a field day of speculation. What no one had expected, not Nicole, not her father, not Tony Dragoni, not Chris, was that the text of the arrest warrant was a surprise. John Manly was being sought not only for questioning with regards to the death of Mitchell Bierman but he was wanted for questioning with regards to the disappearance of his own daughter.

Tony Dragoni called Bill's contact with the FBI and asked for a meeting. He sent Nicole. She would command their attention.

The next morning Jennifer was waiting at the airport at five. Long before the sun came up a private jet carrying 14 passengers touched down and taxied to customs. With Jennifer was a single FBI agent and Bill. The agent had explained to Nicole why John Manly was a suspect in the kidnapping. Nicole was horrified. The agent was told that they had a lead on where Kyle might be.

The entire entourage was moved in the pre-dawn hours to the Manly townhouse. It was conveniently empty. The FBI had asked the staff to take a vacation while they searched the premises.

Jennifer and Kyle hugged. Both of them talked. Neither of them listened. Kyle left the others at the townhouse and went with the FBI agent and Jennifer to the courthouse. They were let in quietly through a back entrance and went directly to the Judge Williams' chambers.

The FBI agent called the judge at home and asked her to come in early. He said he had evidence on the kidnapping.

When court began, there was the usual crowd of spectators and press. Nicole rose. The courtroom was excited. It was expected that Chris Krail would take the stand. Nicole faced the judge who knew what was coming and wondered if her knowledge was unethical. Judge Williams thought that after the FBI statement she was doing the right thing.

"Your honor, we expected to ask Chris Krail to testify this morning. He will in a few minutes. First, we have a surprise witness." The prosecutor was on his feet objecting that he had not been told. "I am sure the prosecutor will not have a problem with this witness. May we approach?"

The prosecutor was told and could hardly object. "The defense calls Kyle Manly." The courtroom erupted.

Judge Williams banged her gavel. "Everyone will have to sit down. No one may enter or leave. The doors have all been sealed while this young woman testifies. You will all please sit. Mr. Krail that includes you."

Kyle entered but went directly to Chris and kissed him on the cheek. She was then sworn in. Nicole got to go first. This was a defense witness. "Good morning. Could you state your name?"

"Yes. I am Kyle Manly."

"Have you been kidnapped?"

"No."

"Are you missing?"

"No. I'm right here."

"Everyone has been concerned about you. Why did you leave school without telling anyone?"

"It was the middle of exams. I was a little stressed. Chris had found out I had grandparents. Would you believe it. My father kept it from me. So I went to meet my grandparents."

"Didn't you read the papers? Didn't you know everyone was looking for you."

"Well, it's really exciting meeting your grandparents for the first time. And they took me to Europe. Nobody told me I was missing. I feel badly about missing a semester of school. I just hope they'll let me come back."

"Your witness."

No questions. The state withdraws the charge of kidnapping.

Kyle was led out through a side door. She was whisked away to the FBI headquarters with her mom. Tony Dragoni left Nicole to run the trial and went with Kyle and Mary. He brought Maureen and Jennifer. They would need support. Nicole and Chris would bury what was left of the opposition. Bill opted for the FBI office. He wanted to meet the surveillance expert he had knocked cold.

At FBI headquarters, Mary and Kyle found out why the FBI thought John Manly might be directly responsible for the disappearance of Kyle.

In the investigation of Mitchell Bierman's death, they had found a gold mine. Mitchell Bierman had long prepared for the fact that the only man he had to fear was his lifelong friend, John Manly. He had put together an insurance policy. The former agent, turned surveillance freelancer had helped Bierman wire his own life. Indeed, his murder had been videotaped from two hidden cameras and transmitted to a secret taping station. There was no doubt about who had killed Bierman. The FBI thought the tapes were one hundred percent authentic.

Both Mary and Kyle declined to watch the tape in its entirety but both confirmed the identification of the murderer from stills. The FBI felt that Manly had chosen the direct approach to murder since the two would obviously meet frequently alone. Manly had apparently thought that the suicide would pass inspection. All other ways to eliminate Bierman would have involved other people or would have been too transparent. Manly was caught when the first bullet bounced inside Bierman's skull. Pure bad luck.

When the announcement came that the cause of death was not suicide, John Manly had disappeared off the face of the earth. Here Tony Dragoni had a suggestion. Why not assume that Manly was also the victim of foul play. Then when he didn't turn up, and the police couldn't find him, all his assets could be turned over to the family. Mary and Kyle would gain control of his assets. Did he have a will? Tony Dragoni would file all the appropriate papers.

Mitchell Bierman had sought advice and help from two people. One was the former FBI agent, the other was his driver. Bierman's driver was a former safe cracker who understood the nuances of how rich people could hide personal possessions. He had helped Bierman construct several well hidden personal safes in various places in Gotham. The most useful for Bierman was the one hidden in the ceiling of the lavatory of the private jet that was part of his escape scenario. He was going to take his insurance policy with him. Bierman's driver and the former agent were beneficiaries in Bierman's will. By contributing to resolving his murder they would both receive large amounts of money.

Hidden in his private jet was a log of John Manly's criminal activity. More valuable was an entire folder about Kyle. John Manly had several contingency plans to keep control of Kyle's stock. There were well thought out plans from challenging the written agreement with his brother to forcing Kyle to write a will overriding the agreement. There were no scenarios that were in Kyle's best interest. Almost all John Manly's plans ended with the death, disability, or disappearance of his daughter. In every scenario, Bierman was the agent to carry out the plan. After reading the file, John Manly had become the prime suspect in Kyle's disappearance. The FBI was relieved that Kyle had fled. Several agents felt that if she had not fled, it was only a matter of time before her father would have found a way to steal her assets and dispose of her person.

While a worldwide manhunt was being mounted to find John Manly, others thought it might be better if he were never found. Tony Dragoni went to the police and filed a missing persons report on behalf of the family. Nicole's father was thoughtfully engaged in a game of cat and mouse. Chris had found some assets that had turned out to be useful. More importantly John Manly had unknowingly set up his escape route in the backyard of an extremely powerful man who had a delicate daughter and whose name no one would mention.

Nicole called Chris Krail to the witness stand. It had taken the court a few minutes to settle down after the testimony of Kyle Manly. Judge Williams wondered why the defense didn't ask for the charges to be dismissed. It was pretty clear they were going to win. By now, Judge Williams realized the defense had an agenda. There was more here than the acquittal of Chris Krail. The trial had already destroyed John Manly and his chief of security. How many more she wondered?

Nicole led Chris through the usual and expected questions. He confessed to many activities that were not crimes. Yes, he knew about Kyle Manly before she ever appeared on campus. Yes, he frequently had dinner with Kyle. Yes, he had sent Kyle to her grandparents because he thought it was about time she met them. Yes, he had moved countless amounts of money by computer. No, he had never stolen any money from Global.

Chris was led through his history with Dr. Roberts and Mitchell Bierman. He discussed how he with the help of his friend Bill had taped all the conversations and had come to the conclusion that for some reason he, Chris, was being set up. Bill had suggested the taggant approach. He gave a short repeat of Mark Allen's comments about tagging the money.

"Chris" asked his attorney. "Do you know the total amount of money missing from Global?"

"Well in excess of $12 million. There may be much more but I was only involved in moving about $12.5 million."

"Do you know where it is now?"

"No."

"Can you find it?"

"Every penny."

Nicole turned to the judge. "With the court's permission, we would like to set the courtroom up with some computer equipment. There will be monitors for the jury, the prosecution, and the court. We would like to ask Chris, working with Mr. Allen who can represent Global's interests to see if they can track the money that is apparently missing from Global."

Judge Williams looked at the prosecutor who seemed to be lost in thought. "Any objections from the prosecution?"

A recess was called until the following morning. The judge met with the prosecution, Nicole, Chris, and Mark Allen to discuss the logistics. The prosecution wanted to be sure that all the equipment would stay in place until he had a chance to cross examine.

Chris and Mark Allen shook hands. They were both pleased to be working with the other. The judge pointed out that from the standpoint of the court, Chris was still testifying and Mr. Allen was there to represent the interests of Global. The prosecutor had reluctantly let Chris go through the computer disks confiscated from his office. Chris had said that while he could reconstruct his taggant key, it would be faster to use the existing one.

Chris and Mark Allen both put there keys into the pilot program Chris had created for the taggants. When they were ready, Nicole took advantage of Chris' strength as a teacher.

"Chris, would we be endangering Global if you told us what you are doing?"

"Basically, I will outline for you the standard approaches I am using but I will leave out some of the details. What I am about to tell you will not increase the risk that Global faces every day from the average hacker."

Dr. Roberts mentioned that I like to spoof. Spoofing is just a technique that convinces a computer or a network of computers that you are entering the network with approval. You claim to be someone that you are not. My favorite technique was to claim that I was Dr. Roberts or Mitchell Bierman and hence I had preapproval. Once I was on the network, I then altered the networks authorization codes so that my home computer was always accepted as an authorized part of Global. What we are doing here is simple. Mr. Allen and I have configured this demonstration setup to look like my portable computer. Global still thinks that my home computer is part of Global's own computer network. Simple. It's a spoof."

"Once we log on, we will essentially have master control authorization to change anything we want. This is because I gave my portable computer the same authorization codes as Mr. Allen has on his. Since Mr. Allen is the senior computer wizard at Global, this is a convenient way to travel. We won't need to enter Mr. Allen's personal passwords, I have bypassed them. While Mr. Allen has known for some time how I got into his personal configuration and passwords, I am going to spare the court. What I did is hopefully not repeatable. Mr. Allen and I have shut down the portal I used to invade his desktop computer but I don't want to take a chance and let anyone else experiment with this."

Nicole interrupted. "Mr. Allen, do you agree with everything the witness has said."

"Yes, he has so far not told the court anything that is not common knowledge. I agree that he and I have hopefully built a firewall around my authorization so no one else can invade it."

Chris continued. "Let's look at how we can review the events. There are logs recording every transaction. They are redundant. Back when I started it was possible to alter these logs. Again Mr. Allen, his two senior programmers, and I, have hopefully prevented the possibility of altering the logs in the future. While we have made it tougher, I think it can still be done. At the time I moved Global's money I was completely able to bypass the logs. Hence the logs at Global are of no value."

"Because I altered Global's logs, if I had moved the money into someone's private account, that person would not receive any notification from Global and Global would not report it to the IRS. Very convenient for whoever is receiving the money."

"Let's review my first withdrawal. I was asked by Dr. Roberts to see if I could remove $100,000 from Global and put the money where it could be returned."

Nicole interrupted. "For the record the defense notes that Dr. Roberts denies that he made this request. There is no acknowledged tape recording of this first request."

"It was very easy. I divided the money into two parts. The first $20,000 I took as CASHcards. ®"

Nicole again. "For the record we are submitting that $20,000 as evidence."

"I should never have erased the bank records showing how I did this but I thought it would be harder to find the trail. What can I say? It was over a year ago. I was young then. The importance of these cards is not only that I can return them to Global but they also encode the date of the original transaction. Mr. Allen has examined them and can confirm what I say."

"As I mentioned I was young and I wanted to show off. So I put the other $80,000 where I was sure Dr. Roberts would find it and I thought he would be proud of me for my technical expertise. I fully expected to be congratulated. Apparently Dr. Roberts never found the $80,000. But I did put it right under his nose."

"Your honor," Nicole rose, "this is a subpoena, one of several we obtained directly from the state Attorney General. It gives us permission to access from here several different parts of the personal accounts of Dr. Roberts."

"Object," from the prosecutor, "Chris is on trial, not Dr. Roberts"

"Your honor, I did advise Dr. Roberts, on the court record, to obtain an attorney. If the defense cannot demonstrate where Chris put the money, how will we ever establish his innocence?"

Judge Williams looked at the subpoena. "This subpoena was requested by Mr. Allen? I will take a fifteen minute break to consider this subpoena." Judge Williams returned. "I have called both the Attorney General and the executive vice president at Global. I left a message for Dr. Roberts notifying him. We will proceed."

Mark Allen activated a macro which accessed Dr. Robert's personal accounts while Chris continued the explanation. "What we are doing looks simple but is actually quite complicated. Global's computers need to be able to communicate with every financial institution to whom Global transfers money. I then spoofed the brokerage firm where Dr. Roberts invests and gave Global and myself access to Dr. Roberts accounts. You will see that in his retirement account, on the same date I took $20,000 in plastic, there is an $80,000 deposit which clearly is indicated as a transfer from Global. I was very proud of this. I was sure that at soon as he got his monthly statement, he would laugh and congratulate me. At first I thought he was just absent minded and didn't read his statements. Later, I realized there was something more sinister..."

"Objection!"

"Sustained. Mr. Krail you may show us evidence you may not speculate about motives."

Chris continued. "As everyone can see the $80,000 is still here. Dr. Roberts can call Global and say there has been a mistake. He can return this $80,000 any time he likes. That is the story of the first $100,000 I took."

Nicole rose. "For the record, your honor, Mr. Krail was not accused of taking this $100,000. He was never caught. Until today no one at Global except Mr. Allen knew this was missing. Chris, what happened next?"

"When no one noticed the missing $100,000, I was approached by Dr. Roberts who introduced me to Mitchell Bierman. I told them I had taken the money but not how or where I had put it. At the same time I had met with Mr. Allen and his corporate computer security group. I thought it might be prudent to tell the story privately to Mr. Allen. Since first meeting Mr. Allen, he and I have maintained a dialog. While technically I was doing research in the university department, my best work was done privately with Mr. Allen."

"What do you call your best work, Chris?"

"The taggant system suggested by my friend Bill was developed by Mr. Allen and myself. While I may have done the bulk of the work, the system would never have been possible without Mr. Allen's assistance."

John Manly was not happy. He should have known that Bierman would want revenge. He should have bribed Bierman into disappearing. Too bad that first bullet had bounced. Manly had been forced to use his escape route. It was predicated on assuming a different identity. Once in his new identity he would lay low for a year or two and then gradually try to get even. He had hidden enough assets under his phony identity that money would never be an issue. It was getting even that he cared about.

He was heading east on a large private yacht. Another day would find him in the Mediterranean. He would change to a slightly more modest boat and then assume the persona of an obscure but wealthy middle-aged playboy. He had purchased an estate on a small island off the coast of Italy. It had state of the art electronics and communications. It had a deep water dock. It had a heliport. He just needed to keep his head down until things blew over.

Bierman had been a loser. Bierman's advice was that when you run you don't plan to come back. Living well is the best escape. Revenge is risky. How much are you willing to lose to get even? Everything was Manly's opinion. Bierman had suggested Cuba for his friend. Bierman had always claimed he would run to some autocratic emirate where he would live in security eating well amidst a harem until he died of some disease related to one indulgence or the other. Bierman had been a loser. Bierman lost. Manly won.

The boat change was done just outside the Gates of Gibraltar. There was a new crew but Manly thought his captain would be coming with him. The captain said he would join Manly in the next day or two. A special license was needed to land the larger yacht which was big enough to cross the ocean. Plus he had at Manly's request arranged a possible buyer. The captain said with luck everything would be taken care of within 48 hours and he would rejoin Manly in the port at Monaco.

The captain thought about the $100,000 he had been paid to abandon his boss. Actually, he was grateful. He had no trouble believing that Manly had killed Bierman. The captain knew he was lucky to get away unscathed. He had never been disloyal to an employer before. Whatever fate awaited John Manly was not undeserved. He watched as the smaller yacht disappeared as it headed east.

Nicole spoke directly to the jury. "I am now going to ask Mr. Krail to trace the first million dollars that are the root of the indictment against him. Mr. Krail will explain as he goes through the process."

"Mr. Allen and I are entering our encrypted taggant keys. This simply allows us to activate the taggant program. As you can see from your screens, after entering our keys we are confirming with independent passwords. Look at your screens we now have access to the program and a menu to select from. Mr. Allen and I can choose to see the final resting place of the money or we can trace each transaction."

"Neither of us yet know the outcome of this search. Mr. Allen, I would prefer the trace procedure, it will have more information. Do you approve of that approach?"

The representative of Global nodded.

"First we have to find the initial account from which the money came. I took it from Global's general cash fund, altered the logs, and placed it in the personal account of Global's own security chief. I did tell Mr. Bierman that he would see the million dollars appear where he might be able to find it. At the same time I made it look as if the money were in my personal account. Since Mitchell Bierman kept his money within the Global employee bank, with Mr. Allen's permission we are now going to look at this account. We go to the date of the transfer. Isn't this interesting, there is no million dollar transfer in or out. We better look at the log."

"The log shows no evidence of our million dollars either. So let's look at the code that controls the log. Hmm! Now this is interesting. Ms. Milocellio, I think at this point I should defer to Mr. Allen. Since he represents Global perhaps he should take over here."

Nicole looked at the judge who nodded. "Mr. Allen, why has Mr. Krail suddenly deferred to you?"

"The logs have clearly been altered. The million dollar entry took place and was deleted, the log was then reconciled. It is however clumsy. Whoever did this either did not have a fine touch or wanted to get caught. I think this is just clumsy, and it really doesn't matter because we are still going to find the money."

"Mr. Allen, you mean despite the fact that the million dollars isn't there, you think you can still find it?"

"I would be very surprised if we can't find it. Let Mr. Krail run the trace program."

Chris was only too pleased to take the next step. "I am going to ask the program where the money was on the following date. It should just take a second. And look, we have the number of an account at the Gotham Center Bank."

Nicole handed the judge another subpoena. "The state Attorney General was nice enough to provide us with a subpoena to look into the banking records of any account showing a taggant flag. Mr. Allen at Global was nice enough to join us in requesting this subpoena."

Chris took the trace program forward. The owner of the account became apparent on all the courtroom monitors. The money had been transferred into another of Mitchell Bierman's personal accounts. Chris then asked the program to continue tracing the money. On the day after the arrest of Chris $250,000 had been transferred into the retirement account of Dr. Roberts.

Nicole spoke to the jury. "The defense is willing to let this tracing program be submitted to any scrutiny that is acceptable to Global Financial Transfer. It is very important to remember that Mitchell Bierman had control of two accounts from which money was transferred. Dr. Roberts could not prevent the money from being transferred to him and may have been totally unaware of the transfer. But the key is that Chris deliberately showed he could take money. When he hid it in another Global account, he had no idea that the owner of that account would steal it. Mitchell Bierman apparently is the person who really stole this million."

"Please note that this last transfer took place at a time that Mr. Krail was in jail and did not have access to a computer. Let's look at the other million."

John Manly was satisfied with the second yacht. It had been leased under a phony name which he would soon abandon. He was well fed. The captain seemed congenial. He went to sleep knowing that he would awake in a safe harbor.

At three in the morning the crew of the yacht had a silent rendezvous with a fishing trawler. The crew of the trawler loosely tied up the crew of the yacht. The yacht was put on autopilot on a heading that would be safe until the crew got loose. Mr. Manly was taken at gunpoint with a bag over his head and put in a fish locker on the trawler.

A short cryptic radio signal confirmed success. In was only nine in Gotham.

★ ★ ★ ★ ★

The prosecutor rose. "Your honor, I would like to cross exam Mr. Krail on the theft of the first million dollars before we move on. Since he admits he stole over $12 million, I would like to look at each theft individually before we move on."

Nicole looked at the judge. "The defense has no objection, except of course, the defendant denies stealing, only moving money at the request of Global."

"Mr. Krail, as I understand your discussion, you are admitting you stole $1 million from Global. Is that true?"

"No, I did not steal any money from Global."

"Then what were you planning to do with the money. It is clear that if you could put the money into Mr. Bierman's account, you could also take it back out. We have no way of telling whether Mr. Bierman put $250,000 in Dr. Roberts account or whether you did. The state has, from the beginning, accepted you as an expert in this area and considered you dangerous. How do I know that you didn't set this all up to make Mr. Bierman and Dr. Roberts look like the culprits? How do I know that the next million won't turn up in the account of one of the jury members?"

"Is the prosecutor making a speech or cross examining the defendant? He needs to let my client answer."

Chris began. "Unfortunately there is no sure way to tell who authorized each transfer. While I can assure you that none of the secondary transfers were mine, I can't prove it. No one else can prove it either. But I was in jail without a computer when the secondary transfer took place."

"So you admit you put the money into the accounts of people you wished to embarrass?"

"No, I always tried to put the money in a clever, visible place. I admit to deliberately tempting Mitchell Bierman. I wasn't real sure about his motives. He kept telling me that he couldn't find the money I moved. So we played a game. He had no idea about the taggants. Only Mr. Allen, his two senior programmers, and I knew we were doing it."

"The point is you took a million dollars and planted in the accounts of two people you wished to embarrass." The prosecutor wanted to hammer home the point that Chris was always in control.

"No. The point is I put the money where it could be recovered. I was asked to take millions. I was told that they didn't care where I put it as long as I could give it back. I put this first million in a Global account that Mr. Bierman controlled. Trust me. I have no idea how the money got into other personal accounts but if you authorize me, I can give it back to Global. More importantly, I can prove it is Global's money."

The judge called a short recess. Chris talked quietly with Nicole and Tony. "If this first million is any example, there is no telling where we will find the rest of the money. Could be a lot of very embarrassed folks. You want to march through it all and see where it is or just call it a day saying we've made our point."

"What are you worried about?"

I always tried to tempt Bierman and Roberts. I always tried to put it some place they were watching. Once I put a million in a joint checking account belonging to Kyle and Jennifer. The money wasn't there ten minutes. It's not where I put it. It's who they tried to bribe with it. Suppose Bierman put it into one of the juror's accounts. Or worse yet, suppose he put it in the prosecutor's retirement account."

"Since Bierman knew who was defending you, do you think he could have put some in our law firm?"

"Don't worry, they had no sense of humor."

"Chris, I see your point. I'll ask to meet with the judge and the prosecutor. Justice will be better served by a little mystery. But we will put you back on the stand. Just insist we can recover the money no matter where it is. Then we'll get Mr. Allen to testify this is just what Global wanted you to do. Then we'll decline to bring Dr. Roberts back. We'll say it would be unfair since he may be charged with a crime."

"Nicole is right" inserted Tony. "We will also offer your full cooperation if the state wishes to investigate where the money went in its travels. Of course every recipient will claim they had no idea where the money came from."

Dinner at the Manly residence had grown to a nightly catered affair. Mary took charge of handling temporary staff. Bill and Bob were helpful in providing security and checking the staff. No serious conversation took place until after dinner when all the non-members of the group had been dismissed.

After dinner Bill and Bob, the resident electronic experts swept the room again. They had become extraordinarily cautious. Bob and his parents, Mary and her parents, Chris and Kyle, Bill and Jennifer, Maureen Martin and Tony Dragoni all waited for Nicole.

"How did you find John's escape route?" Mary asked the young man who was never far from her daughter.

"In general people who try to fool computers either need to hire an expert or they make the same stupid mistakes. Mr. Manly tried to set up his escape route without apparently even consulting Mitchell Bierman. In retrospect, it is clear he didn't trust Bierman but one still has to wonder. Beginner's always try to use passwords and tricks they will recognize. Before he changed his name to Manly, he had authentic documents and he actually used these. Incredibly visible."

Kyle interrupted. "What do you mean before he changed his name?"

Chris pointed to one set of grandparents and laughed. "What have you all been talking about all this time? Kyle, meet Mr. and Mrs. Manlowitz. I assume you also know Mr. Bob Manlowitz, their other son. Anyway, then he did the predictable, he used Berkowitz. Kyle, that's your grandmother's maiden name. And then, he was so sure of himself that he didn't keep the money transfers clean. He did direct transfers from one account to another. Plus, of course, Nicole's father made some very shrewd guesses. Since his Manlowitz passport was a clean document, he used that identity far too much in Europe."

"But his worst mistake was that he didn't really want to run. If he had to escape he wanted to come back for revenge. You could see it in all his planning. Setting up accounts all over and small condominiums in important places like Gotham. If he had hired someone to help him run he might have made it. He should never have thought of returning."

At this point Nicole returned. "Bob, are you one hundred percent sure this is secure or should we go somewhere else."

Bob smiled at Nicole and said. "Bill and I have checked this house. Two rooms are set up to record. We disconnected those. We even swept the whole house again after dinner to make sure no caterer left any recording device. This is as safe as it gets."

"It is up to all of you." Nicole smiled. She knew what the answer would be. "John Manly does not like being poor. Last night he was put into a run down farm house outside a small fishing village on a rural island in the Aegean. He has no running water. He will get his meals delivered daily by the villagers. He has no access to a phone and they even took away all his mirrors so he can't signal a passing boat. Trust me when I tell you there is no one he could possibly bribe. If he hurts anyone he will answer to local laws. He has been told all this very clearly. He would have to be superman to get off that island."

"You have a choice. We can notify the United States government that we have located a fugitive or we can let him learn to be a farmer. If we bring him back we will be in court for years and he may be dangerous even while in prison. If we leave him, Tony and I will declare him a missing person and we will eventually get control of all his assets, no matter what name he put on them. All those assets will go to Kyle making her one of the wealthiest women in the world. Mary will officially be a widow."

Bob had always negotiated for his parents when John was involved. "Doesn't he have a will? Why will his assets go to Kyle?"

"You are going to love this, Bob. We actually contacted his lawyer and a will does exist. The lawyer gets a cool ten million just to be executor. He left everything he had to Mitchell Bierman. Unless Bierman was in any way implicated in his death or disappearance. If that were true, all his money went to his brother Bob." She hesitated, looked up, and smiled at Bob who was stunned.

"But don't worry Bob, there was another clause. If Bierman was already dead at the time of his death, then all assets go to his only child, Kyle."

Bill spoke up. "I guess I don't have to ask if the security arrangements for Mr. Manly are really tight."

"Actually Bill," Nicole was glad to be reminded "there are a couple of other things. First, he has no shoes, only sandals, he won't get far. Not even a young man could swim off this island, and he was also given an electronic ankle bracelet. It doesn't look like much but he won't get lost. He has no identification. He is learning to grow his own vegetables. And my secret sources tell me that if a charity were created for the villagers, say about $100,000 each year to the local church, it would go a long way. Chris I will need your help to launder that money. No criminal activity, just nice clean untraceable cash."

Kyle answered for the group. "Nicole, tell the mysterious angel who watches over my father that the Manlowitz family trust would be pleased to provide whatever the church needs to succeed in its holy mission. And I for one am grateful that my father is at peace living a simple life in retirement. It's a shame he had to fake his own death to escape."

The next phase of the trial was a negotiation about whether it was in anyone's best interest to pursue the taggants in a public forum like the courtroom. Mr. Allen made it very clear to the judge, the prosecutor, and the defense that every penny would be followed and any money that was identified but not recovered would be an issue for the Gotham District Attorney unless the DA were involved. Then it would go to the state.

Nicole and Tony wanted to trade this discretion for completely dropped charges. The prosecutor wanted to plea bargain. That was unacceptable to the defense. The defense then asked the judge for 48 hours to trace all the money and prepare a list for recovery. It might even be possible to recover all the money before the end of the trial. The prosecutor objected. The judge ruled for the defense and a 48 hour recess was called.

On the first day back in court, Nicole asked the judge if the testimony of the defendant could be interrupted to allow Mr. Allen back on the stand. The judge allowed this.

"Mr. Allen, court has been in recess for two days to allow you and your Global staff to pursue the tagged and missing money. Would you tell us how much you found?"

"Essentially what we did was to find the end locations of all the money carrying a Global tag. At this point in time, any tagged money is by definition missing from Global. We are indebted to Mr. Krail."

"We gave each recipient of missing money a phoney name using the alphabet. We found money in the accounts of 25 individuals, hence we have Mr. or Ms. A through Y. We had our legal department call each of these recipients. Each recipient was told that a mistake had been made and a certain amount of money had been accidently transferred to his or her account. We have already been able to contact over half the people on the list and without exception each readily agreed to help us correct the error."

Nicole knew it was improper to ask about the list. Chris would probably tell her eventually anyway. But she would have bet anything that the lead prosecutor was on the list.

Mark Allen continued. "At this point it is safe to say that we will certainly recover not only the two million identified as missing but much more. It may be helpful for the court to know that many paths lead back to Mitchell Bierman. As you know he is no longer with us and we will be reorganizing our department. In the future all aspects of Global computer security will report directly to me.

As the trial wound to a close, notable events occurred as part of the fallout. Bob Manlowitz met with each of the existing members of the Board of Directors of Global Financial Transfer. Ten resigned. For most companies this would have been a disaster. However, when this was reported in the paper, there was a ten percent one day surge in the value of GFT stock. Bob now had temporary control of much of Kyle's stock and could literally control the company. Acting with her consent and the consent of the rest of the family, he took control of the company.

At Athené, three members of the Board of Trustees resigned as did Dr. Roberts. President Edmund Burrows made a statement to the press. In the future corporate grants would be more closely scrutinized and there would be substantial controls put in place to see that no abuses would ever again take place. The university would emerge untarnished. He concluded with the following statement. "As for myself, I wondered if funny money would be found in my personal account. There was none. I am gratified. However,

I have come to the conclusion that I made so much effort on behalf of help Global that they must have thought I was too stupid to need a bribe."

Chris and Nicole's father continued Operation Robinson Crusoe. They tracked down five different identities that John Manly might have used. This was all turned over to Tony who began the process of claiming that John Manly was legally dead. All assets would go to Kyle.

The jury deliberated for twenty minutes. Chris Krail was acquitted. On the steps of the courthouse he turned to Kyle and took her hand. "So?"

"I'd like to finish school" Kyle responded. "Let's go back to Athené."